PRAISE FOR M. L. BUCHMAN

A fabulous soaring thriller.

— *TAKE OVER AT MIDNIGHT,* MIDWEST
BOOK REVIEW

Meticulously researched, hard-hitting, and suspenseful.

— *PURE HEAT,* PUBLISHERS WEEKLY,
STARRED REVIEW

Expert technical details abound, as do realistic military missions with superb imagery that will have readers feeling as if they are right there in the midst and on the edges of their seats.

— *LIGHT UP THE NIGHT,* RT REVIEWS, 4 1/2
STARS

Buchman has catapulted his way to the top tier of my favorite authors.

— FRESH FICTION

Nonstop action that will keep readers on the edge of their seats.

— *TAKE OVER AT MIDNIGHT,* LIBRARY
JOURNAL

M L. Buchman's ability to keep the reader right in the middle of the action is amazing.

— LONG AND SHORT REVIEWS

The only thing you'll ask yourself is, "When does the next one come out?"

— *WAIT UNTIL MIDNIGHT,* RT REVIEWS, 4
STARS

The first...of (a) stellar, long-running (military) romantic suspense series.

— *THE NIGHT IS MINE,* BOOKLIST, "THE 20
BEST ROMANTIC SUSPENSE NOVELS:
MODERN MASTERPIECES"

I knew the books would be good, but I didn't realize how good.

— NIGHT STALKERS SERIES, KIRKUS
REVIEWS

Buchman mixes adrenalin-spiking battles and brusque military jargon with a sensitive approach.

— PUBLISHERS WEEKLY

13 times "Top Pick of the Month"

— NIGHT OWL REVIEWS

Tom Clancy fans open to a strong female lead will clamor for more.

— *DRONE*, PUBLISHERS WEEKLY

Superb! Miranda is utterly compelling!

— *BOOKLIST*, STARRED REVIEW

Miranda Chase continues to astound and charm.

— BARB M.

Escape Rating: A. Five Stars! OMG just start with *Drone* and be prepared for a fantastic binge-read!

— READING REALITY

The best military thriller I've read in a very long time. Love the female characters.

OSPREY

A MIRANDA CHASE ACTION-ADVENTURE
TECHNOTHRILLER

M. L. BUCHMAN

SIGN UP FOR M. L. BUCHMAN'S NEWSLETTER TODAY

and receive:
Release News
Free Short Stories
a Free Book

Get your free book today. Do it now.
free-book.mlbuchman.com

Other works by M. L. Buchman: *(* - also in audio)*

Action-Adventure Thrillers

Dead Chef
One Chef!
Two Chef!

Miranda Chase
Drone*
Thunderbolt*
Condor*
Ghostrider*
Raider*
Chinook*
Havoc*
White Top*
Start the Chase*
Lightning*
Skibird*
Nightwatch*
Osprey*
Gryphon*

Science Fiction / Fantasy

Deities Anonymous
Cookbook from Hell: Reheated
Saviors 101

Contemporary Romance

Eagle Cove
Return to Eagle Cove
Recipe for Eagle Cove
Longing for Eagle Cove
Keepsake for Eagle Cove

Love Abroad
Heart of the Cotswolds: England
Path of Love: Cinque Terre, Italy

Where Dreams
Where Dreams are Born
Where Dreams Reside
Where Dreams Are of Christmas*
Where Dreams Unfold
Where Dreams Are Written
Where Dreams Continue

Non-Fiction

Strategies for Success
Managing Your Inner Artist/Writer
Estate Planning for Authors*
Character Voice
Narrate and Record Your Own
Audiobook*

Short Story Series by M. L. Buchman:

Action-Adventure Thrillers

Dead Chef

Miranda Chase Stories

Romantic Suspense

Antarctic Ice Fliers

US Coast Guard

Contemporary Romance

Eagle Cove

Other

Deities Anonymous (fantasy)

Single Titles

The Emily Beale Universe
(military romantic suspense)

The Night Stalkers
MAIN FLIGHT
The Night Is Mine
I Own the Dawn
Wait Until Dark
Take Over at Midnight
Light Up the Night
Bring On the Dusk
By Break of Day
Target of the Heart
Target Lock on Love
Target of Mine
Target of One's Own
NIGHT STALKERS HOLIDAYS
Daniel's Christmas*
Frank's Independence Day*
Peter's Christmas*
Christmas at Steel Beach
Zachary's Christmas*
Roy's Independence Day*
Damien's Christmas*
Christmas at Peleliu Cove

Henderson's Ranch
Nathan's Big Sky*
Big Sky, Loyal Heart*
Big Sky Dog Whisperer*
Tales of Henderson's Ranch*

Shadow Force: Psi
At the Slightest Sound*
At the Quietest Word*
At the Merest Glance*
At the Clearest Sensation*

White House Protection Force
Off the Leash*
On Your Mark*
In the Weeds*

Firehawks
Pure Heat
Full Blaze
Hot Point*
Flash of Fire*
Wild Fire
SMOKEJUMPERS
Wildfire at Dawn*
Wildfire at Larch Creek*
Wildfire on the Skagit*

Delta Force
Target Engaged*
Heart Strike*
Wild Justice*
Midnight Trust*

Emily Beale Universe Short Story Series

The Night Stalkers
The Night Stalkers Stories
The Night Stalkers CSAR
The Night Stalkers Wedding Stories
The Future Night Stalkers

Delta Force
Th Delta Force Shooters
The Delta Force Warriors

Firehawks
The Firehawks Lookouts
The Firehawks Hotshots
The Firebirds

White House Protection Force
Stories

Future Night Stalkers
Stories (Science Fiction)

ABOUT THIS BOOK

RUSSIA TEETERS ON THE BRINK OF COLLAPSE, SPOILING FOR A *battle to end all wars. All it needs? One thin excuse.*

World War I began with the assassination of Archduke Ferdinand. World War II launched with the invasion of Poland. Russia's invasion of Ukraine didn't do it—yet.

A Russian flyby of an American CMV-22 Osprey tiltrotor goes desperately wrong over the North Sea. Will the tipping point for World War III break the moment a favored daughter of the Oligarchy goes down in flames?

When the NSA's secret military base at Menwith Hill in the UK can't handle it, they call in Miranda Chase. She and her elite team of air-crash investigators must avert a crisis like none before. A crisis that unravels her past, batters at her autism, and threatens to crush her team in the ultimate grinder of East vs. West.

A list of characters and aircraft may be found at:
https://mlbuchman.com/people-places-planes

NOTES

The opening prologue is as accurate as possible based upon the 341-page NTSB report #AAR-00/03 adopted August 23, 2000. (And for you total geeks, like me, read the second part of the prologue before pinning down a key error in the first part.)

The plane crash mentioned as occurring July 16, 1996, the day before the crash of the opening prologue, was moved 34 days earlier for the purposes of the story, but is otherwise accurate.

The other incidents are fictitious but, the author fears, only too possible.

PROLOGUE

July 17, 1996
8:17 p.m.

THE SUN HUNG LOW AMONG THE TOWERS OF NEW YORK CITY casting final shadows across JFK International Airport.

At 2017:18 Eastern Daylight Time, Trans World Airlines Flight 800 from New York to Paris was instructed to hold short of JFK's Runway 22R. A landing 757 had kicked up some heavy wake turbulence that would take half a minute to subside. The 747-100, with two hundred and ten passengers and eighteen crew members aboard, held their position for a minute and three seconds.

While idling at the edge of the runway, the cockpit flight crew remained focused on completing the pre-takeoff checklist. The flight hadn't gotten off to a good start and the four men were all glad to finally be on the move.

The 747 had landed from Athens on schedule at 1631 hours. For cabin comfort, the APU—Auxiliary Power Unit, a small engine used as a generator to power the plane's systems—was kept powered up to run two of its three air conditioners to mitigate the heavy heat of the July sun beating down from the partly cloudy skies over New York.

Three of the crew had over sixty thousand hours combined flight experience, much of it in the 747. The fourth was relatively new to the 747, a trainee flight engineer. At twenty-four years old, he had over two thousand hours of flight time as an engineer, but only thirty of those were in a 747. His trainer on this flight was two years from retirement and did his best not to think how much he'd miss the big plane that had dominated his forty-year career.

Over the previous two and a half hours, the plane had been emptied, serviced, and reloaded with passengers and their luggage.

Rather than departing for Charles de Gaulle at 1900 hours as scheduled, there had been multiple delays.

First, a service vehicle had broken down, blocking the plane at Gate 27 until it could be towed clear.

Once it was clear, there was a further delay as gate personnel insisted that a piece of luggage had to be pulled from the hold because the passenger hadn't boarded. Eventually the luggage and its owner were both located. The owner sat already aboard the plane, seriously considering several scotches once they were aloft. The overexcited high school French class looking forward to their first trip to France were boisterously annoying. It was going to be a long damn flight and scotch was definitely in order. Despite the delays, he'd still be in time for his lunch meeting. The French would just have to take him in whatever state he was in.

The bag was returned to the hold.

Of only slightly more concern, the captain's weather

radar wasn't working properly. Maintenance marked it as inoperative and, per regulation, ordered service at the next opportunity within ten days. The copilot's radar was operative, so the flight was finally cleared for departure.

At 2018:21, the tower transmitted final wind conditions and cleared TWA 800 for departure. They rolled down Runway 22R and lifted into the air well before midfield as they carried only two-thirds capacity. The final fuel load had been adjusted downward to avoid carrying any extra weight across the Atlantic. As a result, the large central wing tank sat mostly empty.

Over the next eleven minutes, as air traffic control routed the flight east to higher flight levels through the typical clutter of jet traffic, there was only one unusual comment captured by the Cockpit Voice Recorder.

At 2029:15, the captain remarked, "Look at that crazy fuel flow indicator on Number Four...see that?"

There was no follow-up comment captured by the CVR.

A minute and fifty-seven seconds subsequent to that remark, at 2031:12 after the flight was cleared to climb to fifteen thousand feet, the CVR abruptly ceased operation. For just over a tenth of a second before it did, a *very loud sound* was recorded.

It stopped recording because a frayed fuel gauge wire, probably chafed by a sagging air duct, sparked. The spark occurred inside the nearly empty central wing tank, now primarily filled with a highly combustible fuel/air mixture. The mixture had been further heated and concentrated during the overlong wait on the tarmac by the heat exchangers for the air conditioning units—mounted directly below the tank.

When the fuel/air mixture ignited, an intense explosion

sliced the airplane in two, immediately ahead of the wings. This severed the wiring to the flight recorders as well as killing many of the passengers instantly—mostly by snapping their necks. Those who survived in the main body of the aircraft died from inhaling the burning air rolling through the cabin like a roiling wall of death.

Approximately five seconds later, the nose of the plane—including the flight deck and first-class passenger section—broke free and began its long, eighty-three-second fall to the ocean. Based on ocean water found in their lungs, some of these passengers may have survived long enough to attempt a breath after the impact with the Atlantic off East Moriches, Long Island, New York.

The main fuselage and wings of the 747, abruptly lighter in the nose, tipped steeply upward. With the engines still driving ahead at climb thrust, it ascended an additional three thousand feet over the next thirty-eight seconds before the wings broke free from the shattered central wing box that had enclosed the fuel tank. No one aboard remained alive as it too began its long tumble toward the ocean.

During the next four years, the largest investigation in the history of the National Transportation Safety Board recovered over ninety-five percent of the debris and all the bodies from the Atlantic. The plane was reassembled in a hangar piece by piece to determine the causes. Over forty recommendations were sent to the FAA by the NTSB, including several changes to all 747 wiring harnesses.

The most important? All future jets—civilian, military, by every nation—would eventually be redesigned to pump inert nitrogen into their fuel tanks as they empty to prevent the accumulation of a highly explosive fuel/air mixture. With that single design change recommendation, it is estimated that the National Transportation Safety Board has saved tens of thousands of lives globally.

———

July 17, 1996
8:55 p.m.
CIA Headquarters
Langley, Virginia

"TURN ON THE NEWS."

Ron Klemens looked up from the file that was causing him such misery to glare at his assistant as he hustled into Ron's office.

Bert ignored the glare and hurried over to the television.

Ron must be losing his touch.

The set came alive with a bright red *Breaking News* banner. Some passenger jet had crashed into the ocean less than thirty minutes ago.

What the hell was it with planes going down all of a sudden? His two top agents, he resisted the urge to look down at the file spread before him, had gone down yesterday under conditions that could never be revealed. How was he supposed to explain their deaths?

Even as the Director of the Russia Desk for the CIA, one didn't stroll into the Director's office and announce such a thing without having a solution already in place. The bastard was too busy declassifying the Cold War and damaging the CIA in all sorts of creative ways. Ron couldn't fight back, but he couldn't let *this* get out. No, he wasn't going to the Director until this one was locked down and fully in the bag.

Wait. Did he have to explain it?

He flipped to the front of the file. Damn it. They had a kid, insurance policies, property, any number of loose threads that could never be allowed to be questioned.

The real tragedy? Nothing could be done to plug the massive intelligence hole that their deaths created. They were irreplaceable.

He stared at the screen as dribs and drabs of information were gathered about the air crash.

Explosion.

A dead 747 plunged into the water off Long Island.

A French class field trip on its way from JFK to Paris.

"Survivors?" the news anchor asked.

After an explosion high over the ocean? Ron thought the man should be shot for offering false hopes. Nothing but death and confusion would result.

If only he could hide his agents' deaths there, then—

"Bert!" he shouted so loudly that the man less than five feet away jumped.

"Sir?"

"Was the flight full?"

"What flight?"

Ron jabbed a finger toward the screen.

Bert twisted his head like that green Muppet frog-thing, first to the screen, then back. Then he glanced down at the file on Ron's desk that had been giving them both headaches all day.

He bolted for his desk.

He was back less than five minutes later, and he was smiling. "The flight wasn't full. Two hundred and ten people and about three hundred and sixty seats."

Ron felt like a bit of a ghoul as he returned the smile—

just another day at the CIA. "Make it two hundred and *twelve*. Get them confirmed aboard. Alter paperwork, flight manifests, all of it. Fast, before they can absolutely confirm the number."

"Assign seats. First class, I think. Fabricate some luggage and sink it in the recovery area…" Bert kept talking to himself as he hurried away. It was the kind of deep cover that the CIA had a whole department dedicated to creating.

TWA Flight 800 would now have two hundred and *twelve* passenger deaths, not two-ten. The agent's bodies should be repatriated within twenty-four hours. Divers from a Special Activities Division team could quietly insert them into the wreckage, even snap their seatbelts.

He could always wait for the next director before reporting it so that it stayed hidden; the current idiot couldn't last much longer. If he was careful, that director might well be him. Then he could add their stars to the Memorial Wall with no one in the wider world any wiser.

Ron flipped to the first page of Sam and Olivia's file. The emergency contact was some live-in nanny. Close enough.

He dialed the number and listened while it rang in the hell-and-gone Pacific Northwest.

As the call was answered, Ron glanced down to find the surviving kid's name: Miranda.

1

2,349' (716m)
High on Great Shunner Fell
North Yorkshire, England
Today

"JUST LOOK AT THAT."

Miranda Chase did. Again. She still failed to feel the excitement in Andi's voice.

She did feel the cold of the quartering headwind that had been lashing her face all morning. Was her right cheek tingling from incipient frostbite due to windchill on a sunny day—or simply from being battered for the last four hours?

They had spent the whole morning climbing the rocky path up the south face of Great Shunner Fell in England's Yorkshire Dales National Park. Nothing here grew higher than her knees. No bushes or trees. Only scrub grass, brown bracken not yet recovered from winter, sandstone rock (most of it converted to tall walls to border sheep pastures), and the beaten-down footpath often thick with mud.

Many of the stretches were worn calf-deep, which made the grass thigh high rather than knee high. Other stretches were paved with sandstone or limestone blocks, she couldn't tell which, a meter square and ten centimeters thick. She'd measured several and found little variation.

She pulled out a notebook and added Hydrochloric Acid to her list—after she'd turned her back to the wind to stop the panicked flapping of the pages. If she ever came back, she'd be sure to bring a dropper bottle of it. Even a few drops of HCl would fizz on limestone but not on sandstone offering a definitive identification.

Miranda then attempted to calculate how many people must have walked these paths to wear the trench she trudged along. An average human weight would be easy enough to assume, courtesy of the FAA. They provided average combined weight for passengers and carry-on luggage based on gender and seasonality (five pounds more clothes in winter) for aircraft loading estimates.

Should she downgrade the FAA's allocation? Only the more fit people would attempt this hike. Though hikers would be carrying packs: lighter day packs like their own or heavier packs for those hiking self-contained around the four-day circuit of the Herriot Way. No, she'd use the FAA standards: males at a hundred and ninety pounds and women at one-seventy-four. That was inclusive of clothing and typical carry-on weights.

Ratio of males to females? Based on their own group, one-to-three. Mike and Holly were already at the top of the peak. She and Andi were yet a hundred meters from the top. But were they typical? Perhaps a one-to-one ratio would be better. Or were men more likely to set out on the fifty-two-mile walk? She'd have to ask Mike, he understood people better.

Without soil density measurements, calculating the impact of each step upon soil compaction or erosion would be—

"Is something wrong?" Andi had come back down the trail to stand in front of her.

Her hiking pants had a pocket for her phone along the outside of her thigh. That looked very convenient. If she did that, then she'd be able to carry additional items in her vest. "I need pants like yours."

Andi looked down at them, then back at her.

"That's what's wrong?"

"Oh, no." After Miranda had explained the problem with soil erosion and trail-wear mathematics, Andi offered one of her understanding smiles.

"It's been worn down as much as it has by people enjoying themselves as they walk along. Maybe that's all we really need to know?"

Miranda always marveled at Andi's clear view of the world. She herself was far too likely to overcomplicate things. She never remembered to tell her autism to calm down when in the midst of overthinking something. Andi now did that for her.

Hands clasped, they walked up to join Holly and Mike, their boots shushing along together through the taller grass that carpeted the top and blurred the final part of the trail into invisibility.

The top of Great Shunner Fell was marked by a crossed pair of stone walls, high enough to block the wind and let her assess that she wasn't suffering from incipient frostbite. That appeared to be the one great constant of the Yorkshire Dales, a powerful wind. It had measured fifteen to twenty knots, gusting to thirty, since they'd climbed out of the ancient town of Hawes. During each major gust catching her along the steep path, all she'd been able to do was brace in position and wait it out. To lift a foot was to be sent staggering aside.

The air reminded her of home in the Pacific Northwest. Most places she'd been, the air had distinct scents. Of course, at plane crash investigation sites, it was typically the sharp tang of spilled kerosene-based fuels or the char of the fire that had followed. Thankfully, the roasted meat smell of corpses in post-crash fire typically dissipated by the time her investigation team arrived.

In Washington, DC, at NTSB Headquarters, the wind felt as if it had been breathed and rebreathed by every person from the outermost Caribbean islands and up the whole East Coast, starting at the Florida beaches. Humidity and a greasiness like too much sunscreen hung on the air—she never felt clean in DC. At home, the wind off the Pacific Ocean tasted as if it had never been breathed by anyone, scrubbed clean and born anew before sweeping down from the Gulf of Alaska.

The Dales air had that same quality, fresh and clean. No scent of ocean or grass or the sheep they had walked past. That was the other great constant aside from the wind: sheep. Thousands of them. There were no sheep here atop Great Shunner Fell, but she could see whole hillsides dotted white ranging off in every direction.

Walking around the crossed stone walls, Miranda looked in each direction to assess the countryside. Above hung a blue sky peppered with small clusters of scudding clouds, several of which had dispensed a few raindrops on them before hurrying away to the east.

At ground level to the southwest, there was a small clump of trees in a deep valley—*dale* she corrected herself. Around here they were called dales. Just as a hill was a *fell.* To her ear they sounded backwards. A dale sounded high and a fell low, but the ancient bards of Old Norse had never asked for her opinion.

Nothing but vibrant green grass-covered dales and fells were visible along the other seven points of the compass— she resisted the urge to inspect the sixteen or thirty-two points of the compass as being excessively OCD. She patted herself on the back.

"What was that one for?" Mike was the one who'd taught her to remember to congratulate herself every time she made progress on any task—but especially on living better with her own autism—with a literal pat on the back.

Andi often had to point out when she'd achieved one, but she no longer had to remind Miranda to pat her back once she understood.

"I'm working on limiting excessive observation segmentation to improve speed of capturing an overview."

"Nice," Mike offered a nod and a smile.

Holly laughed. Her laughs were always friendly, or at least Miranda had chosen to decide so when they were directed at her, and were easy to join in.

"Well done, you," Andi whispered and squeezed her hand.

Miranda scanned the more distant horizon. Nothing but more dales and fells, green below yet still brown along the tops, geometrically crisscrossed by long stretches of rock walls dividing all of it into sheep pastures. The temperature a consistent fifty-three Fahrenheit—eleven-point-six *Centigrade*. She was in England after all. But the wind, still incongruously measured in miles per hour, hadn't slackened here at the peak of Great Shunner Fell. The wind chill factor kept them well bundled up.

"Why are we here again?"

"Vacation," Andi reminded her.

"I thought you said it was so that you didn't have to go to your family law firm's hundred-and-sixtieth anniversary party. Aren't you and your mother getting along anymore?"

"No, we're fine. I guess. Finer than we've been since I was a kid, which isn't saying much. Besides, my grandmother bought out the Chens in 1952, renamed it Wu and Wu Law, and changed everything, including firing all the Chens. The whole anniversary thing is phony."

"But it's family. I don't have family anymore. Are you sure you shouldn't have gone to be with yours?"

Andi's face looked...Miranda pulled out her personal notebook and flipped to the emoji reference page...*pained?*

"We're on a vacation," Andi declared in a tone that Miranda didn't recognize but didn't feel inclined to argue with. Like it hurt Andi's throat or something.

"I've never had one of those before." Miranda tucked the notebook into the appropriate vest pocket. She'd done her best to prepare a vacation vest—based on her NTSB work vest because she had no other reference.

Some parts had converted well, like the notebooks and weather instrument. She'd brought along the Herriot Way trail guide and the OL 30 Ordnance Survey map, as well as installing it on her phone. The RSPB's bird guide and laminated quick ID card had only been marginally useful. Even with her binoculars, she'd only logged six species so far: crows, two gulls, ring-neck pheasant, blackbird, and one lone black-and-white wagtail, fishing along a stream in the first mile of the hike. Her sheep reference had only given her a single entry so far, the Swaledale with its white body and black-and-white face.

"You've never been on a vacation?" Mike squinted at her as if surprised. Or perhaps it was against the wind. It was hard to tell because of the floppy beige sunhat he wore over his dark hair. Holly wore her Matilda's Australian soccer team ball cap over her own gold-blonde, which she'd recently hacked off again to shoulder-length with the kitchen shears. Holly looked rugged as ever. Despite the floppy hat, Mike still looked as if he belonged in an upscale hip bistro...*pub.*

There were benches on the inside of each corner formed by the stone cross.

They chose the angle of the crossed walls that faced the warm sun but protected them from the wind. Wooden benches had been placed across stone supports built into the wall's structure. Mike and Holly were tall enough for their feet to touch the rocks below, she and Andi were left with their feet swinging in the air.

Miranda didn't know why *not* having a vacation would be unusual. There was always another crash, more information on a prior one, or older reports to study. The aircraft manufacturers also never stopped innovating, and each change required careful consideration and cataloging against a future investigation.

When still thirteen, she was supposed to have had a vacation, meeting her parents in Paris after her horse-riding camp was done. They'd gone ahead early but died when their plane went down.

"Well, Jon and I spent an extra forty-eight hours in Hawaii after a crash investigation, visiting the Air Force base mechanics and—"

"Not a vacay, mate." Holly's Australian accent thickened, which meant whatever she said next would be a tease. "When me and Mikey spent that week there, we spent it on the beaches—"

"And in the bedroom," Mike nudged her.

Holly nudged him back in a way that apparently meant something to the two of them. "Visited a volcano or two. Ate too much good food." She rubbed her stomach as if it yet bulged months after their trip. With Holly's workout schedule, that would be very unlikely mere *days* after their trip. She claimed it was the soldier in her who needed to always be ready to fight or fight. Apparently *flight* was not in the vocabulary of a former SASR soldier.

The top of Great Shunner Fell was at seven hundred and sixteen meters, barely a foothill to Washington State's Cascade Mountains. Her own Washington island rose to a hundred and fourteen meters if she didn't add on the fifty-meter-tall Douglas fir trees. Here atop the fell, the highest point was the head-high crisscross wall of rocks.

"I don't see any beaches, volcanoes, or places to eat food."

"This is more of a hiking vacation. And there's a pub in Keld, or at least there's a restaurant." Mike sounded less than certain.

The trip had come about because Miranda had mentioned she liked watching *All Creatures Great and Small*. She'd read all the James Herriot books, at least the parts about the animals, long before she first spoke at age six. They all watched it together. She wanted to fast forward to the animal parts on the show too, but Andi and the others had protested, leading to them watching each episode of the show in its entirety. She mostly worked on metallurgy reports during the people parts.

At times like that she missed Jeremy. Before he and Taz had left for Washington, DC, to work at NTSB headquarters and the Pentagon, she and Jeremy would often discuss technical details. Holly understood explosives and structure. Mike understood people. And Andi was an expert in helicopters and flight operations. But that left her alone when she had a technical question she wanted a second opinion on.

With Andi on the team, there'd been no need for Jeremy to remain, but that didn't stop her missing him. He would have taken solving the human-footprint-impact analysis of the hiking trail as a challenge. She looked down the path and felt...wistful?

She pulled out her emoji reference page, but none of them were labeled wistful. Besides, she didn't have a mirror to check her own expression for comparison. She tucked the notebook away.

But she'd enjoyed the television show, and Andi had decided that they should go out on Herriot's favorite walk. Now called the Herriot Way, it ran in four stages through the Yorkshire Dales, each leg—still discussed in miles, not kilometers—was twelve to thirteen miles long. The verticals were referred to in meters by most locals.

The English had a very peculiar system. Part metric and part imperial; the latter made her think of the Roman and the *Star Wars* empires at the same time. Even *she* knew that was silly—they used the Hellenic and metric systems respectively.

While still down low on the trail, they had passed occasional farms. Miranda had counted two horses, still wearing heavy winter blankets, and one small herd of seventeen cows. Sheep, especially sheep with lambs, didn't hold still long enough to even estimate a count, but it had to be in the thousands.

The lambs almost always came in twins. Perhaps a lone lamb meant another had died. The thought made her feet heavier to pick up each time she saw a lone lamb—or perhaps it was the amount of mud glued to her hiking boots.

Whenever she started to tally, she'd discover a lamb hidden by the mother. Or a whole pile of them sleeping one on the other, abruptly springing up and racing to find their mothers, bouncing more like rabbits than running.

But *no* friendly veterinarians marched over the heath, offering worried looks but friendly smiles. Not a one who she could ask questions about treating the wild sheep and deer who shared her own island.

Miranda still didn't understand the point of their vacation.

2

A COUPLE HOURS PAST SUNRISE. THE APRIL SUN HUNG ALMOST dead ahead over the eastern end of Runway 08 at RNAS Yeovilton. Commander Josh Osborne appreciated the excuse to keep his helmet's tinted visor down; he'd rather the Yanks didn't know quite how successfully they'd impressed the bloody hell out of him.

The US Navy had sent one of the CMV-22 Osprey tiltrotors to pick him up at the Royal Naval Air Station outside of Bath, England, where the Royal Navy's Fleet Air Arm was also based.

Their plan as well as his commander's? To whisk him from these gentle hills of southern England out to sea for a month embedded aboard one of their supercarriers—along with ten thousand kilos of supplies and mail. Or to make his life hell. He didn't know which, and his commander had offered little illumination.

"Hey, you outrank me, sir." US Navy Captain Dave Walsh explained as he planted Josh in the right-hand command seat. Not that Josh was close to being trained to fly one of these. Dave bumped the copilot from the left-hand seat back to the observer's jump seat but remained the pilot-in-command—at least Josh bloody well hoped so or the Royal and US Navies would be writing very sad letters to all their respective parents in the immediate future.

Somewhere in the back, a pair of loadmaster / side-gunners were probably playing a fierce game of Happy Families or whatever cards young Yanks played. They had to be at least eighteen, but they both looked like they were twelve. He refused to let that make him feel grumpy in his late thirties. Of course it was hard to embrace such a mood with the prospect of flying, in any aircraft, on such a lovely day.

"I've been nineteen years flying Her, and now His Majesty's finest helicopters. A decent helo has nothing to do with this Osprey." Josh's protest was ignored.

He now sat in a strange land where everything fit like a slightly strange yet well-worn set of football kit—he'd been the top-pick goalie back at the Royal Naval College. Except these Yanks had slipped a raucous Hawaiian shirt over his head when he wasn't looking. It was still a shirt. It still had buttons. But it made no sense in the real world.

His gray AW101 Merlin was the heavy lifter of the entire Fleet Air Arm. And his baby maxed out at a third of the load and half the speed of this beast.

"Ready for the fun?" Dave Walsh asked once they were cycled up and had received clearance from the tower. Josh's helmet dampened the six-thousand-horsepower turboshaft engine roaring away a half dozen meters out his right window—down to the contented background hum of a rabid dog about to break his leash.

"Bring it on." Looking upward, he could see the flat

whirling disk of the massive starboard rotor. The engine was pointed at the sky and the... "What do you call those damned things anyway?"

"A proprotor, one word," Dave laughed. "And I can't believe that's your first question."

"Believe it," one of his young niece's favorite phrases—one he was rather proud of teaching her much to his sister's dismay.

It earned him the laugh it always earned her. Perhaps not the best lesson to reinforce in a precocious five-year-old, but that wasn't going to stop him egging her on. It was an uncle's duty to make his little sister's life as tough as possible. The boys would never be ready for Dori the Warrior Princess when she started First Year in a few months.

The *proprotor* was spinning overhead like a lethal twelve-meter-wide umbrella. Two of them if he looked out Dave's side.

"Hand on the TCL," Dave pointed at the...*thing* by his left hand. So absolutely *Hawaiian-shirt* wrong.

Every helicopter he'd ever flown had two hand controls: the cyclic placed between his knees for the right hand to control, the collective mounted to the left side of the seat like a car's pull-up parking brake. The first controlled the direction of flight with a bit of help from the rudders, the second the bite of the blades—up on the collective equaled more lift and a faster climb. Then tip the cyclic forward to turn the climb into forward flight.

No collective.

Not even when he looked down at his left hand flailing about to find it.

In its place, the TCL, Thrust Control Lever, was mounted on a fore-aft slider in front of the left armrest. The head of the control, instead of being a mass of buttons on the head of a stick, form-fit his hand like the perfect video game controller with the additional keys at his fingertips.

The aircraft didn't even smell right. His Merlin had seen a decade aloft, much of it on anti-submarine patrols with the occasional search-and-rescue or transport mission thrown in. The scent of sea, sweat, and the occasional splash of hydraulic oil had penetrated it like a medal for valorous duty.

Not new, but this bird smelled like...a freshly starched and ironed Hawaiian shirt. Spotless like no working bird should ever be.

"I know. I know." Dave must have seen his face; never should have raised his tinted visor to look around. "VIP transport last week. Three-star admiral came out to the boat. Long talks with the Old Man."

In anyone's Navy, Old Man meant the one-star admiral in charge of the strike group.

"You'll never guess who drew the short straw."

Which they both knew meant that Josh's team were the carrier's A-crew—not that anyone in any service, British or Yank, would admit to such a trite emotion as pride under the circumstances.

"No need to melt your runway..." Dave nodded to Josh's left hand, "roll the thumbwheel forward to initiate proprotor transition."

That was a real problem with the design of the Osprey—one of many things he didn't like about the bird. He wondered for the tenth time if that's why he'd drawn this assignment, his well-known distrust of the aircraft. Had someone chosen him to make sure this evaluation failed? Focusing on being impartial didn't help. Something else would have to get him through this, which he had a month to find.

The tiltrotor concept aimed the proprotors aloft like side-by-side helo rotors, one at the end of each wing. Then, once aloft, they tilted them forward so that the Osprey flew like an airplane—one with ludicrously large propellors. When still on the ground they were far too big to start facing forward. But they could be partly tilted, enough to gain some forward momentum, without battering the blades against the ground like the world's most expensive trench-digger.

The Bell Boeing design didn't hinge the proprotor itself. Instead, they'd mounted the engine at the very end of the wing and rotated the whole engine-proprotor assembly. Therefore, during VTOL—vertical takeoff-and-landing—operations, the rotor and engine were aimed straight up. This aimed the blazing hot engine exhaust straight down. In the early days, it had melted runways, started grass fires during field landings, and even warped the decks of several aircraft carriers before they learned ways to mitigate that.

Initially, they'd had to put down thick steel plates any time an Osprey wanted to land. Now, when down, the engines were programmed to oscillate a few degrees back and forth so as not to melt the metal decks of ships. Over tar, the answer was to ramp up power *after* you were already in motion. He still didn't know how they didn't start grass fires when landing in the rough.

Josh nudged the knurled knob under his left thumb forward for half a second. The machine responded to the tiny motion of his thumb by angling the seven-meter-long engine—topped by the spinning twelve-meter proprotor—forward about five degrees. Another half second, another five degrees, and she began to roll. He *could* get to like this. A

Merlin's collective gave no such sense of childhood superhero dreams come true.

"I am become a Viking God." He and Sis had done one of those genetic tests and learned they were about half Viking. Sis had insisted she was Norse, not Viking—a trader not a farmer-warrior. Josh only had to point to his niece to refute that, ready to wield the full power of her beribboned fairy wand at the least chance.

Josh had worn his blond hair Viking-long until Britannia Royal Naval College had shaved it close. He'd even managed —leveraging a little underhanded dealing with a school rival who thought it was a put-down—to get tagged with *Viking* for a call sign.

"Viking God, you say?" Dave laughed. "Odin or—"

"Thor. I bring not only the hammer and the lightning, I bring the thunder! Check the helmet." He pointed at the image on the side of his flight helmet, a Viking helm with a lightning bolt slicing between the sharp-tipped horns.

"You want thunder? Feed some power and you'll feel that for real."

All of his instincts said to pull up on the left-hand control, but there was no *up*. Dave gave him a clue by nudging his interlinked TCL forward ever so slightly.

With a bitter moment of chagrin not befitting Thor in the least, Josh continued the motion. The blades shifted their angle to bite the air more deeply, and she began to roll down the runway. The aircraft might weigh fifty-five thousand kilos for this trip, but it lifted with the ease he'd expect from a lightweight training bird.

"Continue to roll the thumbwheel forward and keep easing in the power."

Josh did. It was a single coordinated motion that felt completely natural.

By the time he thought to look down, they were already past midfield and gaining altitude fast. The outer marker was there and gone so fast it made his head spin. A thousand rotorcraft departures from this field hadn't prepared him for how fast the Osprey left it all behind.

Twelve seconds flat had turned the up-pointing helicopter rotors into forward-aimed airplane propellors. Proprotor indeed. Shuffling aloft at two hundred-and-fifty knots—already a hundred faster than his Merlin's top speed —and climbing like a house afire? He *had* become the Thunder God. *Take that, Ironman.*

"Bloody hell, Yank." He knew why the Fleet Air Arm had given these birds a pass fifteen years ago. In their infancy, the teething problems had been horrendous, frustrating mechanics and killing too many pilots. Now? Perhaps he was getting a taste for Hawaiian shirts. "You're going to ruin me for life."

"You said it, brother. Ready to defect to the Colonies?"

"If you can guarantee me a seat in one of these lovely birds, we'll have to talk."

Dave laughed aloud, then called out an altitude and heading. The transition from helo to fixed-wing flight had been both effortless and notably efficient.

The advantages of both in a single aircraft wasn't playing fair. Josh reminded himself that he hated and mistrusted these things. He'd lay down a fiver with the bookmaker that the Osprey merely chose to bide its time before killing him.

"Control is yours."

"I have control," Josh responded, pleased that he didn't squeak like his young niece. In addition to having a warrior's confidence, Dori was the age where nothing was merely delightful, it was always super-cali-fantastical delightful. She lived in a world of rainbow-unicorn wonder no matter how mundane the moment. Someday he'd find the right lady and they'd have a Dori of their own. *Sooner rather than later* he sent a quick prayer to Odin the Father God before focusing back on the feel of the Osprey—though Odin had been an inconstant bastard. Maybe...

With the hydraulic controls, it was very light to the touch with only minimal feedback to the pilot. He would never admit to his relief that Dave kept his hands riding on the controls, lightly but there.

Still, putatively controlling the Osprey was seriously squeal-worthy.

A helicopter was often described as "a hundred thousand parts that just happened to be flying in the same direction"—and they felt that way. Always juddering about like awkward teenage males at their first dance.

In forward flight, all of that smoothed out and this girl ripped ahead like Freyja, Norse Goddess of War and Beauty, while bearing a serious grudge. Even Odin messed with her at his own peril.

As they slid northeast over the Cotswolds at fifteen thousand feet climbing to twenty-five, Dave talked him through standard flight and emergency procedures, a comfortably familiar pastime among pilots. They blasted high above his hometown of York. Josh's Viking ancestors had turned the large town into a key trading center over a thousand years ago—and lost it a century later, leaving a *lot* of half- and full-blood Viking farmers and their babies scattered all over Yorkshire.

He waggled the Osprey's wings to wave at his sister. She

wouldn't see, of course, but he'd promised he always would every time he flew this way. The body motion felt wrong during the wave. In a helicopter, the body of the helo swung a little side-to-side like a pendulum under the rotors. In this contraption, he was at the center of rotation. He lodged a complaint with Dave, which led to a discussion of flight characteristics during transition modes from helo to airplane and back.

At a cruising altitude of twenty-five thousand feet, they followed the direction of his retreating kinsmen out over the North Sea.

"Where's your boat?" Josh hadn't thought to look up where the US Carrier Strike Groups were.

"The USS *Gerald R. Ford* is off Stavanger, Norway."

A hard four-hour flight in his Merlin, most of it over water—which was never a comfortable place to be in a helicopter. The Osprey would knock it out in under two.

The next thought? Far less comfortable and had nothing to do with the Osprey or his Merlin.

The Yanks had eleven of those fearsome aircraft carriers.

Britain's second one had failed shortly after commissioning while trying to cross the Atlantic to visit the Yanks for a training exercise. Even now it remained in drydock eight months later while they replaced the bent propellor shaft and all the damage that had caused. Bloody *Prince of Wales*. He'd never been a fan of the now King, a leftover from a childhood crush on Princess Di and his mum's devastation at her death.

He kept his mouth shut on that point; graduates of Britannia Royal Naval College weren't supposed to be staunch Republicans. The more vocal anti-monarchists in the service often tangled with the upper ranks who'd proudly served a lifetime under the Queen—tangled and lost. Outside of the family house and the voting booth, he kept his politics to himself.

The Yanks rotated their eleven carriers through nine Carrier Strike Groups—the other two passing through phases of scheduled maintenance. A CSG was a daunting collection of missile cruisers, destroyers, submarines, and an entire Air Wing. But they only sent those CSGs into the world's hotspots, three always around North Korea and Taiwan, another one or two off the South China Sea, and another in the Eastern Med.

What the hell was the newest and most powerful of those boats doing in the North Sea? And one of the Yanks' vice admirals had just paid a visit to the boat? That coincidence wasn't some friendly inspection tour.

An old itch said that evaluating the Ospreys might be the least of his worries on this assignment.

3

"Again?" Captain Natalia Ivanovna's attempt to not sound bitter failed even to her own ears when the flight engineer called out the reason for an ordered course correction.

"Again, Captain." Senior Lieutenant Viktor Arsenyev had been with her long enough to not take offense or threaten to report her to the Gromovo Air Base commander for unseemly behavior—again. His tall console directly behind her seat kept them from exchanging meaningful glances.

She cocked a hand out into the area between the pilot seats where he'd be able to see it and made a flat-palmed tapping motion as if her throat was there. *Fed up with that to here!*

Natalia could hear Viktor's double chest-thump over the intercom, *Truth.*

She was less sure of their new copilot seated to her right. Three weeks aboard, Lieutenant Sergei Balakin had yet to speak one word that wasn't required. Yet every time he didn't think she was looking, she'd caught him staring at her. Why couldn't she keep a copilot past a few months?

Natalia was used to the stare. A woman pilot in the Russian Air Force was rare. One with bright red hair billowing down to her chest was a startling oddity. But there was something else in his look that said maybe he was a spy sent to catch the day she crossed the line.

Or perhaps he was one of her father's spies. His role high in the *oligarkhi* had protected her this long but it also made her a target. Party power no longer counted to any but the unseemly masses. The modern currencies of success in the Russian Federation were wealth, power, and having a nose of the color brown, as the Americans called it. Her father's had been rammed up the President's behind probably since he'd had to open the man's diapers to do it.

Of course, she'd never be stupid enough to say that out loud, because there was no safety in Russia since the time when Rurik had first ruled Ancient Rus' twelve hundred years ago. Instead, she'd walked away from the life of parties and politics—to which she was being groomed as little more than a prize for whatever grand connection Father wished to forge with her life and body.

She'd taken her mother's maiden name and the Air Force had taken her in. Changing her name couldn't hide who she was, which had one advantage: until her family fell out of favor and was forced to flee, she remained untouchable. Mostly. The base commander remained very cautious of her connections—not a big fan.

Not that she blamed him. She wasn't spoiled—gods, she'd seen enough oh-so-groomed daughters to not ever be that. But a sense of humor held a high-level risk factor in the service of the Motherland.

"I wonder if that's why they always send me."

"Why what?" Balakin had control of the plane and was following the new vector that Viktor had given them, not that the Antonov AN-74MP Cheburashka needed much attention. The airplane's resemblance, with its close-aboard engines on the high wing, to the big-eared cartoon character made the nickname unavoidable. The recent release of the most successful film in Russian history—named for Cheburashka—only reenforced how annoying everyone could be about her sweet plane. The crass Americans, with no understanding of the subtleties of...anything, had called her sweet bird the Coaler, like a dumping truck.

She'd love a chance to show them what the MP stood for. Marine Patrol meant she also carried a twin-barrel twenty-three-millimeter autocannon. And the AN-74 meant she was the Artic capable version of the AN-72. But for the moment it wasn't the Americans who held her attention.

That simple question, *Why what?,* was perhaps the first time Balakin had spoken without a direct question. His flight hours were painfully low, below typical for even a junior officer. He was automaton perfect in every maneuver, like a beginner terrified of making a mistake, but had no feel for the aircraft. She wondered how that perfection of flight-school skills would survive a real-world test.

Like her own flight instructor, she actually worked to train those behind her to be better pilots—instead of the more common practice of hogging all the flight hours to herself. Only time would tell her Balakin's weaknesses.

Command, of course, never treated a weakness as a training opportunity, but rather as a weapon to hold over a pilot's head. She was sick of the games. Fed up with the superior officers of inferior intellect. Annoyed that they never let her near one of their precious combat jets. Just...*done.* Fine! She threw caution to the wind and spoke the truth for a change.

"They always send me for their stupidest games. Maybe it is because I play games well or—"

"You scare them to death," Balakin said over the intercom.

She traded a surprised silence with Viktor. Balakin *never* offered an opinion on anything.

"Me? How do I scare the Americans?" An Antonov AN-74MP simply wasn't that scary a plane. Useful, yes. Scary?

"Us. The Russians. It's your father."

Everyone knew who he was, of course. They weren't supposed to, but if a low-ranker like Balakin knew, then everyone probably did. Secrets sold faster than vareniki in Russia.

"They keep waiting for you to use him like a hammer and anvil, and you keep not doing it. That makes you terrifying. If you can control that urge every time they give you a crappy assignment or a stupid order, what would happen to them if they *do* cross some line with you?"

"So, they send me to scare the Americans why?" They'd been ordered to do a close flyby of a US Navy flight. At some point Russia would finally plumb the depths of the Americans' patience and get swatted down for doing it.

"You're the scariest thing in our commanders' lives— worse than their wives meeting their mistresses. I don't even think it is conscious. They get the order to spook the Americans and the first pilot to come to mind is—"

"That Natalia Ivanovna girl with the powerful father. If we're lucky, the Americans will shoot her down for us."

Balakin briefly bobbled the flight controls. If her hand

hadn't been following his flight on the linked yokes, she might have missed it, but it was there. The first sign there was more than the flying robot he chose to show. Anything short of being shot should never transmit as much to the controls; it was a sign of his inexperience.

Didn't think of that, did you, Balakin? Flying with me puts you in the line of direct fire.

"What do *you* think?" She raised her voice in question.

There was a shrug's worth of silence from Viktor.

"If you're shrugging back there, Viktor, I can't see it." She was half tempted to release her harness and lean out far enough over the central console to look back at him. Maybe offer a gesture questioning his manhood.

"A shrug is as good an answer as I have." His tone implied much more; that it might be something deeper.

Was Balakin setting a trap? Natalia couldn't ask Viktor's opinion on that over the open intercom. She removed her hand from the yoke, no longer liking the connection to the unknown beside her.

Did Lieutenant Sergei Balakin hope to entice her to speak ill of command or Russia in general so that he could report it and ruin her to promote his own career? All those stupid political maneuverings. That's why she'd run away from home to join the Air Force; well, that and the flying. She *loved* the flying. Now if she could find a man who fit her even half as well as her Cheburashka...

"How long?" she asked for a subject change.

"Direct target acquisition in one-five minutes," Victor reported.

Balakin's tone was wry as he added, "That's if the reported satellite tracking is even a little accurate for once."

Natalia twisted to inspect him. Joking and disloyal to the

Party? Was it possible her new *robotizirovanny* copilot was human after all?

He kept his attention carefully on the flying.

Fly more, worry less?

Da, that was a fantasy life she'd never achieve.

She kept her attention on Balakin. "What's your sad story?"

4

Sergei Balakin knew exactly why Natalia Ivanovna terrified him. And *that* defined his sad story.

He had been a nobody at Lomonosov School where most of the Moscow elite attended; Natalia had been the czarina. The volleyball captain driving the team to league victory four years in a row. There wasn't a male in the entire school who missed a chance to watch her win the school track meets with her long legs and her hair streaming behind like she was sticking a giant red tongue out at all the runners who couldn't keep up.

That her father was one of the President's closest advisors only added to the mystique.

Balakin had paid numerous bribes to be assigned to her plane. Rather than paying commanders, which would drive the price up, he paid other copilots to ask for transfers until the position was labeled as cursed. The bribe cost fell precipitously over time. When he'd—grudgingly—agreed to take the seat, his commander had been so smug about finding someone for the *cursed* position of Balakin's own creation that he'd half expected his commander to bribe *him*.

Balakin knew that he'd never be worthy of such a woman, but right now he was the one who served with her and that was worth any price. Her mastery in the air—even in the unassuming Cheburashka patrol airplane—shone fire-bright. She was a flame that drew him as undeniably as any moth.

Natalia might think that flybys on the Americans were mundane, but it was his first.

He swallowed against a dry throat and monitored the radar. No sign of anything. Perhaps Moscow *had* gotten the Americans' vector wrong, he could always hope.

5

AFTER TWO YEARS AS THE LEAD IMAGERY INTELLIGENCE analyst—IMINT—at Menwith Hill, Ian Faulkner didn't need the alarm to notice the course change of the Antonov AN-74. Any Russian flight that passed west of Helsinki was automatically tracked by the NRO's satellites.

The National Reconnaissance Office had more birds in orbit than all other global intelligence services combined. And the bulk of those were tracked through the three big intelligence sites: Buckley Space Force Base in Colorado, Joint Defence Facility Pine Gap in the Australian Outback, and Royal Air Force Menwith Hill here in the Yorkshire dales. Each had dozens of radio dishes, safe inside giant geodesic domes like great white orbs scattered on the heath, aimed at the satellites—both friendly and not—watching the world's communications up above.

Despite their pretty names, they were all owned and run by the Americans' National Security Agency. The NSA called all the shots, which had included Ian's own assignment to the UK.

Up until now, the Russian plane had been flying an unremarkable route. They'd eventually emerged west out of the Baltic after a careful slalom course between Danish, Swedish, and Norwegian air space. This far from home, they were either on a training run or hurrying some hardware out to yet another broken submarine. Since the collapse of the Soviet Union, flight training had fallen to miserable levels to conserve fuel and aging aircraft.

He'd been following the Antonov's passage with occasional check-ins in case it turned out to be another reactor meltdown or a drifting ship that would eventually need a tow—but only after Russia once again proved their inability to service their own fleet in distress.

After holding steady out to sea for twenty minutes, the aircraft altered its heading by thirty-seven degrees to the south.

A quick scan of assets in the area answered why.

They hadn't turned toward the USS *Gerald R. Ford's* carrier group, which lay almost due north of the Antonov's westerly emergence from the Baltic Sea. Instead, they were headed southwest, on an intercept course with a Navy COD flight. Carrier On-board Delivery aircraft had never been the target of a Russian flyby before that Ian had ever heard.

"SIGINT, IMINT," Ian called out over the headset.

The Menwith Hill Ops Floor included the leads for each area of operations. In other rooms, each of them had a team monitoring every aspect of information gathered by the US and UK intelligence satellites. Technically Canada's, New Zealand's, and Australia's as well, but those were few and far between in orbit. The Five Eyes Alliance depended heavily on its two primary members.

Among the leads on the floor, they ran an open intercom, which included the Mission Director.

"SIGINT," Verity responded from two seats to his right on the middle arc of desks. She had one of those lovely West Country accents that impossibly made even Signals Intelligence sound sexy. It was always a pleasure to listen to, even if she was plumpish and happily married with three teenage kids.

"Any transmissions related to Russian flight currently tracking…" he read out the coordinates and heading.

The Mission Director glanced toward him from her desk in the middle of the floor. Like NASA's Mission Control, the desks were arranged in three long arcs behind her. To the front, there was a massive central screen with multiple slightly smaller displays to either side.

Astrid was actually the Chief of Facility, the top National Security Administration person in the UK. Where was David anyway? The normal Mission Director was a no-show today. Sick, reassigned, or locked up for some violation of site security? Mere operators would never know if it was the last of those. Then he remembered: a very pregnant wife. Wouldn't it be nice if today some good news hit the Ops Floor for once.

The MD's glance was enough of a question.

Ian explained. "Antonov AN-74MP Coaler, Russian designation Cheburashka, altered course sixty seconds ago to direct intercept course with CMV-22 Osprey Number Three-four-one out of RNAS Yeovilton bound for USS *Gerald R. Ford.*"

She nodded. No need to respond, but she'd be keeping an eye on it now. He flipped the tracking onto a front screen about the same time SIGINT replied.

"I have a course-change order confirmation from the AN-74," Verity announced with that voice of hers. Ian *really* needed to get out more. But with the protocols of a Menwith Hill security clearance, that was a royal pain. By the third date, the lady would have to submit to a seriously intrusive background check—not exactly a charming icebreaker with civilian women.

Despite his two years at the desk, Ian couldn't resist flipping the surveillance satellite tracking on his third monitor. The Orion satellite, USA-311, was the largest in orbit by any nation. The three-hundred-and-fifty-foot diameter radio dish currently flew thirty-five thousand kilometers above them in geostationary orbit. Even from there, it could pick up a cell phone signal that wouldn't reach a cell tower thirty kilometers away. This morning it had been tasked with monitoring the area around the *Ford's* carrier group.

A glance at the log made him wonder how in the hell Verity and her team managed to sort through all that noise. It had gathered an immense amount of chatter from the carrier group itself. Most of the rest of today's information were location pings from various shipping and a mess of—very slow—ship-to-shore cruise line chatter. From all that noise, they and the supercomputers had plucked out the Antonov's reply to their new orders.

He waited. The next part wasn't merely magic, it was outright alchemy as far as he was concerned.

Thirty seconds later, Verity was back. Somehow, one of the big radio dishes here at Menwith Hill had been monitoring the correct Russian satellite at the correct time. The original order had been located, decrypted, translated, and Verity now read it out.

"The Antonov has been ordered to alter course to

intercept and shadow the Osprey flight. Full text is on your screens."

Ian clicked the icon that popped up a window. The encrypted gibberish, the decrypted Russian, then the translated English. He read the Russian more out of habit than any doubt of Verity's translation.

He looked up the Osprey's command frequency and keyed the mike.

Less than two minutes had passed since the original course change issued by the Russians.

6

"CHARLIE MIKE VICTOR TWO-TWO THREE-FOUR-ONE."

"Three-four-one," Dave answered the radio call with the CMV-22 Osprey's tail number.

Josh found it a little curious that the operator didn't identify himself on the radio. He whispered his question back to the copilot.

"Not normal," Dave whispered back because they were all on the same intercom. Now he was appearing foolish in front of the Yanks, and Josh liked that even less.

"Tracking in-bound Alpha-Nancy Seven-four Marine Patrol. Range eight-zero and on intercept your position from six-four degrees in one-seven minutes."

Josh tried to remember the last time he'd heard about an AN-74MP Cheburashka transport plane out this way. The Chebbie was fifteen hundred kilometers from the nearest Russian air base. The only reason they came out to the North Sea was for an urgent drop to a Russian sub or ship.

"Intentional?" Dave asked the unidentified dispatcher.

"Roger. Altered course zero-two minutes ago and settled

on course for direct intercept. Origin..." there was a fast clatter of keys "...looks to have been Gromovo Air Base."

Josh stared hard at the radio. It had taken the operator mere seconds to trace the origin of a flight fifteen hundred kilometers from its base. He glanced west.

They were far enough out over the North Sea for land to be out of sight, but a boy didn't grow up tramping through the Yorkshire Dales and not know about Menwith Hill and its two sister stations. The three sites, and their dozens of giant radio antennas, controlled and monitored all the West's spy satellites—and most of the East's. Everything from cell phone traffic to, he consciously unclenched his jaw when his tongue began throbbing, unscheduled flybys.

Neither Dave nor the copilot had looked to the West. It wasn't his place to start talking about RAF Menwith Hill.

"Toward *me?*" Dave asked the Menwith operator. Russians shadowed missile cruisers and destroyers, not Osprey tiltrotors.

"'Fraid so," the operator unwound enough to reply.

"Understood, keep advised, Three-four-one out."

"Will do. Out."

Dave frowned at the radio as if trying to solve who had called him.

"What's up?" Josh had followed the content of the call well enough. Even though he knew the origin, the content didn't make a whole lot of sense. "An AN-74MP, really?"

"That is a little odd," Dave admitted. "Usually if they're going to do a close flyby, the Russians use a Sukhoi fighter or one of their monster bombers to appear intimidating. I've heard of Coalers flying alongside some of our radio trawlers, but not much else. And as far as I know, the Ruskies never harassed an Osprey before and not with a patrol aircraft. But she's the AN-74MP variant, has a 23 mm twin-barreled autocannon, so let's not piss her off."

"I'll try to remember that. And it's *he*," Josh corrected. "Russians call their planes and ships *he.*"

Dave rolled his eyes but didn't argue.

"How far to the carrier when they catch up to us?"

"Still another two hundred klicks. I didn't think we were inside the carrier group's awareness range yet, but we must be."

Nope, but they were in Menwith Hill's, which was global.

"Definitely not in the hundred-kilometer no-fly zone around the carrier yet," Dave mused aloud. "Normally we don't enforce that but the disaster in Ukraine has us at DEFCON 3, so we're a little jumpy."

"DEFCON 3? Your Air Force is set to fully mobilize in under fifteen minutes?"

"Navy, too. Whole European theater and North Pacific. Ever since Russia put nukes on the table in their fucking Special Military Operation. Then add in the Chinese wargames around Taiwan and the South China Sea—those could be a weekly spectator sport. And North Korea's boss who thinks his tiny prick can be replaced by stuffing a bigger nuke in his pants. I tell you, it's nuts out there. So don't mess with us right now, Josh." He kept his tone light though Josh could see by the set of his jaw quite how pissed the pilot felt.

"Sure thing, Dave. I'll just give the PM a jingle at Number 10 and let her know. What about them?" Josh nodded off to the northeast where the Russians were inbound. Unlike a helo, in airplane mode the CMV-22 didn't skitter aside with his merest body motion.

That killed Dave's friendly smile. "Never been a part of one of these flybys. *Ford* will have a couple of fighters up just in case they try to get closer. We once let a bomber come within ten klicks of one of our carriers, but that was three years ago. They played it like good PR back home at how close they'd gotten to our boat, never mentioned the three F/A-18 Super Hornets we had wrapped around her...sorry, *his* ass. Included a SIGINT Growler who stripped every bit of data and capabilities out of their system without them noticing. What happens if they try that at DEFCON 3? Way above this boy's pay grade. I have no idea."

"Standard protocol?"

"Straight and level, brother. Straight and level." Dave slid his hands back on the controls, which he'd removed earlier without Josh noticing. That was fine with him.

7

"I HAVE NEVER SEEN ONE EXCEPT IN PICTURES," BALAKIN announced over the intercom.

Natalia wasn't impressed. As oddly cute as her AN-74MP looked, the CMV-22 Osprey still looked ridiculous in comparison. A tiny wing supporting huge propellors off to the sides? More like their Mickey Mouse than the mighty raptor bird it was named for—and that mouse was never as cute as Cheburashka.

That an aircraft barely half the size of hers could carry the same payload was annoying. At least she could outpace it; having three times the range made her feel a little better too.

The Americans had showed no reaction to their arrival, flying straight on. One pilot had done little more than glance in her direction as if thoroughly bored. The other had watched and waved. He didn't smile but he waved. She returned the gesture.

Up here we're all just pilots. Only down there are our commanders so crazy.

They flew close enough for Natalia to see that the side of his helmet sported a Viking helm complete with tall horns. *That's* what she needed. Not some party hack vying for her father's favor, but rather a fellow warrior. Of course, he was probably a loser-boy *rogatii kozyol* from New York City, suffering from delusions of manhood while his wife cheated on him.

"Video is running?"

"Yes, Captain," Viktor replied.

"Balakin, do a slow circle horizontally and vertically. Not directly in front or behind." Neither aircraft wanted to eat the other's turbulence.

"Understood." He didn't push back at her beginner's instruction, which spoke to his nerves matching hers—or his lack of meaningful flight experience.

They'd arrived to the right of the Osprey, giving Natalia the best initial view. Now Balakin swung under so that they were looking up at the aircraft's belly, then to the port side.

From below, she could see the joints where the wings could be folded up so that it could be stored in the smallest space on an aircraft carrier. Not an MV-22, but the carrier-modified CMV-22. She didn't think one of these had been photographed this close before. But that meant there was one of those monstrous American aircraft carriers about. Command hadn't seen fit to mention that lethal detail.

Shadow the Osprey. But how long? Until she was in the carrier's gunsights?

It was the first time in eight years of flying that she might rather be at one of Father's parties, being assessed like a heifer at a cattle auction by his fellow *oligarkhi* seeking to tuck her into their beds. Pigs! The same ones who would happily order her little plane into the lion's jaw without giving her decent orders or warning of the risks. *"Zhri govno i zdohni!"*

"What did I do?" Balakin twisted to look at her.

He wasn't the one she wanted to snort his own shit and die. It was her father's...

Then Lieutenant Balakin's inexperience revealed itself in all its horrid glory.

Beyond his shoulder, she could only watch as her AN-74MP slid to starboard in reaction to him twisting his hands to support the turning of his body. Not much. A single wingspan. Thirty meters. A distance she could run in four seconds, a sliding drift of a half a heartbeat at five hundred kilometers an hour. A span they covered before her hands were halfway from her lap to the yoke.

They'd have been okay if it was a normal airplane. No more than a wing tap.

Except the Osprey was not normal at all.

That big rotor, propellor, whatever the hell the Americans called it, stuck six meters past the end of the wing like a giant sawmill blade. The entire plane shuddered with the pounding vibration like an out-of-balance clothes washer the size of a building.

A blast of shattering steel filled the cockpit as the propellor sliced into their wingtip.

If the propellor rotated from the bottom up, it would have slammed their wing upward and they'd have naturally turned away from the Osprey. But it didn't, the outer tips rotated from the top down to the outside.

The impact drove their Cheburashka's starboard wing down. As the wing dipped, it forced them to turn further into the Osprey's flight path.

8

_____

"I HAVE CONTROL!" DAVE TOOK IMMEDIATE COMMAND, NOT waiting for Josh's acknowledgement of giving up control.

Looking at Dave let Josh stare out the window beyond the American pilot. The portside proprotor was pounding against the wing of the Antonov airplane with a truly thunderous roar of abused metal. The lashing split open a fuel tank, which began spilling prodigious amounts of TS-1 jet fuel.

He winced instinctively but couldn't look away.

Helicopter rotors were hard and stiff. When they broke, they shattered and threw large shards outward in a lethal sweep toward anyone in the vicinity. But with the proprotors aimed forward like propellors, they would heave those shards into the fuselage of their own aircraft rather than spewing them outward overhead like a deadly umbrella.

Only when they didn't immediately die did he recall that the designers had specifically designed the proprotors to shred rather than shatter for that reason.

Emergency procedures, he reminded himself. They'd

just been reviewing them. The Osprey could fly on one engine, but he couldn't recall if it could fly on one proprotor.

That was the second thing he hated about the design of these aircraft, the wing was tiny, slender and utterly dependent on a lot of airspeed to create lift. Nothing was going to make these birds glide to a graceful landing with a survival rate above one in a thousand.

"Feather Proprotor One," Dave called out.

Josh grabbed for the control and pulled it back, not that there was much left to feather.

With the portside forward thrust neutralized, the still spinning starboard proprotor drove the right wing ahead. It's forward drive, now all on the right side, twisted them to the left and into the Antonov. No one had ever thought of this scenario when creating those emergency procedures. He grabbed for the feather control on the starboard proprotor— far too late.

The Osprey pithed itself on the Russian plane's battered and leaking wing hard enough for Josh to lose his focus as his neck was nearly snapped by the force. The Ukrainian-designed aircraft was stout. Rather than crumpling, the robust wing spars punched into their Osprey's still running portside turboshaft engine.

The impact crumpled the containment casing into the engine's fan blades. Spinning at twenty-one thousand rpm, the titanium-alloy compressor fans shattered. The damage to the Osprey engine's safety housing proved too drastic to stop the spray of fan-blade fragments. Like a great circular shotgun blast, ten times worse than any shredded proprotor blade, the fragments fired outward in all directions.

Josh regained awareness in time to see the copilot seated in the jump seat die instantly.

Captain Dave Walsh's body shielded Josh, but his hands slid off the controls as he set about the serious business of bleeding out from a hundred impacts and lacerations.

Under the influence of a massive adrenal rush, Josh didn't notice the dozen small cuts and injuries he'd sustained.

On the opposite side of the engine, the same spray of shattered titanium fan blades sliced into the Antonov like the pounding of a large-caliber machine gun. The blinding fire that the blast sparked in the AN-74's fuel stream was the least of the problems.

Flight Engineer Viktor Arsenyev also died instantly. The Osprey's Rolls Royce engine flung only one fan blade into the forward cockpit of the Antonov. It removed the last hopes of Senior Lieutenant Balakin's fantasy of bedding Natalia Ivanovna, slicing through the top of his right thigh, castrating him, then embedding into his left thigh—it was never going to happen anyway.

Natalia attempted to swing the Antonov free, but the right wingtip had caught on the Osprey's left engine frame.

Josh remembered his hand on the feather control for the starboard proprotor, but he had missed the chance of any meaningful action. It still drove ahead at full power, dragging the Osprey into a tight turn even as he backed it off.

Still moving at over three hundred miles an hour, the two aircraft pivoted together around their snagged wingtips like a pair of scissor blades swinging around the central bolt.

For a brief moment, as the noses of the two aircraft swung together, Josh came face-to-face with an utterly stunning redhead, whose eyes were probably as wide as his. The very image of Freyja the Goddess of War—the embodiment of all his dreams.

Almost close enough to touch, they cried out in unison as the forward-looking radars and comm equipment mounted in the nose of both aircraft were driven into their respective cockpits by the force of the head-on impact. Heavy structural frames crumpled across both their legs.

In some instinctual form of desperation, they reached out for each other before their aircraft finally tumbled apart.

The last one alive on the Osprey, Josh fought the controls all the way down. But his instincts didn't have the right training to change dive into glide during his thirty-one second fall toward the frigid North Sea. The safe glide parameters of the heavy-loaded Osprey and the slender wings required a precise airspeed and angle of attack, but they hadn't gotten to that emergency procedure yet. He tried —but the correct answer was *not* spinning out of control at three hundred knots with no rudder control because of his pinned legs.

Nothing much larger than his Viking-emblazoned helmet remained after impacting the ocean.

Natalia could barely see through the pain of her crushed legs, but she was in a wholly familiar aircraft and the instincts that had made her a masterful pilot continued to function. She fought her way out of the spin, without rudder pedals, and managed to stabilize in something approximating straight-and-level flight.

Radar and autopilot gone, she turned east. Toward the sun still east over the horizon.

Across the Baltic.

Home.

It was the only thought she could hold through the agony.

Despite the damage, no arteries had been cut. If she

could land the plane, her life might be saved, though there was no hope for her legs. It felt as if every bone from her knees down had been shattered—an accurate assessment.

It was fourteen seconds before she recalled the flaming wingtip—*her* flaming wingtip.

Natalia grabbed air where the Engine Two fire extinguisher handle normally hung overhead. The cockpit's deformation had moved it. Her vision, tunneled by the pain, couldn't spot it.

The starboard fuel-tank cutoff valve had also made a journey of its own to lands unknown.

Natalia flew on, mesmerized by the flames erupting from her plane. She maintained level flight by aligning the burning wingtip with the thin line where blue met blue, ocean to sky. Her mind remained incapable of more.

Sixty-two seconds later, nine kilometers from the collision site, the AN-74MP Cheburashka was struck by an AIM-120 *Slammer* AMRAAM—Advanced Medium-Range Air-to-Air Missile. Fired at a range of eighty kilometers by an F-35C Lightning II fighter jet launched from the *Gerald R. Ford* super carrier, the missile was traveling at Mach 4 when it reached her plane.

The twenty-kilo warhead was unnecessary. Her right wing exploded in flames an instant before the missile's warhead detected a sufficiently close approach and triggered the explosive charge.

The twin explosions guaranteed Natalia a proper fiery funeral as she plummeted to share a watery grave with the warrior, Josh *Viking* Osborne. If the Hall of the Slain of Norse mythos existed, perhaps they would meet in Valhalla.

9

Ian Faulkner stared at his screen in disbelief as the aircraft collided. That it was happening hundreds of kilometers from Menwith Hill did nothing to abate the shock. He'd seen a lot of bad shit on his feeds, but a Russian downing an American Osprey? That was a whole new world of hurt.

The room's main screens and most of their attention had been diverted to a new terrorist strike against a French embassy official's home in Mali. He was at work, the kids were at school, but the wife was still unaccounted for.

He ran back the collision and replayed the scant seconds between first contact over the North Sea and disaster, selecting zoom and image enhancements.

He ran it again, overlaying the aircraft radio chatter. Nothing from either of the involved aircraft. SIGINT showed some data had been captured, but he didn't have time to ask Verity and wait for answers.

Once more, he let it run and pasted in the feed from the

aircraft carrier's air wing. His playback was under thirty seconds behind real time.

"This is Weasel Two-three. Our bird is going down. I repeat, going down. Bogey is departing the area. Request permission to fire." Ian's display identified the F-35 Lightning II and the pilot, if he'd cared. He didn't.

"Confirm status of CMV-22," the carrier asked.

"Non-responsive. In high-speed spiraling dive. Estimate one-five seconds to water impact."

Ian could actually see that the Osprey was still maneuvering, but not effectively. The jet pilot's assessment of impact was sufficiently accurate.

"You are cleared to engage."

"Fox One," the jet pilot called out, announcing the launch of his missile. "Time to target fifty-eight seconds."

Ian slapped the red call button by his desk as he watched the missile race toward the departing AN-74. Limping—he could see the heat plume of the burning wing. The whole review process had taken less than a minute—the missile was still in flight. His slamming the button overrode the least critical feed from Mali on the Ops Floor's large front screens.

"Talk to me, Ian." Astrid Underwood answered immediately over the intercom as she stared up at the images Ian flashed to the front of the room. It was still jarring to have the Chief of Facility at the Mission Director station, just one more whacked thing about this day.

"Screen Three." Ian didn't take his hand off the keyboard to point.

Menwith Hill intercepts were rarely good news.

A drone strike on a jihadist's convoy in the depths of the Syrian Desert? Menwith Hill had provided the surveillance, tracking, target ID confirmation, and optimized the strike timing to minimize collateral damage aka civilian casualties. The drones flew for final observation and weapon delivery, long after the Menwith Hill satellites and operators had performed the bulk of the heavy lifting.

Chinese overflights of Taiwan? Menwith Hill and its two sister sites intercepted and decrypted the commands from Beijing, telling their pilots to not fire unless fired upon—and passed the information to Taiwan's high command telling them don't rise to the bait.

India put up a new bird? Menwith Hill had it imaged and intercept frequencies set up by the time the orbit had been stabilized.

The three NSA sites processed thousands of satellite intercepts every day, culled from the millions of gathered communications around the globe and preprocessed by some of the world's fastest supercomputers.

The number of aircraft downed by another country outside of a war zone like the one in Ukraine during any typical year? Zero.

Number of times an operator smacked the red alert button in a career? Not much more often.

Ian felt as if his hand had been burned. The last time he'd pounded that button had led to warning the Ukrainian Special Forces to rush an action team to Antonov Airport outside Kyiv. They'd foiled the surprise Russian attack. Russia's *Special Military Operation* would have been decisively won if the Ukrainians hadn't succeeded in keeping the airport from Russian control. Oh, the bad boys had captured it, but only after days of fighting and the destruction of men, equipment, and runways had kept reinforcements from landing.

It had been a close call. In the year since, slamming that

button on the first day of the Ukraine War had become one of Ian's proudest moments.

This time? Perhaps the first step of a Russian-American shootout? The room's temperature seemed to have dropped twenty degrees in as many seconds.

The entire Ops Floor went quiet as everyone watched. The analysts in this room all had the highest security clearance the NSA maintained below Mission Director.

In the room, only Astrid had that level of clearance.

Before the video was over, Astrid picked up a phone, punched the topmost button, and said, "We have an issue."

Ten seconds later the British Deputy Chief of Facility was in the room.

Then she punched the button for the Pentagon.

10

A NEW FIVE-POINTED STAR HAD BEEN CARVED INTO THE MARBLE of the Memorial Wall. The Wall formed the north side of the CIA's Old Headquarters Building lobby. The interior of the palm-sized star-shaped cavity had been painted black. Only time would turn it to gray as the marble absorbed the pigment until it matched its precursors. No number, no name, no other marking, only the star showed another agent had died in the line of duty.

A fucking awful way to start the day. But at least the unveiling ceremony was done, the few words she'd said hadn't choked her to death, and the small crowd of agents were dispersing to their desks.

With a perimeter guard formed, CIA Director Clarissa Reese had only one more task, unlocking the inch-thick glass case containing the *Book of Honor*. The calligrapher would add a gold star to the book's index page. Some stars were followed by the agent's name, this one never would be.

Every star on the CIA Memorial Wall was matched by a star in the *Book of Honor*. Each star represented an agent killed in the line of duty. A quarter of the stars were followed by no name in the book because to disclose the name was to disclose a secret CIA operation or invite retaliation from the country where the agent had died. As was the case this time.

Clarissa felt hollowed out as she looked at the page.

Her husband, former Director of the CIA turned Vice President, was the most recent entry in the book. He had no longer worked for the CIA when the terrorists attacked his Marine Two helicopter, but he'd died in the line of duty and should be honored. The Honor and Merit Awards Board had voted unanimously that Clark deserved a star, sparing her recommending the inclusion of her own husband.

And now, who to be awarded a star on the Memorial Wall immediately after her dead husband? The head of CIA's Special Operations Group.

Why had she insisted that Kurt handle this mission himself? Because he was the best qualified. Even he had agreed that if he couldn't do it, no one could.

Well, they'd answered that question now. Kurt had managed to keep his secrets in the hell of Hyanghari prison. The *resort* prison, so called for all the former North Korean political officials sent there to die under torture. The place was far worse than even the reeducation gulags and political concentration camps. Kurt hadn't succeeded in creating a massive accident at North Korea's nuclear facilities—the perfect excuse to cleanse that particular thorn in everyone's ass.

If she could take back the suggestion, would Kurt still be gracing her bed? Aside from being the best lover she'd ever had, he'd been her greatest ally inside the CIA. Absolutely loyal to the agency and the Director since before she'd come on the scene. And the most lethal operator in a team of trained assassins. There was a reason he led the deepest layer of the CIA's Black Ops division, the Special Operation Group.

Now she'd have to replace him. There was little question with who but, no matter how good he was, she didn't like Emil Chavez. A former Marine Force Recon team leader, he'd serve the SOG well but didn't think much more deeply than most Jarheads.

The calligrapher finished the gold star.

Clarissa stepped over to turn to the blank page after her dead husband's. There the calligrapher would record the star number and the sparse description of how he'd died—transcribed from the handwritten sheet Clarissa now passed over.

Tortured and fed to starving dogs while still alive. Hyanghari Prison, North Korea. He never spoke a word. And the date. All the epitaph Kurt would ever have. No body, no ashes, no grave. No one to contact for personal reasons except Clarissa herself, and she was the only one who knew that fact as well.

Once locked in its glass case, only the next D/CIA could ever see this page.

Clark was gone.

Kurt was gone.

She was—

Clarissa didn't know anymore. Adrift in a way that made her body feel as foreign as if it belonged to someone else. Had she become some form of a black widow spider that killed anyone she risked caring about?

The calligrapher finished the work with his nib pen, blotted the page, and returned the sheet of information to Clarissa. She would burn and powder it personally rather than trusting to the burn bag. She waved him away.

When she was alone within the cordon of outward-facing guards, she wrote Kurt's name at the head of the page, leaving a thin line of heart's blood with each stroke of the pen. Damn him! The bastard was supposed to be alive and at her side, helping her make the CIA the most indispensable arm of US foreign relations.

But he wasn't—and never would be again.

No guard would be able to report any tears if they turned around, she was careful to shed none. She would not fold in on herself as she had when Clark had died. Kurt was ten times the man her husband had been, but it was Clark's death that had almost destroyed her. Years of maneuvering to put herself in line for the Presidency had died with him. If it hadn't been for Rose Ramson, she might well have lost everything, including her role as D/CIA.

She'd show Rose that she could do this herself. Of course, now she *had* to. It had been Clarissa's destiny to sit in the Oval Office—until it wasn't.

Yet the same events that denied her chance had brought Rose to President Cole's attention. Widow and widower. The President and the First Lady of DC's social scene, now the First Lady in title as well. The perfect power-couple. Rose might not rule from the Oval, but her voice would be heard there for the remainder of Cole's second term.

If Clarissa was to share the truth of Kurt Grice's final mission with Rose, would that information then travel to President Roy Cole's ear? It wasn't a risk she could take. Not since President Herbert Hoover's friendship with the unrelated J. Edgar Hoover had the Executive Branch been comfortable with the clandestine services. Even Roosevelt and the OSS had often been at odds.

No, once again, Clarissa was wholly on her own. She

would draw strength from that...on some day other than today.

She lifted the book from the small desk that had been provided for this ceremony.

The black goatskin cover was rough against her palms as she returned it to the display case. The texture was smooth, but the contents— They hurt, scraping her raw.

A hundred and forty-one stars now. Two dead since she'd become Director. She'd been prepared for that. An average of two a year and she'd made it through four years as D/CIA with only the two. But she'd never suspected how personal those new stars would be. What of the next star and the one after that? How was she supposed to survive those?

She felt a sudden affinity for Miranda Chase; her parents' stars were on this wall. Numbers...

Clarissa's hand froze on the key before she turned the lock to seal the book once more into its glass case.

They had died as passengers on TWA Flight 800 in 1996.

As *passengers*.

The very first person to be killed in the service of the CIA, just a hundred and ten days after the founding of the agency in 1948, had died when an Air France DC-3 had gone down. Yet Jane Wallace Burrell had no star on the Memorial Wall, because she'd died, as a civilian, on a commercial flight. Her death wasn't because she'd gone into harm's way; it was because her plane to get there had crashed.

Not like that utter loser who'd committed suicide after a year in Afghanistan targeting al-Qaeda leaders. She and Clark both agreed the woman should never have been included on the wall by the previous director.

If Jane Wallace Burrell didn't have an entry in the book, then why did Miranda's parents? Because they'd been friends of Clark? No, they'd died back in 1996 when an honest-to-God mechanical fault had caused the Boeing 747 to explode shortly after takeoff—long before Clark's time as D/CIA began.

Of their own accord, her hands began flipping through the entries. Not browsing, seeking.

Seeking Sam and Olivia Chase. Their names didn't appear on the index pages—they had blank star names. Or were they even here? Had their inclusion on the Memorial Wall been some comforting fiction that Clark had made up for Miranda's peace of—

There. Facing pages.

The entries were no longer than the one she'd written for Kurt.

They were supposed to have fallen from the sky aboard a 747 close off the shore of Long Island, New York on July 17th, 1996. The book said they'd died in a Russian military plane crash on the 16th.

On a *Russian* plane?

Then how the hell had their bodies ended up on TWA 800?

11

_____

MIRANDA ACHIEVED SOME CLARITY ABOUT THE MULTIPLE aspects of a vacation on their second day of hiking.

Mike had added a layover day to the four-day circular hike. Last night and tonight they were staying in the smallest enclave on the entire route. Keld was little more than a half dozen B&Bs and two restaurants to serve the hikers—and a lot of sheep grazing over the hills and even on the town green. The hikers were also called _walkers_ or _ramblers._ She made a note of the three words with apparently identical meanings.

Their walk for the layover day made even less sense than the overall plan itself as it had nothing to do with the Herriot Way, but she was looking forward to it the most.

After a lazy morning that let her read the latest issue of _Aviation Week and Space Technology,_ they hiked up the road.

As with apparently everything else in the Yorkshire Dales, it was required to descend before ascending. There were no level paths here.

The only discernable difference from yesterday was that

the paved road was far surer underfoot than the trench-and-boulder trail up Great Shunner Fell and the subsequent Kisdon Hill. There was a distinct downside: the chances of death by speeding cars on the narrow road was only mitigated by their scarcity.

Kisdon had been a rude surprise. Such a great amount of the guidebooks' texts had been dedicated to the challenges of the hike up and over Great Shunner as the third highest point in the Yorkshire Dales that it seemed to be the whole challenge. After the descent, and a cup of tea in the Thwaite tearoom, they'd ascended Kisdon Hill. Though a third the height, it was far steeper than any section of Great Shunner. The daily runs with Andi around her own island hadn't prepared her for that.

Last night, curled up together in Keld Lodge, both of their legs had stunk of salve as they cramped and twitched for hours before finally allowing sleep.

This is fun? she'd asked.

Andi's response had been fun enough to let them forget about their legs for a while.

By comparison, today had been easy, if only because the limitations of cars had forced the road to have a lesser grade to the highest pub in the entire United Kingdom. For reasons unknown, it was at 1,732 feet, not 528 meters.

Tan Hill Inn, like most buildings in the area, looked to be built of gray fieldstone. Here it was the *only* building in the area, sitting alone high on Tan Hill, not Tan *Fell*.

Am I the only one bothered by all of these inconsistencies? she'd asked the others. Then, as usual, she'd been forced to explain what she meant and received little more than shrugs.

She kept the next thought to herself. Because they were in England, was its proper morphological name *grey* fieldstone rather than *gray?* Or because it was stone should she be considering its proper *geomorphological* designation?

The building sat alone; she knew that much. And the air was very clean based on the heavy growths of gold and green lichens clinging to much of the outside surfaces.

Inside was also heavy stone. The base of the bar was a hip-high stone wall. Walls between each section were heavy stone, their doorways spanned by massive lintels that must have taken ten men to lift into place.

They managed to get a table close by the large gray...or *grey,* stone hearth and she appreciated the fire's efforts to replace the warmth that the wind had remained so intent on sucking out of her.

A dog lay curled mere feet away, also happy in the wash of heat. She certainly didn't pet it, but she also no longer had the childhood fear to shy away from it either. That too was progress.

She paid little attention to her food order. The pub was too busy to allow clear thinking. There were heavy beams supporting the ceiling. Were they the same ones installed five hundred years before when the place was built? There were pictures hanging from the interior walls, at least those made of wood and plaster. Each unfamiliar, each clamoring for her attention. The tables were three-quarters full of hikers (*walkers, ramblers)* like themselves, cyclists, people who had driven in, and even groups from an array of motor homes (no, *caravans)* that were parked outside.

At least it didn't have the noise levels of an American bar. She missed being out on the Yorkshire fells, out in all that nice silence with only the roaring wind and sheep to listen to. Even Andi created her own version of noise simply with her presence. Now that she lived on the island, Miranda's only alone time was when she slipped from their bed in the middle of the night.

She would take rings of dried apple that she prepared every autumn and go visit the places she knew the deer liked to sleep. Many times she fell asleep with them, only to wake up alone in her own little circle of pressed grass.

Here on the high fells as on her island, a lamb, woken from a nap, would call for its mother. A distant answer. An excited bleat of recognition and then a race to rejoin. To nurse. To find comfort and safety. She could have watched them all day, but the others had remained intent on the hike up to the pub and she'd followed along.

Up here at the Tan Hill Inn, they seemed to be above the altitude of most sheep. The meager grasses had drastically thinned the number of sheep per acre. They were still too hard to count accurately because of the rolling landscape; lying down easily hid them from view.

She'd done her best to estimate by area.

As the lambs were still nursing rather than foraging themselves, Miranda felt that dismissing them from the calculation of supportable sheep per acre was a reasonable assumption. Of course, their nursing would require the mother to forage more to not deplete her body. Miranda amended her notebook heading to *Nursing sheep per acre* for greater specificity, though the numbers still remained far too vague for more than first-order estimates.

The pub's fish and chips at such an inland location seemed counterintuitive—though the numerous black-headed seagulls they'd spotted would argue that point. Nothing in England was particularly far from the ocean, a curious concept. Her own island of Spieden in Puget Sound lay as far from the ocean as the centermost point of England.

Despite the gulls' presence indicating the appropriateness of fish and chips, she selected the chicken-and-ham Yorkshire pie and began the difficult task of imagining herself elsewhere than she was.

This afternoon as they hiked back from the pub, they would leave the road and descend along the trail passing through Ravenseat. It was a sheep farm where a television show called *Our Yorkshire Farm* had been filmed. It lay high in the Yorkshire dales—well, the dales and fells, as by definition the dales were low not high. Yet people always referred to the region of the *Yorkshire Dales* as up (*the uplands*). Yet another confusing inconsistency. Even the landforms were loud here.

There was far more about tending the sheep and cows in the show than there was in *All Creatures Great and Small,* so she rather enjoyed watching that—the practical rather than the veterinary. Especially when she imagined spending an extra few days helping out in their lambing barn. She wouldn't, but she could imagine it.

If she did, she'd then be much better able to tend the herd of Mouflon sheep that inhabited her island. This spring they'd been left to fend for themselves far more than usual.

There were contractors on the island—right now tearing down the burned-out hangar, house, and garage. But with no home, she hadn't been there to regularly patrol the island for any animals in distress. There had only been a few animals that she'd had to put down after the lightning-strike fire burned half the island. Most had escaped to the safety of the southern end. But it would be months before she'd be living full-time on the island again.

It was...wrong for other people to be there—not her.

She thought of wandering among the sheep and deer.

Petting a new lamb by the old rose bush, feeding dried apple rings to her favorite deer family of Rudolph, Bambi, and Thumper. Then—

"What's that?" Andi called out.

Miranda slammed back into the present with a hard visceral shock that knocked the wind from her lungs. She hadn't been paying attention to the others' conversation.

Andi was looking up from her beef brisket hotpot, squinting toward the heavy timber beams that supported the ceiling. Some sounds were so very distinctive.

"AgustaWestland 109. One of the newer ones, I think, with the upgrade PW207C engine." Miranda listened a few moments longer, which helped as it came closer to the inn. "Yes, the AW109S with the new rotor-blade tips."

Mike looked at her. "I'd still like to know how you do that."

Miranda had never known how to answer that type of question. To her the surprising thing was that other people couldn't; it was there for all to hear. Yet even Andi, a former Night Stalker helicopter pilot, tilted her head one way and another like one of the crows in the sheep pastures puzzling at a sound that might be a worm under the soil.

"Listen for the secondary harmonic in the upper register."

Andi stopped tilting her head, but after a long moment simply shook it. It always bothered Miranda when she discovered something Andi couldn't do. It was like a piece of the world didn't quite fit. Of course, Andi was so much better at a wide variety of things that Miranda could never hope to match. Yet...

"Are both of us broken?"

12

"ARE WE *WHAT?*" ANDI TWISTED TO LOOK AT HER, ALMOST knocking over her half-finished beer into Miranda's lap.

She went to shift aside, but the dog still lay to her other side and Miranda didn't want to move any closer.

Mike tipped his head quickly to one side and made a face that she was fairly sure was a wince, but she didn't know why he would do that. Holly hadn't elbowed him hard. In fact, since their Hawaii trip, she was positively mellow where Mike was concerned.

"Broken," Miranda repeated herself. It seemed a simple enough question. Though the rising volume of the approaching helicopter was somewhat distracting, it wasn't loud enough to drown out her words.

"Am I...broken?" Andi whispered. The look on her face was one Miranda had never seen there before. Fear mixed with something that eluded her.

"Well, we know I'm a failure at being normal."

"You're not!" Andi snapped back to life. "Other-abled. *Not* a failure."

Miranda still thought of herself as broken when she looked at neurotypical people, but she didn't want to get into an argument and managed to move on to the next part of the topic after only three deep breaths.

"And *you* can't identify the secondary harmonic of the rotor blade despite your training."

The helo was loud enough now that most patrons were moving to the windows to see what was going on. Miranda could hear the tone change that said it would be landing shortly. Once it did, they'd be able to inspect it at leisure. No one appeared to realize that. Were they all broken in some way as well?

"That's what you meant?" Mike huffed out a breath and rolled his eyes at her. He'd been watching her closely and not Andi, so she couldn't ask what Andi's expression had meant.

"What did you think I meant?"

Mike scrubbed at his face.

Andi seemed very interested in her own clenched hands.

Holly said on a half laugh, "That our favorite pint-sized American-born Chinese helo pilot is still suffering from PTSD."

"Are you?" Miranda turned to Andi.

Now Andi looked...relieved. "I don't think so. But, uh, sometimes I have nightmares that I still am." Her voice was certainly steadier than a moment ago.

"Oh. My nightmares aren't like that."

"What are they like?" Andi asked quickly, perhaps... glad...to have herself no longer be the topic of conversation.

"That I wake up one day and you aren't there with me."

Andi's eyes went wide and her mouth fell partway open.

"Aww. So sweet." Holly reached across the table and

thumped a fist hard enough into Andi's shoulder to knock her sideways into Miranda.

Miranda planted her elbow firmly enough in her French fries—no, *fried chips*—to make the silverware on the table clatter. The English language was already overelaborate, why did there have to be multiple versions of it? Because of the Soviet-era school system, Russia was one language with one dialect from border to border. The many disparate states that became Italy had settled on a single national dialect chosen for its beauty, that of Dante Alighieri. Yet English varied between countries, regions, states, and even—

There was a loud disturbance by the entrance, followed by a deep silence throughout the pub—*inn*. With the door open, the heavy beat of the rotors and the whine of twin turboshaft engines of the AW109S flooded the room. The rotors were set to neutral attack but still spinning at full throttle rather than idling down now that they'd landed. They weren't planning on staying long.

"Excuse me, folks. Is there a Miranda Chase here?" A man called out as soon as the closing door blocked the worst of the racket.

"Yes," she answered. After all, there was at least one, and it was her.

As all heads turned in her direction, a man walked over to their table. He had four bars on his uniform.

"Ms. Chase? I'm Group Captain Raymond Fielding of His Majesty's Royal Air Force. I would like to ask you to accompany me."

"Are you sure I'm the right person? You only asked, nonspecifically, if there was *a* Miranda Chase here. There could be several of us in the room. It does seem unlikely as I'm the only me I've ever met, but it is possible."

He looked down at her. "Are you an investigator for the United States National Transportation Safety Board?"

"I am."

"Then, ma'am, you are the correct Miranda Chase."

Everyone in the pub to the farthest table and even the staff were as frozen as the cards during the trial at the end of *Alice in Wonderland*. If she shouted *You're all a pack of cards*, would they burst into the air to flutter down like leaves? It was possible, she was in the English countryside after all. Where had Lewis Carroll told his tales to Alice Liddell as he rowed her and her sisters along a river? Not here. The rugged Yorkshire dales (and fells) were not an area given to lazy rivers. Besides, there were no trees this high on Tan Hill for leaves to flutter down from. She decided against testing if they were indeed a pack of cards.

"Why? We haven't half finished eating, mate." Holly made a show of picking up a piece of fish, dredging it in tartar sauce, and biting deeply. "See? Plenty of good nosh to go and I still have me a half pint to drain. Hate to waste any Black Sheep Bitter. Take a load off, mate, and have a pint. It's a proper brew."

The group captain, the equivalent of an American lieutenant colonel, ignored Holly. She was so dangerous that Miranda felt it was an ill-advised attitude.

"How can the team help, Group Captain?" Mike cut off Holly's next round before she could start it.

The man's gaze flashed around the table and then returned to her. Miranda turned her focus back to her own plate to avoid looking at his eyes. Eyes were intensely uncomfortable, sometimes even Andi's were hard to look at. It was like Miranda could see right through them to all of the emotions and turmoil behind them and it always—

"Your *team,* ma'am?"

"Yes," Andi replied for her.

"If you could *all* come with me, then. Immediately, ma'am."

Miranda had never liked sentences like that. It started as a question but somewhere before it reached the end it twisted like a mouse's tail and became a statement. There was scant comfort in knowing it would puzzle little Alice as much as it puzzled her.

"On whose request?" Holly made a show of toasting him with her half pint before she began drinking.

"I'm sorry, that's classified," he said aloud.

Holly tried to laugh in his face and drink her beer at the same time, succeeding with an ease that Miranda had long since identified as a uniquely Aussie skill.

Until he very quietly set a small slip of paper in the middle of the table.

Andi and Holly leaned in together.

Prime Minister Olivia Whitaker.

Holly spit out a cloud of beer in Mike's face as he turned from the group captain to look at the paper.

"Hey!"

"Miranda, have you met—" Holly looked at Miranda as she pointed at the paper, then lowered her voice so that only those around the table could hear. "Let me guess, first-name basis?"

Miranda nodded. "Did I forget to mention that I saved her life a few months ago? I told Andi, didn't I?"

Andi nodded, so she hadn't failed to notify at least one team member about that assignment.

Group Captain Fielding twitched as if he'd...twitched.

No good metaphor came to mind. She was disappointed. She thought she finally had better control of those.

"She has the same first name as my mother. She was very nice."

"Well, dip me in sheep shit."

Andi reached across the table and thumped Holly hard on the arm. "Aww. So sweet that you'd do that for the team."

13

"I'm not sure that we can," Miranda explained as the officer snapped on a cigarette lighter to ignite the paper bearing the Prime Minister's name and dropped it into the last quarter of Holly's beer.

Holly frowned and pushed the beer aside.

"Ma'am?" Group Captain Fielding's tone...

"Does his tone sound like a question or a threat?" she asked Andi.

"A bit of both actually."

Miranda reached over her shoulder. But most of the way to patting herself on the back for getting it right (even if there were two answers each only partially correct), she noticed the French—the *fried chips* smushed into the elbow of her fleece jacket and worked to brush them off.

"Ma'am?"

The farther reaches of the pub had turned back to their own meals and the low hum of conversation rebuilt slowly but with many continued glances in their direction. The nearer tables weren't watching them, at least not directly, but either they were listening—or they really were no more than a pack of cards frozen to stillness and trapped with Alice in a place called Wonderland.

"Oh." Unsure how to answer both tones, Miranda decided to answer the question rather than the threat. "We're on vacation. I've never had one before, so I looked it up. According to the Merriam-Webster Dictionary, a vacation is *a period spent away from home or business in travel or recreation.* This is further supported by Definition 2b, which states that it is *a period of exemption from work granted to an employee.* As we're on vacation, would I be in violation of the word's very meaning if I were to accede to your request?"

Group Captain Fielding looked around the table once more.

Holly held up her hands palm out with a don't-ask-me gesture, but she was laughing.

Mike was struggling with something that contorted his face in a peculiar fashion.

Andi was smiling, but she rested her hand firmly on Miranda's forearm.

Miranda knew that was the gesture she used before she explained something. With her free hand Miranda pulled out a notebook, ready to write down the explanation.

For a moment she considered graphing the rising conversation levels as time-variant without any further excitement at their table adding a factor...but decided that would be significantly off topic.

Instead of explaining, Andi asked a question. She did that more and more lately. Miranda had yet to decide if she was comfortable with that. It was always nicer when someone simply gave her the answer about situations involving people.

"Miranda, considering the source of the request, do you think we should declare a hiatus in the vacation?"

"*An interruption in time or continuity?* An interruption in a vacation, which itself interrupted work in the first place? That strikes me as rather circular reasoning. And if we are then asked to interrupt *that* process? Will we become trapped in some meta-space of iterative breaks in cognitive sequences?"

She drew a quick process flow diagram.

In the first rectangular process box she wrote: *Vacation.*

From that an arrow down to a second process box, which she labeled: *Crisis.*

Below that a diamond-shaped decision box: *Crisis ended?*

Then an arrow out either side of the last to the prior two boxes. She labeled one arrow: *No.* That arrow led them back into the *Crisis* box. The *Yes* arrow led them back to the *Vacation* box.

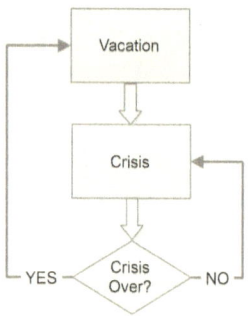

"What is the testing frequency for the iterative Crisis-not-complete loop? A second is too fast. But is ten minutes? Or ten hours? And what if the crisis is ongoing? Do we become trapped in an infinite Do-loop of *Crisis over? No. Crisis over? No.* And so on. That's very dangerous in programming. What if there was never an *End Crisis* trigger? Then it's possible to be permanently stuck in the Do-loop. How many iterations would be necessary before throwing an error code and an escape sequence? I don't know how to think about this."

Andi slipped the notebook and pen from Miranda's hands and made a drawing before handing it back. She was the first person other than herself to ever write in one of her notebooks. Andi had made notes about the new island house in a notebook once, but that had been a fresh blank one. This was her active personal notebook. Mike had once given her pages of emojis to help her identify people's emotions, but she'd been the one to paste them in.

It was a small diagram of three boxes connected by arrows: *Vacation – Crisis – Vacation (continued)*. Nothing else. No iterations. No timelines. A clean, linear progression.

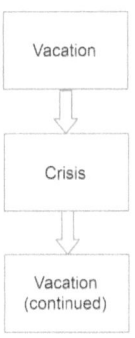

She leaned forward and kissed Andi. Now she understood.

After carefully crossing out her own diagram, Miranda made a quick note: *Andi drew this,* then tucked away the notebook.

Miranda turned to the group captain. "We're ready when you are."

He opened his mouth, apparently thought better of it, and closed it again. Instead, he stepped aside between two other tables and waved for them to proceed him toward the exit.

Miranda hadn't thought to put her decibel meter in this vacation vest, but it seemed conversations were now at a level above the sound level prior to the helicopter's arrival. She couldn't imagine why.

Oh. The Pratt & Whitney engines on the helicopter had drastically added to the background noise level. That precluded any accurate assessment of conversation volume change. And they did keep looking her way. Were they talking about her? She didn't like that thought at all.

She inspected Group Captain Fielding standing between the tables and again waving her ahead.

"Doesn't he trust us to follow him?" she whispered to Andi.

"Maybe he's being courteous. He is British, after all."

Before Miranda could ask him, Holly had risen to her feet and hesitated for only a moment in front of the group captain. "Don't forget to pay the bill, mate. Spoiled the last of my brew, so the tab's on you."

She led the way out and Miranda followed.

14

Major General.

Major General Artemy Turgenev brushed his fingers over the lone star on his epaulet. He had to stop doing that—soon. Mustn't let it become a habit because doing so in front of others would show a weakness. To reveal any chink in his armor could prove lethal—Russia was always about moves and countermoves.

He had played every card perfectly so far and now the AARI was his. All Russian operations in the Arctic and Antarctic landed within his purview. Which made him the target of every little career climber. Not unlike himself.

That *dikaya suka* Aloysha had given the star to him—not intentionally, but still her doing. She'd willingly self-destructed to take out the prior major general of the Artic and Antarctic Research Institute. All he'd had to tell her was that Yugov was the one whose misguided policy had killed her husband. It hadn't mattered to her that it was actually the President's irrational policy to secretly militarize

Antarctica and Yugov had merely been implementing his orders.

Like a praying mantis, she'd fucked him and then bitten off his head—well, decapitated him with a straight razor. Crazy bitch Aloysha indeed, she'd finally gone truly mad. Unable to handle her—apparently she'd attacked Yugov's security team naked and covered in Yugov's blood—they'd put her down on the spot. Too late to save Yugov. And one of the guards would never be having sex again.

Artemy's pity for her was mitigated by the deep relief that, with her death, no one could connect his name to Yugov's fall. Also that she hadn't decided to kill him the last time they'd fucked. A year ago she'd only been half crazy, so he'd been safe. Besides, he'd been useful to her.

He rubbed his star again, for what he promised himself was the last time ever.

And now? Inessa, his lovely Inessa, had agreed to become his guiding hand after the death of her *grebanyy pridurok* husband. Colonel Romanoff was *such* a fucking moron that he'd not only lost most of Russia's Antarctic stations to the Chinese in a period of forty-eight hours, but he'd gotten himself killed in the process.

Inessa had the old-world sophistication he himself lacked—and that Romanoff had never understood at all. Not Old World like the Soviets but like a throwback to the tsarinas. When she walked into a room, even that rabid-dog President paid attention. And now she entered on Artemy's arm.

That *too* was power.

On her advice, Artemy had oh-so-carefully turned down Major General Yugov's physical office when he'd taken over the position. He liked the symmetry of remaining in Romanoff's former office and marrying his widow.

Inessa was correct, of course. It was a statement: *My power doesn't lie where it is visible.* It lay in the fact that he had become the right-hand man for General Murov. Murov wasn't the four-star general of the Army nor the Marshall of the entire Russian Federation. Murov merely ran the FSB— personally. He'd made the Federal Security Service even more feared than its predecessor, the KGB.

And Artemy now had direct control of one of the lone prosperous sectors remaining in the whole of Russia—the Artic. As long as he kept the oil exploration on track for the ice-bound fields of the north, he could do no wrong.

There was a discreet knock on the door.

"Knock like you mean it, Shirinov," he called out.

Shirinov knocked solidly this time.

"Enter." Six months ago he himself had been a lowly lieutenant colonel. Now he had one as his assistant.

The man entered and snapped a salute.

"Enough of that, Shirinov," Artemy decided. "Save it for when others are here."

The man nodded.

They'd already had *The Talk.* Artemy had made two things clear.

Unlike any of his own former commanders, Artemy told Shirinov that ten percent of anything that came Artemy's way in terms of bribes and profit-skims would go to Shirinov for absolutely loyal service. That this would probably exceed his official salary by a factor of ten purchased significant loyalty. He didn't even ask for a reciprocal courtesy as he knew from experience how meager the pickings for a lieutenant colonel could be.

The second thing he had assured the man was that if *anything* happened to Artemy, Shirinov wouldn't be touched. But his family would be sent to work the deepest mines in Siberia—and he'd never see them again.

At Inessa's insistence, Artemy would take only half of what might flow his way. That counted as supreme honesty in New Russia. That too would worry those around him—again power. And the other half would be routed upward to his own commanders—trustworthy and useful.

"Sir..."

"Just spit it out, Shirinov. Let's not waste time between us."

"Yes sir. The Americans just shot down an AN-74MP Cheburashka surveillance plane during a close flyby." The man looked to be on the verge of puking.

Artemy tried to speak, he really did. The AN-74MP were specially configured for Arctic missions, which meant it was one of his. The Marine Patrol designation meant that it carried an autocannon and could be loaded with bombs to blast annoying spy trawlers into tiny pieces. It could also deliver emergency cargo anywhere—to a submarine or the North Pole.

"It is still unclear what happened. They were ordered to do a flyby of an American aircraft."

"Not by me. And those bastards shot down our plane?" Artemy pushed to his feet. It was the worst possible scenario —a declaration of war. A war that Russia would have no hope of surviving. The *Special Military Operation* in Ukraine had taught him that if nothing else. Mother Russia couldn't even win against US weapons in the hands of underfed Ukrainians.

Shirinov's face paled. He didn't look down at the paper

crumpling in his hands. "We don't know. One of their planes was destroyed as well."

"What lame-dick declared war on the United States of America?" Even the President wasn't that goddamn stupid. Was he? Could be. He'd started this whole *Cleansing the Nazis from freedom-loving Ukraine* bullshit-show personally and now, thanks to his incomparable ego, Russia was stuck with it.

"That isn't the problem, sir."

Artemy propped his fists on the desk to keep himself upright as he leaned forward. "Then what is, Shirinov?"

"The pilot..." he looked down at the paper he held, now rattier than a week-old *Pravda* wrapped around a street bum's vodka bottle. Shirinov stepped forward to lay it on Artemy's desk and smoothed it out as well as he could before turning it for Artemy to read.

Artemy looked down at the wrinkled report. Little more than the few details that Shirinov had already conveyed.

Lieutenant Colonel Shirinov's finger was shaking as he pointed at the pilot's name.

Captain Natalia Ivanovna.

He didn't know her. He'd taken over the AARI in full only a week ago and couldn't be expected to know every pilot who...

Natalia Ivanovna?

He slowly raised his gaze to meet Shirinov's. "Is that..."

Shirinov nodded. "She uses—*used* her mother's maiden name."

Artemy collapsed back in his chair. His shiny new star would be his for less than a week.

He was a dead man.

15

AT THE SOFT KNOCK ON THE DOOR, ARTEMY CALLED OUT, "Come" before he had a chance to reconsider.

What if it was General Murov? He wasn't ready for that yet.

Inessa stepped in with a bright smile that he tried to return. She was so beautiful. Three decades before she'd been runner-up to the last-ever Miss USSR. *I refused to play the sexy vixen. That cost me the win.*

She hadn't been disappointed. Instead, Inessa had proved that her major assets lay far deeper under her lovely tan-dark skin. She'd started a business, taking advantage of the collapse of the USSR that she'd witnessed firsthand from the beauty-pageant stage. She became the first large-scale importer of Western fashion and built that into an empire that reached far beyond clothes and deep into influence. Inessa wasn't an advisor to generals or political leaders; she was confidant to their wives and mistresses.

Her thick brunette hair was draped over her shoulder in

a loose braid, her cream slacks and blazer highlighted her athletic figure, medium complexion, and dark eyes.

Eyes that dimmed as she assessed the mood of the room.

"What brings you by, Inessa?" Then Artemy remembered himself and circled his desk to embrace her.

"It is time you were seen. I have reserved a table at Buro TSUM."

Artemy barely repressed a comment. Buro wasn't the most expensive restaurant in Moscow, but it was close. He'd never been able to afford it—as a mere lieutenant colonel. Now, he had a general's salary and was married to a woman far wealthier than he'd ever imagined possible—she was one of the few self-made *oligarkhi*. Her parents had been rich before her, but she'd surpassed them long before they died.

Buro was a good choice, next door to the Bolshoi and equidistant from the FSB's headquarters in the Lubyanka Building and the Kremlin. Located on the fifth floor of the TSUM department store, it was very easy to be seen there.

The only impressive thing, he supposed, was her power to simply *reserve a table* on such short notice at Buro. What underling had just lost his reservation?

The only problem? "I can't."

She arched one of her exquisite dark eyebrows.

"We have..." he glanced toward Shirinov and the crumpled paper on his desk, "...a problem."

"Tell me."

Shirinov blanched white. He reached for the paper, hesitated, then withdrew his hand as if he'd be burned.

Artemy, finding his own unwillingness to touch it running deep, finally pointed at the transmission report.

Inessa rested long fingers on his chest for a moment, then stepped over to the desk. She circled to stand before his empty chair and looked down at the report. The only reaction she showed was raising a hand to press it to her heart. She looked at it long enough to read its horrid message ten times over.

"Colonel Shirinov, is he in his office?" Inessa asked without raising her eyes.

Shirinov nodded. Would Artemy have thought to check that detail before delivering the bad news? Perhaps yes, if only to delay the inevitable a few moments.

"Artemy, he must be told."

"But—"

"Now." Inessa didn't need to raise her voice to make it a command.

"How—"

"Just the facts. No conjecture." She turned to his aide. "Colonel Shirinov, we need to contact flight operations at—" she didn't even look up. "Go, Artemy. Now. We have dinner reservations in an hour."

He hurried out the door of his own office wondering if he'd still be alive when it was time for dinner, or would they be serving his head on a platter.

16

THE HALL HAD NEVER SEEMED SO LONG. IT WAS UNSEEMLY FOR a general to take the stairs, but the Lubyanka elevators were notoriously fickle. Major General (for such a brief time) Artemy Turgenev forced himself not to race up the flight to the next floor and moved calmly down the hall to General Murov's office.

Trying to take a lesson from Inessa, he kept his voice even as he reached the two aides in the outer office. "Is he in? It's important."

Faster than he was ready, he was standing in front of the general's desk. It was large without being ostentatious. Dark wood that matched the wall paneling. The April afternoon light streamed into the room as if the sun had been created for no other purpose than brightening General Mikhail Murov's office and striking luster in the rich woods.

"Yes, Turgenev?" Murov didn't even look up from the report he'd been studying.

Artemy looked at his own hands, but they were empty. He should have grabbed the report, if only for something to hold. Experience had taught him that General Murov was not a patient man, so he didn't delay more than time to gather his breath. Regrettably, it didn't burst his lungs and kill him to preclude the next moment.

"Sir," Artemy resisted taking the time to swallow. Instead, he took refuge in the same instruction he'd given to Shirinov not ten minutes ago and started in quickly. "I have a report of a flyby we performed on an American naval aircraft in the North Sea. Details are unclear, but apparently both aircraft were destroyed."

Murov looked up very slowly until his palest-of-blue eyes bore into him like a pair of ice drills. "The North Sea, you say?"

Artemy nodded.

"A flyby in the vicinity of the American carrier strike group off Norway?"

He didn't know anything about the American carriers, but he knew the typical areas of operation of AARI and it was one of the few areas that would overlap. "I believe so, sir. My staff are working on the details."

"But you felt it was urgent enough to report it to me before you knew what had actually happened." He didn't make it a question.

Should Artemy admit to that or... "It's about the pilot, sir."

"About the..." His voice trailed off and his preternaturally light skin paled—did the man never go outside? Murov whispered, "The pilot was an AARI pilot. A female one?"

"Yes sir," Artemy took a deep breath and decided to take the final plunge before his nerves scared him into tongue-tied silence. "By the name of Captain Natalia Ivanovna. We have no word of survivors. I'm very sorry, sir."

General Mikhail Murov looked at him without reaction. Was it a death sentence? Would he be locked up in the parts of Lubyanka Prison that were rumored to still occupy the fifth floor of this very building? Would the general shake off his paralysis, leap over the desk, and drive a letter opener into his heart for delivering such news?

"Natalia," Murov mouthed but made no sound.

"Yes sir. It's—"

Inessa hurried into the room. "Oh, Mikhail. I'm so sorry. I stopped by to take Artemy to dinner and heard the horrid news. You must go home and tell poor Raya. Oh, such a horrid way to lose a daughter. I know she was a troublesome child, but she never deserved this."

Shirinov knocked, stepped into the room, handed a piece of paper to Artemy, and stepped back out.

The timing was too perfect—Inessa had orchestrated it, of course.

Murov's baleful eyes focused on him. Artemy started reading aloud without scanning the contents first, to avoid looking directly at his death sentence.

"Our tracking shows a normal approach. The two aircraft flew close together, briefly merging into a single locus on our satellite imaging. The AN-74MP flown by Captain Ivanovna, your daughter, and the American aircraft may have collided. The American crashed into the ocean from fifteen thousand feet."

Murov leaned forward. Inessa, who had circled into the sacrosanct territory behind his desk, rested a comforting hand on General Murov's shoulder. Tears were trickling down her face.

Artemy gasped as he read the next sentence. "Losing half her altitude, Captain Ivanovna recovered partial control of her own aircraft but was shot out of the sky shortly afterward by an American fighter jet from their aircraft carrier. I will order—" the next words had been written just that way in Inessa's handwriting, so he continued reading them "—her commanding officer from Gromovo Air Base to be here in Moscow by eight a.m. tomorrow to provide details in person."

"Have him brought by armed guard," Murov whispered. "Our people."

"I wouldn't handle it any other way, sir." At least not after he'd been told. It was only now becoming clear that in supporting his ascension, the FSB had taken over direct control of the AARI. And with that, opened a channel to the vast cash flow represented by Artic oil. He was useful; he knew more about managing Artic operations than any man still living in Russia. Maybe he would survive this. "Again, please accept my—"

Murov waved his condolences aside.

"Raya," Inessa whispered. "Mikhail, you must be the one who delivers the news to your wife."

"Yes. Of course." Murov rose and Inessa helped him into his jacket.

At the door, he turned and looked straight at Artemy.

Here comes my verdict.

"Top security. I don't want word of this getting out to anyone. Not even the President. Keep your staff on the details. But nothing that draws attention. Your wife says that you are expected for dinner. Go once you have seen to Gromovo. For the moment we will behave completely normally. Let's keep this compartmentalized inside the FSB and AARI."

He had closed the report he'd been studying but left it on his desk rather than locking it up.

When Artemy pointed to it in question, Murov had merely grunted, then turned to go as if in a daze. Already in his sixties, he looked as if he aged a decade in the last two minutes.

Artemy glanced at the report's cover page: *Threat Analysis of US Carrier Strike Group—North Sea.*

Had Murov purposely left the report out for Artemy to see? To understand the delicate moment that was the present? No wonder he wanted to keep the news internal to the FSB. Even in his grief, General Murov had considered the risk of his close friend the President learning about this. There was a dead girl—a daughter of the elite. World wars had started with little more impetus.

That news to *this* President? He'd get a hard-on to nuke Washington, DC, in retaliation—and this was a President notorious for following wherever his ego and his dick led him.

He looked up. Murov hadn't left, hadn't been in a daze. He watched Artemy closely.

Artemy offered his best nod of surety. Yes, he understood. Yes, Murov could count on him no matter what.

General Murov barely tipped his head before stepping out of the office.

Once he was gone, Inessa wiped her eyes and slid a hand through his arm. "You did that wonderfully."

"I'm still alive, so something must have worked. You're perfect," he waved the note at her, before sliding it through the slot into Murov's locked burn bag.

"Is that why you married me?"

"Must be." Artemy had liked Inessa for years, perhaps

even falling in love with her over that time though she'd been married to his superior officer. But not once in the year since Romanoff's death or the month since their marriage had he appreciated her as he did at this moment.

"Good. You can tell me all about my perfection over dinner. We older women need to hear that on occasion."

His scoff earned her brief smile despite the tears that were slower in stopping than he'd expected. She wasn't proof that fifty was the new forty, she was the living embodiment of why women should be eager to reach that refined age.

"And I will tell you the sad tale of Natalia Ivanovna Murov. You'll need that to make it through the next few days."

"Better than perfect," he kissed her cheek and led her downstairs to order the arrest and transport of the Gromovo base commander before escorting his wife to dinner.

17

SHE'D BEEN WRONG. MIRANDA HAD THOUGHT IT WAS AN AgustaWestland AW109S Grand; it was an AW109SP GrandNew. The difference was slight, undetectable without actually looking at the cockpit electronics or thumping her knuckles on the nose skin to determine that it was carbon fiber rather than aluminum, but the mistake bothered her. Maybe that's why all of Tan Hill Inn's patrons had been going to the windows to look at it, just as they were now gathered again to watch their departure. But looking wouldn't have distinguished the differences. So what had they been looking at?

She closed her eyes, wishing the world would slow down for a moment, be quieter. The crowds in the pub. The new experiences of the Yorkshire Dales (and fells), which each needed observation, comprehension, and cataloging. The whirlwind of information that—

Miranda opened her eyes and yanked out a notebook as the helicopter eased into forward flight. She didn't need to record the VVIP interior with its heavy sound insulation and the deep leather of its six facing seats placed behind the two pilot seats; those matched the manufacturer specifications she'd studied on the AW109S' release in 2005. No, but the opportunity to gather *aerial* data on nursing sheep density per acre—per *hectare* here in the UK—oh, variant by elevation above mean sea level was something she hadn't previously considered.

It was a hard blow that airborne observation proved little better than walking along the trail. The helicopter had soared up to five thousand feet, making the dot of a lamb indistinguishable from a white rock or a clump of daffodils. Daffodils were blooming everywhere in the dales. Not up on the windswept fells much, but definitely down in the dales.

"Where are we going?" Mike was looking out the window.

Holly had stretched her feet out to rest them on the empty seat between Miranda and Andi. "Catterick Garrison lies to the east. Did a bit of play there when on exchange with the British SAS back in the day. Biggest Brit Army base in the world."

"We're headed south-southeast," Mike pointed at the sun.

Group Captain Fielding had sat in the front with the pilot, clamped on a headset, and gave no sign of any interest in conversing.

Andi leaned in and said in a strange thin voice that didn't fit her at all. "We should have asked before we came aboard. Do you think we're being kidnapped by the British Army? Fed nothing but bangers and mash until we swear loyalty oaths to the King?"

"Made to sit in comfy chairs and be poked with soft pillows?" Mike also made his voice odd and...

Miranda flipped open her emoji page and studied it. *Spooky?* Oh, she hoped so. Because if they were being spooky, then it was the first time she'd ever identified that one. She showed it to Mike and received back a thumbs up and a big smile.

She entered a tiny checkmark next to it and tucked it away while Andi patted her on the back in congratulations. Of course that didn't answer *why* they'd used a spooky voice.

"The nearest British base along this vector is Menwith Hill." Her own attempt to sound spooky didn't sound right to her ears, but maybe it worked anyway. The reactions to her statement were certainly varied and Miranda suspected would have told a different person far more than it told her.

Andi raised her eyebrows in surprise, then looked pleased. Perhaps at Miranda getting it right, though she didn't pat her on the back this time.

Mike looked puzzled.

Group Captain Raymond Fielding twisted sharply to look at her, then looked as quickly away.

Holly's reaction she didn't understand at all; she went as white as a ghost.

Miranda liked that—she'd found that metaphor without any effort at all.

18

"MAN, THAT'S A LOT OF OVERSIZED GOLF BALLS." MIKE WAS looking out the window.

"Thirty-seven radomes," Miranda understood the analogy without having to ask! Back pat. "There are presently thirty-seven at Menwith Hill."

The white golf-ball-shaped radar domes varied from fifteen to fifty meters in diameter—most of twenty stories tall.

"I think it would make more sense if their arrangement was less haphazard. RAF Menwith Hill covers six hundred and five acres—two hundred and forty-four hectares. That's one radome every six-point-five hectares, which seems alarmingly inefficient. Though those numbers are shifted because of several operations and security buildings, sufficient for the two thousand staff needed to operate the site, they can obviously function in much closer proximity."

The white radomes themselves were transparent to radio signals. Inside each one would be a large radio dish antenna for communicating with various NRO satellites and for eavesdropping upon those of other nations. The radomes would keep them out of the weather as well as masking where the antennas were aimed. Miranda approved of the dual purpose in design.

She made a note to think about that in the design of her new home. The old hunting lodge on Spieden Island had, in retrospect, been alarmingly inefficient in its layout before it burned down. Its destruction created a chance to rectify that. It was perhaps the first positive to come from the disaster.

Mike continued staring out the window as the helo landed.

Miranda decided to assume that meant a continued interest. "The National Reconnaissance Office runs these sites for the National Security Agency. They link to all of our surveillance satellites. The more sensitive satellites can pick up and track cell phone communications from orbit. They can also intercept worldwide radio satellite communications. Oh, and there are several links to the global undersea cable network."

"That's a lot of data."

"It is. There are five to six billion people who are awake at any time of day. Even if only one in a hundred is on the phone at any one time—"

"That's a hell of a lot of phone calls."

That was the point Miranda would have made if she'd been allowed to finish her sentence. At least she understood now that once the point was made, she no longer needed to finish the sentence. Its brokenness still bothered her, but at least she understood.

"Do I want to ask what they do with all of this?"

"Probably not with Group Captain Fielding listening in,"

Andi pointed out; she too must have noticed his earlier reaction. "We don't know his level of clearance."

"Bloody well higher than you lot," he spoke for the first time since they'd boarded. Then he made a face that said he wished he hadn't.

Andi's laugh didn't sound very nice or friendly.

"Assumptions, Captain. Be very careful of assumptions," Mike warned him.

He looked unhappy but returned his attention to the landing.

Miranda stared out at the base. "I don't understand. It seems unlikely that there is an aircraft accident here at Menwith Hill; they have no runway. Why would they call me here?"

"Because," Holly's voice barely sounded in the cabin despite the heavy sound insulation, "this is the place where the end of the world begins."

Miranda tried to detect any hint of the broad Strine in Holly's voice that would mean she was joking—but couldn't.

19

GROUP CAPTAIN RAYMOND FIELDING HATED BEING AN ERRAND boy. He was the ranking British officer at Menwith Hill, the Deputy Chief of Operations, except the Yanks could overrule him and the entire British Ministry of Defence whenever it struck them as amusing.

However, Prime Minister Whittaker had made it clear. This woman, with sheep shit on her boots, mud splattered up to her knees, and a worn daypack twice the size that was needed for any day hike, required his personal escort. A brainless mission in which he mustn't fail. She'd declined to explain herself.

The three companions, *her team,* were even more unlikely. The little Chinese, the blustering Aussie (he certainly knew that type all too well). He'd done his time in Pine Gap—deep in the middle of the Australian Outback— their counterpart to the Menwith Hill installation. Their arrogance was unbelievable. The only one with any hint of manners had been the man who carried himself with a proper sense of subtle self-deprecation, yet he had the most American accent of them all.

They knew about Menwith Hill, which the average person didn't. And details, the odd little woman who'd argued about dictionary definitions of vacations, she knew details which she shouldn't. Nothing top secret, but details nonetheless.

The pilot settled the helo at Menwith Hill's grassy heliport and began shutting down the aircraft.

When Fielding tried to lead them toward the operations center, the blonde stopped him with a grab of his jacket's collar.

"What the bloody hell?"

"Just give it a sec, mate."

Miranda Chase had stopped and set her daypack on the ground. From it she extracted a many-pocketed vest very like the one she was already wearing. She transferred several items from the one she wore, but not all of them. Then she switched vests. She looked from one to the other as if checking the dumbest fashion statement in the world.

"What are you—"

"I wouldn't," the lone man of the group said. "You'll only slow her down if you start asking questions."

As if she could possibly go any slower.

When she held up a birding book and scanned the Menwith Hill grounds, he gave up.

"Now! We're moving now, Ms. Chase. Let's go." He hadn't been told what was so urgent, but the Prime Minister had left little doubt about that.

She acted as if she hadn't heard him.

"Have you gone deaf?" He stepped over to yank her to her feet from where she squatted by her pack.

He only made it one step, his arm half extended. An utterly obscene bolt of pain launched from his chest. Bloody hell! Was he having a having a heart attack just like Father? One moment hale and hearty, the next flopped face down on his bank manager desk.

He couldn't breathe—to do so would hurt far too much to consider. Unable to move his eyes for fear of his head exploding in agony, he could only watch his half-extended arm, frozen in space and time. The scale of the pain utterly precluded any other signals traveling down his nervous system. He could only hope that Father hadn't felt such pain before he died.

Then it eased to merely catastrophic.

A voice whispered close by his ear. A sweetly feminine voice with a thick Strine accent worthy of the deepest Outback in Oz. "You really need to learn to listen, mate. It would vastly increase your life expectancy."

Which had better be less than ten seconds or he wouldn't survive it because—

In a flash, the pain was gone, suddenly no more than the worst memory of his life.

The blonde Australian patted his chest. "It'll clear in a few minutes."

Okay, not gone, but a tenth, a thousandth of the mind-numbing agony of the moment before. A pectoral pinch. With no more than a simple grasp, she'd abused him past reason.

"I'll have you up on charges for—"

"Civilian, mate. You can't touch me." She didn't look the least bit bothered. "And don't go throwing *His Majesty's* government into this. We Aussies aren't exactly huge fans of the Commonwealth."

He was aware of the breath still wracking in and out of his own lungs like a steel rasp. The pain definitely wasn't gone; it had only seemed that way for a moment after the sudden release.

He'd had enough of all of these people. He'd been called to duty three nights in a row. Nothing major, but enough that he'd had to leave home and spend several hours here in the middle of each night. There was no telecommuting with Menwith Hill data.

Oblivious to everything around her, the Chase woman had finally decided against transferring the birding book to her new vest. As she tucked the other vest into her pack, she turned enough for him to see the fifteen-centimeter letters on her back, NTSB.

And why the NTSB? He'd seen the data and it looked pretty damn obvious to him. If corroboration was required, why wasn't the AAIB the one on call? The Air Accidents Investigation Branch didn't need the Americans any more than he did.

When Chase stood and shouldered her pack, she then went through a ritual of some sort, touching every tool or notebook in every pouch and pocket twice.

The blonde was watching her with an irrational patience. Relaxed, actually paying attention to Chase's ritual.

He went for a solar plexus blow that had put his opponents on the ground several times during hand-to-hand combat training. It had worked splendidly twenty years before during his six months Basic Training at Catterick Garrison just north of here. He would show the blonde Aussie who—

Raymond landed face down in the grass so fast that it knocked the wind out of him. His arm was twisted far up behind his back. He knew if he even breathed it would dislocate his shoulder. Christ! He'd never seen anyone so fast.

"Well, that was a shit-for-brains maneuver." The woman let him go. Raymond continued lying with the side of his face in the grass, wondering if he might need a sling.

Mike knelt until Raymond could see his face. "I tried to warn you because I can feel your pain. Took me a long time to learn to be careful around trigger-happy SASR operators."

SASR? Raymond pushed up enough, using his other hand, to look at the woman now standing beside Miranda. "Who are you people?"

Mike offered him a friendly grimace before helping him to his feet. "Like we said, not sure if you're cleared to know that, buddy."

20

"I'M THE GODDAMN DEPUTY DIRECTOR OF THIS OPERATION."
Group Captain Fielding was speaking far more loudly than
seemed appropriate. "And you aren't leaving this office until
I know who you are and that you have the clearance..." He
appeared to enjoy hearing himself talk.

It was one of Miranda's newer observations. The people
on her team talked mostly when they had something to say,
a joke to make, or communication that they felt to be
relevant to Miranda herself such as comments on their
mood or the mood of others. She'd also cataloged a
moderate percentage of what she could only classify as
pleasant chit-chat.

Some were more taciturn; Colonel Taz Cortez had
demonstrated that consistently when she'd been on
Miranda's team. And her husband Jeremy was consistently
more loquacious, especially when excited by a topic. He
often outpaced Taz by a factor of three times under normal
conditions and as high as a factor of eight when a topic truly
caught his interest.

Group Captain Fielding belonged to a recently defined category in Miranda's *Society-at-Large* notebook: *Talkers*.

She stopped listening and assessed his office at three hundred square f—at thirty square meters. It was nicely appointed, one end filled by a large conference table, the other by a desk and a small seating area. Beyond the window, a wide assortment of radomes could be observed in various sizes implying hidden radio dishes from five to thirty meters. The only sound over forty decibels inside the office was the HVAC system's circulating fan and Fielding's voice.

Without listening to Fielding, the world was finally still enough for her to consider what was happening.

Her team had been extracted from a vacation due to a crisis and she had Andi's diagram to verify that. Then transported to Menwith Hill. The RAF base had no runway, only a heliport, and there'd been no accident there.

She'd been in the White House Situation Room enough times to understand that some investigations were, by necessity, performed remotely. The available data was distinctly different in such situations than visiting an actual wreckage site. She'd found a way to work with that by imagining that it was simply data that led up to the physical incident. Then the physical was skipped over and alternate-source data could be gathered to confirm or expand the variables.

It was an investigator's duty to inspect all pre-incident information before determining causal factors.

None of the physical information would be in this office but a great deal of information and imagery would be.

By the sound of Fielding's diatribe (she'd confirm that descriptor with Andi if he'd ever stop talking), Miranda wondered if the British wouldn't validate her clearance without performing their own investigation—typically a year-long process. She remembered the word *Crisis* from Andi's drawing. That would imply the need for more immediate action.

Crises called for action.

Miranda pulled her phone out of its vest pocket and dialed a number.

"Hey! There are no uncleared cell phones allowed in this facility."

It was answered on the third ring. "Hi, Miranda. How are you?"

Miranda took a moment to assess that. "I'm okay, I think. I was on vacation. We were walking the Herriot Way in the Yorkshire Dales, but now I'm in Menwith Hill with a Group Captain who likes to hear himself talk at length. I find this very confusing."

"Me too," Lizzy answered. "What is the Group Captain talking about?"

"I don't know. I wasn't listening closely because he wasn't communicating any information."

The group captain made a loud spluttering noise like...a burst hydraulic line with a failing pump engaging and disengaging. Was a convoluted metaphor still a viable one? Probably not. She considered creating a chart of complexity verses metaphorical efficacy, but decided that she still didn't have enough insight into metaphors themselves to create a meaningful analysis.

"Let me talk to him."

Miranda reached out to hand her phone to him, but Holly intercepted it. She glanced at the screen, smiled her *evil* smile (Miranda had cataloged Holly's evil smile as being quite distinct from her other smiles), then hit the Speaker key.

"Hey Lizzy! Holly here. There's a sticky wicket here named Group Captain Raymond Fielding. Blighter seems to think being Deputy Chief of Menwith Hill makes him important in some way. I've already kicked his ass twice, but apparently he's a slow learner. You want to go a round with the bloke?"

"Ah," Lizzy said. "Hold a minute." Then she was gone.

"Who the bloody hell is Lizzy and why would I have any interest in what she—"

"Okay, I'm back," Lizzy cut off Fielding. "This is General Elizabeth Gray, Director of the NRO. I'm responsible for all operations at Menwith Hill."

Which, Miranda supposed, was an accurate statement. The NRO ran the site for the National Security Agency. The NSA cared about the data, not the antennas or satellites that conveyed it. So, all operational aspects of Menwith Hill and the two other global NSA sites were Lizzy's to take care of.

Fielding was having some sort of a reaction that might have been the onset of an epileptic fit. Miranda placed her hand on a wooden carpenter's pencil in her vest in case he suddenly needed a wooden bite guard to avoid hurting himself.

"And this is Prime Minister Olivia Whittaker. Hello, Miranda. I'm so sorry for interrupting your vacation but we have a matter of some importance."

"I'm glad," Miranda answered. This statement earned her several odd looks from her team. "That matches my conclusion of why we are here. Except there seems to be some issue about our clearance."

"What's the issue?"

"Group Captain Fielding appears concerned with my and my team's authorization to be present on his base. He definitely has resistance to leading us to the operations floor."

"I will not allow unknowns to wander—" Fielding apparently didn't need her wooden pencil.

Miranda removed her hand from it. In the process, she brushed her ID. "He never checked our security clearances. Perhaps that's the issue."

Holly's laugh sounded very amused by something.

"If you wish to remain in the service, Group Captain," Olivia spoke up, "You will begin by scanning their security clearances and then escorting them immediately to the main floor of the Operations Center. I and their President need answers an hour ago, not an hour from now."

"But Olivia," Miranda protested in some alarm. "An hour ago I was eating chicken-and-ham Yorkshire pie. I couldn't possibly have given you an answer when I still didn't know there was a crisis or—as continues into the present—what the crisis might be."

"It's a turn of phrase," Andi clarified in the silence that seemed to stretch out too long. "It simply means she needs answers quickly."

"Oh."

"Miranda, do you still have my direct number?" Olivia asked.

"Yes." Another odd twitch from the Group Captain. She put her hand back on the wooden pencil as a precaution.

"Good, call me the moment you have any information. Get them moving, Group Captain. Goodbye, General Gray."

Lizzy echoed the salutation, then they both were gone.

Group Captain Fielding checked their security badges in

his system, twice each as if he didn't quite believe what he was seeing. While he did this, a muscle along his jawline jumped in a chaotically arrhythmic manner that resisted all of Miranda's attempts to determine a timing pattern.

In minutes they each wore visitor badges and were being escorted across a wide hallway where they showed their brand-new badges to a security guard. Once he too was satisfied, from behind his thick wall of bullet-proof glass, he pressed a buzzer that opened one of the heavy doors beside his station.

As they stepped in, Miranda was trying to decide which should hang to the front, her NTSB badge or the visitor one. If she chose the latter, it would communicate her status most clearly to any who met her. But if she did that, how was she supposed to introduce herself? With the NTSB badge forward she could always say her memorized greeting, *Hello. I'm Miranda Chase. Investigator-in-Charge for the NTSB.*

There was a quiet, steady cursing beside her. Perhaps Holly too was having trouble with her badge precedence.

No, she was looking at the room they'd stepped into. There was no sign of her evil smile, or any other smile. She did look as if she'd much rather still be eating fish and chips at the Tan Hill Inn. If they had named it properly, the Tan Fell Pub, Miranda would be inclined to agree, but the name disconnect was still jarring.

No, this was a world she understood far better than that place high atop the fell that was called a hill.

21

THE BUZZ OF HER INTERCOM JOLTED CLARISSA OUT OF THE FILE she'd been studying as if she'd been slammed into a wall.

"What? Yes?" Incoherent, but Merle had learned to not take it personally. He'd been so competent as Clark's assistant that she'd kept him on when she'd become director. He was the first assistant she'd ever had who lasted more than a year. She often joked that he was forbidden to retire unless she was dead. A former senior field agent, he knew every trick in the book to block the idiots who wanted a slice of her time. He also knew precisely who to let through.

And when she asked for something or someone herself? He always nodded his graying head like a wise old sage, *Yes, Director Reese.* And in hours, often minutes, whatever she needed would materialize.

"The Russia Desk Director is asking to see you on an urgent matter."

One of the skills that had elevated Clarissa so quickly to being the Director of the CIA was her ability to adapt instantly to rapidly changing scenarios, but she couldn't wrap her head around it this time.

She'd been surprised that the files of Sam and Olivia Chase were Director's Eyes Only classified, then realized she shouldn't have been. Their stars were on the Memorial Wall, of course they'd been into something heavy.

To avoid questions, she'd looked up the file number herself before going down to the archives. The librarian could do that for her, but because the Chases' stars on the wall and in the *Book of Honor* were anonymous, she decided against having the librarian run the query.

The librarian had led her to a locked room that looked little different from those spread down the long underground corridor. Except this one had two locks, not one. They'd each inserted a key, then a code, and Clarissa had entered alone. There were no machines here. No computers, no copiers, no fiche readers. No documents bearing the DEO security classification were ever made electronic.

She'd expected the Chase file to be slim, typical of some low- to mid-level agent who happened to die in the line of duty—it wasn't. It would have filled half a file box. She was certainly not going to read all that in the deep basement. Knowing it was purely psychological didn't matter. This room had full temperature and humidity controls like the rest of the archive, but it had felt as if she was being buried alive in that vault of the nation's darkest secrets.

Clarissa had selected a portable safe box of the appropriate size, dumped in their files, and sealed it. It was unusual for the Director to carry such a large case herself and she was sure it garnered her many curious looks once she was past.

Anyone who saw her carrying a DEO case was welcome to worry what she was up to. A few looked concerned for their very lives. Maybe she should do this more often, though maybe she'd use an empty box next time, this thing was heavy.

Once securely locked in her office, she spread them out on her desk. Sam and Olivia had been recruited as a couple during college—Yale, how stereotypical—and been thirty-eight when they died, leaving behind thirteen-year-old autistic Miranda.

The first quarter of their files were thin reports typical of a successful husband-wife team. It was the height of the Cold War and they'd managed to float back and forth across the Iron Curtain with an ease rarely matched before the fall of the Berlin Wall. They were also among the few agents who had successfully transitioned from the USSR to the Russian Federation.

The purge and power shifts within Russia had been so severe that most established contacts had become useless. Sam and Olivia's contacts had not. In fact, after the fall, Sam and Olivia Chase's files underwent a drastic expansion, not a contraction.

Her intercom buzzed again, but Merle didn't speak from his desk outside her office.

Five minutes. Merle knew that was all it had typically taken to satisfy her late husband when she'd drop in for a surprise round of office sex while he was Director, or he'd dropped in on her once she'd taken control of the agency. Clark might be dead, but the patterns of their lives together lived on.

"Russia Desk," Clarissa remembered. "Right. Send her in. No, give me one minute, then send her in."

Sex in her office had always been Clark's domain.

Before his execution in a North Korean prison, she and Kurt had made love in many interesting places, but her office hadn't been one of them. She couldn't walk past the CIA's indoor firing range or the SOG's armory without a blinding flash of heat surging up her body. Or the indoor track where they had raced naked until they were both drenched with one kind of sweat before another kind had slicked their bodies. Or...

Damn him to Hell for being dead!

She used that minute to tuck all the Chase files regarding a Russia of twenty-seven years ago into the secure case. She locked it at the same moment that her door latch snapped electronically aside after precisely sixty seconds, and Director Valentina Mills strode in.

She was slender where Clarissa was full-figured, several inches shorter, and had a severe chin-length cut to her oak-brown hair. But her knowledge of Russia could be traced back to a childhood passion for her grandfather's stories of escape from tsarist Russia as a boy. He was one of the lucky few who'd been smuggled out. Most of the rest of his family had been shot along a railroad siding for being tsarist supporters during the October Revolution. His granddaughter, a decade older than Clarissa, had a serious hate on for all things Russian. That drive had made her one of the world's leading authorities on the country.

Clarissa didn't imagine leaving her post in the foreseeable future, but if someone had to replace her...

Perhaps it was time to take Director Mills' future in hand.

"Sorry to keep you waiting, Val." Clarissa nudged a foot against the DEO case at her feet, turning it enough for the security panel to be easily visible through the thick glass sheet that was her desk. "Please have a seat."

Val's eyes flickered down, lingered long enough to show interest, then looked up. She didn't sit. "There's a situation that I felt you should be made aware of."

"Please." Clarissa did her best to show interest, but her mind was still preoccupied by the Chases' files. She'd long ago learned to recognize the curve of a pending major operation, and theirs bore all the trademarks. But she hadn't reached it yet. The sheer volume of the file dedicated to the final few years of their lives told her she needed to study the build-up to understand it fully and—

"Wait. What? Run that by me again. A midair collision over the North Sea this morning?"

"Yes, Director. About six a.m. our time."

Clarissa glanced at a clock. Two hours ago.

Val restarted her explanation.

Russian and US? Both aircraft down in the ocean. Near an aircraft carrier?

"Source?" She cut Val off.

Val hesitated. Which answered the question—a deep asset. The kind that was never revealed beyond the senior agent controlling them, not even to the Desk Director or the D/CIA.

"Ours or theirs?" Clarissa asked. She'd done her best to have her agents cultivate...*contacts* within the various intelligence and military organizations of the US as well as among allies. She didn't do it within US Borders, that was the FBI's area of control by the letter of the law. But once they were overseas, she considered anyone to be a fair target.

"Theirs."

"On CNN yet?"

Val shook her head.

Two hours through a Russian intelligence asset. Fully scrubbed of any identity and on her desk that fast meant that their mole and the agent running them at the other end thought this was crucial intelligence. Nothing except the worst news moved that fast through so many protective layers.

Clarissa punched a speed-dial on her phone.

"What do you want, Clarissa?" Drake Nason hated her guts, which was fair as it was completely mutual. But as he was Chairman of the Joint Chiefs of Staff, the highest-ranking officer in the US military, and she was the D/CIA, They worked with it. She did wish that she hadn't used the speakerphone in front of Val Mills, but perhaps it was time to show her how this world worked.

"North Sea. Wanted to make sure you were aware."

He grunted. "A lot going on there at the moment."

"Midair collision. Both down."

"Source?" Drake didn't sound surprised.

"Grab a clue. You know I'm not going to tell you that, Drake. Reliability is—" she glanced at Val who pointed a finger sharply upward "—is considered very high."

Drake grunted.

"Drake? Are we at war?"

There was a long pause. Long enough for her to trade a worried look with her Director of the Russia Desk.

"Not yet. Anything else?"

"Not yet." Clarissa did her best to mimic his dry tone.

"Let me know immediately if there is. Top priority, Clarissa. Reach deep on this one. It's dicey."

"Okay." That meant to risk burning the asset if it provided better intel. An asset, who may have taken years to cultivate, could be thrown away for a single answer if the question was important enough. That Drake had said that told her how serious this was, which told her quite how much *was* going on in the North Sea.

Clarissa glanced down at the locked file box by her feet, holding Sam and Olivia Chases' files. There'd been little mention of their troubled autistic daughter past the Personal Summary page.

"Drake, if it's a collision, you should call Miranda."

"Already done."

Bitch! They call *her* before they call the D/CIA? Clarissa knew it wasn't professional, but she'd love to rip Miranda's hair out.

"Chill the fuck out, Clarissa."

"I didn't say a word!" That Drake knew her well enough to read her silences only made her despise his every living breath even more. No one was allowed to know what she was thinking—ever.

"Their PM called her directly. I only found out two minutes ago. Lizzy called me the moment she found out to let me know."

Clarissa managed a deep breath.

Didn't work.

The order of contact still rankled.

Another breath merely burned in her lungs. "Do you have anything else for m—"

But Drake was gone.

"Bastard!"

Val was eyeing her warily.

Clarissa let herself flop back in her chair. "Welcome to the next level, Director Val Mills. Now," she sat upright once more because she was willing to show frustration but not weakness. "In order: who can we tap *without* destroying the asset? Who wouldn't we mind burning for the right information? And finally, who do we burn if we have to?"

They began discussing the various moles and agents embedded in Russia and Belarus. It wasn't as if the Russian Federation had a whole collection of other allies left since launching their Special Military Operation in Ukraine. The only other real candidates were the Chinese, balancing the East-versus-West knife edge so carefully that they wouldn't know anything—or Iran, a fucked up nightmare—and a couple of small satellite countries so unimportant that no one outside their borders could remember their names.

Clarissa ignored the itch that told her she should be delving more deeply into the Chases' files. She had to be alone to do that. Somewhere in there she'd hit the reason their lives were labeled Director's Eyes Only.

22

A FEW MONTHS AGO MIRANDA HAD BEEN TO THE NRO/NSA satellite station at Buckley Space Force Base in Colorado. She'd entered the Operations Center but had little time to look around due to an imminent assassination attempt of Prime Minister Olivia Whittaker.

This time at Menwith Hill she allowed herself to observe the environment carefully—it might prove useful if any rapid follow-up reactions were called for.

The room was all about computer monitors and dim lights. At the front of the room opposite the entrance, four large displays around a massive central screen were mounted high enough on the walls for everyone in the room to see easily. And while the half-lighting made the large screens easy to read, it turned the room's occupants into half-seen ghosts, each lit mostly by their own array of monitors.

In curved banks, like NASA's Mission Control Center at Houston, were three long rows of side-by-side desks. Each station had a trio of monitors available to the operator. The focus, however, didn't appear to follow the lines of the rows, but rather clustered in sections.

To the right side of the room she identified satellite control, most of the screens displaying orbital information. Behind them, a team focused on communication channels, presumably between ground and satellite. Next toward the center were stations clearly labeled Pine Gap and Buckley—Australia and Colorado. They would manage information flow from satellites presently below the horizon from Menwith Hill, as well as those two teams of analysts.

The left side of the room were the team leads for various countries: Russia, Iran, Saudi Arabia, North Korea, and other leads by continent. The support teams, cryptography, and many other support services would be in nearby rooms, feeding their results to the appropriate desk on the main Ops Floor.

The center of the room included six stations arranged around the single desk of the Mission Director. These were the people who managed the results coming in from both sides of the room and turned it into actionable intelligence —taking action as necessary.

All of the operators wore headsets and a low murmur of chatter pervaded the air.

At their own entrance, it seemed that the chatter level dropped by at least fifty percent. Unlike Tan Hill Inn, Miranda now wore her crash-site investigation vest. She extracted her Castle sound level meter from its pocket and took a reading. It recorded noise levels by frequency in one-third octave increments. When sound levels returned to normal, she'd take another reading and compare them.

Was sound suppression a local effect of her presence? Or perhaps Group Captain Fielding's? It had occurred atop Tan

Hill and also here. She'd never made note of that aspect of her immediate environment before and would now have to quantify it carefully before she could chart possible causal relationships.

Then she focused on the instrument in her hand for a moment.

"Oh." She handed it to Andi.

"What?"

"I just remembered how I learned to recognize the different sounds of various aircraft and their motive elements: engines, turbines, propellors, rotors, APUs, and so on."

Andi turned the instrument over as if the answer might be on the back. It wasn't, so Miranda turned her wrist to show the front again.

"If you observe the different graph profiles on the meter's screen as various aircraft are passing by, you'll learn to recognize them. Here," she accessed the memory feature. "This is an AgustaWestland AW109S; see the strong secondary harmonic at ten-point-three kilohertz? Or this," she pulled up another. "This is my F-86 Sabrejet. Takeoff," she toggled to the next file, "overflight," and again, "landing."

The sound wave graphs on the small screen shifted accordingly.

"It is much easier to see on a larger computer screen, and you'll want good headphones. I'll send the app and recordings to you."

Andi handed it back as if it was about to...bite her? "I think I'll leave that part of it to you." She turned her attention back to avidly studying each screen.

Holly was staring so fixedly at the room that it was hard to tell if she was seeing anything.

Only Mike appeared intrigued. "Ah, the secret sauce of another of your magic tricks."

"I can do magic tricks?"

"Sufficiently advanced science is indistinguishable from magic."

"Arthur C. Clarke," Miranda knew the quote. She'd rather liked the idea that she could do magic and was as abruptly disappointed that she couldn't. She tucked away the instrument as a towering black woman rose from the operations desk, shed her headset, and stepped in their direction. Her skin was so dark that she was hard to focus on in the dimly lit room.

"Who are these folks, Fielding?"

Her tone seemed neutral. Miranda could never be sure, but she'd learned to watch for her team's reactions. No one shifted up onto their toes, leaned forward, or—in the most extreme cases—moved to block Miranda's vision of them. In many situations she was forced to observe the interlocutor over or around the shoulders of her protective team members. Their lack of intercession at least *indicated* a nonaggressive posture from the woman.

"Some team that PM Whittaker asked for. They're—"

"Which one of you is Miranda Chase?"

"My name is Miranda Chase. I'm the investigator-in-charge for the NTSB."

"Chief of the Facility Astrid Underwood, pleased to meet you." She held out a hand.

Miranda had never come up with a good solution for these moments. She didn't like touching others, especially strangers. Andi had cured her of this—but only in the scope of Andi as a single individual—and never for very long except during sex or very strong hugs.

"Uh, hi." Miranda kept her hands firmly wrapped around her sound level meter.

Mike solved it by taking Astrid's hand before she withdrew it and then introducing the others of the team.

Chief of Facility meant that she was the top-ranked NSA officer on one of the world's three largest satellite monitoring sites. She would have a direct line to everyone from the Pentagon to the White House. That might prove useful.

Astrid watched her closely as Miranda carefully tucked away the meter. This took a little doing to protect the microphones. They were a significant portion of the four-thousand-dollar cost of the device. Astrid then eyed her now empty hands, but made no move to offer hers again, so everything was okay.

"I'm told that you can help us with a problem, though I'm unsure how."

"Without knowing the nature of the problem, I don't know either."

"Replay on Screen Two," Astrid called out to the room.

One of the screens at the front of the room flickered. It had been showing an area around a carrier strike group that must be patrolling along Norway's coast, based on the latitude and longitude listed in the corner of the screen. They were well-positioned to block access to the Baltic Sea though Miranda couldn't imagine why someone would want to do that. It provided several countries including Germany, Sweden, and Russia with their primary access to the Atlantic.

Now it was replaced by a view that appeared to be only ocean. Two tracking circles were superimposed on opposite sides of the screen.

"Two and a half hours ago at 1000 local time, we had a

CMV-22 Osprey flight crossing the North Sea from RNAS Yeovilton in southern England to the USS *Gerald R. Ford* patrolling off Norway. At that time the other flight, a Russian AN-74MP NATO designator Coaler, was redirected by Gromovo Air Base to intercept our aircraft."

The left screen began scrolling two columns of text, one in Russian and the other in English. The order to intercept and the AN-74's acknowledgement rolled up the screen. She didn't wholly agree with the translation, but the errors were non-substantive, so she ignored them for the moment.

"They sent the order in the clear?" Andi sounded surprised.

"No," was all Astrid said in reply. That meant that the NSA had broken the current Russian military encryption.

"What the... Oh." Mike was the only one who seemed surprised, until he too figured it out.

Miranda watched the Coaler turn and settle on the new intercept course. Personally she preferred the Russian designator of Cheburashka, but perhaps whoever named aircraft for NATO didn't like small, cute, fictional animals.

"Nothing remarkable for the next twenty-one minutes."

Some operator took that as a cue to scroll ahead to a high-resolution image of the two aircraft converging.

As the image fast forwarded, more text flowed up the screen time-stamped two minutes after the initial Russian transmission. It was a warning sent to the Osprey to be on the lookout for the converging Antonov. It was labeled MWH for Menwith Hill.

Just after that, MWH messaged the aircraft carrier recommending they launch their alert fighters toward the most likely rendezvous point. And their acknowledgement to do so.

By the time the operator returned the display to normal speed, the Antonov flew close along the Osprey's starboard side. It briefly disappeared from view as it passed below the Osprey, then came up to the port side.

They flew in tandem for thirty seconds—then the Antonov sideslipped into the Osprey. The collision and destruction became inevitable from the moment the Russian's wingtip intersected the proprotor's blades. When the wings became entangled and the aircraft slammed nose-to-nose, Miranda didn't need to watch it to know what would happen next.

She was half turned from the screen when something caught her attention.

Facing the screen once more, she watched the AN-74MP recover. *That* was unexpected. She continued watching until it was blown to bits by an AMRAM missile. She'd expected it to freefall into the ocean.

"What was it you said before Holly?" Miranda asked softly. "Well, dip me in sheep shit?"

"Got it in one, Miranda." Holly nodded without looking away from the screens.

"I get it now."

23

Far sooner than she intended, Clarissa chased Val Mills out of her office. Finally telling her to do what she thought best.

Val had looked surprised.

Clarissa admitted it wasn't an instruction she often gave, but she'd finally pinpointed the itch. It was locked away in the box at her feet.

Sam and Olivia Chase's file had listed their network of contacts within the reconstituted structure of the Russian Federation.

The names were the itch.

The file included no list of military, governmental, or business contacts.

But there'd been a list of their Russian social circle that she'd passed by.

Once Val was gone, it only took moment to locate Sam Chase's list of their personal contacts within Russia as of 1995, the year before their deaths. Not a single name in the leadership, then or now.

They were all women's first names followed by an initial. Women.

The Chases weren't a husband-and-wife team, they'd been a *wife-and-husband* team with Olivia Chase as the brains of their operation. How many prior male directors had looked at this unmarked list and dismissed them as Clarissa almost had?

The filed reports made it sound as if Sam Chase had been in the lead, but never identified any of his contacts.

What if *this* list said otherwise?

If Sam had the task of writing and filing the reports about the work that Olivia was doing, that would fit the tone —the arrogant male attempting to take credit for the female's achievements.

Clarissa began searching for the names and initials.

The first one she tracked down? Naina Y. turned out to be Anastasia *Naina* Yeltsina, the wife of former Russian President Boris Yeltsin.

That rocked Clarissa back in her chair. Friends with the President's wife? Perhaps close friends?

Clarissa started working her way down the list. It was a damn long list.

24

WHEN HE'D BEEN GROWING UP ON THIN BORSCHT AND STEWED beef, Artemy had dreamed of meals like this one at Buro TSUM. Or he would have if he'd possessed more imagination.

The ceiling was paneled with great sheets of hand-worked copper. Each table was different. He and Inessa had settled at a round table that was pleasant with two and would be comfortably cozy with four; so artfully made that it took him a moment to find the seam proving it was made from two great slabs of wood and not a single piece from a primordial forest. The next table over boasted an artistic marble slab that could seat eight. The one beyond that looked like hammer-beaten steel and the next different again. Great glass windows captured the April sunlight and showed Moscow at her best. Spring was the best season in the heart of Russia.

They'd arrived early, 1700 hours when dinner would normally be two or three hours later.

He teased Inessa by *not* asking why they were dining so early. It also explained how she'd managed a reservation on such short notice, though he'd wager she could walk in during peak service and find a table had magically opened for her.

As he'd suspected, the reason for the early dinner soon became crystal clear.

Their table, in addition to exquisite craftsmanship, also sat in easy view from the entrance. Not too close, but not tucked away in some corner either.

Many women, and a few men, who had been shopping at the TSUM department store that filled the four floors below them, came to Buro for a glass of wine and perhaps an appetizer before heading home for dinner. And people who could afford to come to Buro were not of the *apparatchik,* the worker dogs. While neither his family nor Inessa's were Soviet-era *nomenklatura*—she'd come from a background as humble as his own—those who flocked to visit their table upon spotting Inessa definitely were.

She made introductions.

Artemy had always had a good head for names and faces, so he was able to greet those he'd met even briefly as old friends. Those he didn't, he often knew their husbands despite his recent ascension to power. Inessa had made him wear his uniform. She'd teased him about being so handsome in it, but he'd bet that after a month or so, when his new rank had become an accepted fact, he would be dining in a suit stating that his rank no longer mattered, his power did.

During a brief lull, perhaps caused by the arrival of his beef fillet with wild mushrooms and truffle and Inessa's

Sakhalin scallops flown in fresh from the Far East and luxuriating in cauliflower cream, Inessa turned her full attention on him.

"You do this very well, Artemy."

"I merely follow your lead, my dear."

Her smile and light laugh were appreciative, perhaps for the audience of others who sat nearby and pretended to have conversations of their own. But her deep brown eyes remained serious.

"It may be time for you to lead."

For a moment his mind blanked. Lead? The country? Oust that lunatic in the Kremlin and his last few cronies to become... Then the absurdity sank in and he almost spit a black chanterelle mushroom into Inessa's lovely cleavage as he laughed.

He sobered at her sideways look—not the sexy one. "Please tell me you don't mean..." He let the sentence dribble out as they were relatively private at the moment but some things shouldn't be said aloud anywhere in Russia.

"No, I do not. You don't have the killer instinct. I thought Nikolas Romanoff did." Inessa poked around a shoot of baby asparagus, sending it wading into the cauliflower cream. "Regrettably, I was too young and too naive. He absolutely had it, but only in the most literal sense."

Artemy reached across the table to hold her hand as she studied her plate without seeing it.

"Well, you freed me of that mistake. Or I suppose he did when he unintentionally killed himself in his supreme act of arrogance. Perhaps, Artemy, you were my reward for surviving him." She squeezed his hand back.

They remained holding hands for a long moment. And

out of the corner of his eyes he could see the effect ripple outward from their table. Among the groups of women who had visited Inessa upon their arrival gathering at other tables, one would spot them, tell her friends, and then they would all glance this direction. Some quick and coy. Some would stare for a moment with a sadness sliding over their faces.

Sadness?

Ah, because their husbands would never think to hold their hand to comfort them. They had married power but only a lucky few had married for love as well.

He could see Inessa stuck deep in the memories of her long years with Nikolas Romanoff. Artemy knew he needed to shake her loose from those. With a final squeeze of her hand, he returned to his meal, slicing a bite from his beef fillet with his fork because it was so tender he didn't need a knife, and then immersing that in the gravy so rich it was more black than brown.

He held it out for her to taste.

When she leaned in, he whispered, "I'm glad you didn't mean what I first thought. I don't think I'd survive it."

Inessa shook off the past. "No, Artemy. You would not. Like me, you still remember what it was to be poor and hungry. None of these," her microscopic nod took in the women around her, "have the least idea. My dead husband never had a heart that hurt. Be warned, the Director doesn't either."

He hoped no one noticed the flash of anger that slid across her face—anger and disgust. But she schooled it quickly.

She took the bite and raised her eyebrows appreciatively as she chewed.

Artemy didn't argue. Moments after his daughter's death, Murov had been testing Artemy's loyalty and speed of thought by leaving that report about the American carrier strike group on his desk. Not opened as he'd been reading it, but closed, and turned enough to make the title easy to read.

"Natalia had a heart, a big one, big enough to dream of a better life."

"But she was from—" again, he didn't say it aloud. But Natalia Ivanovna Murov came from the very peak of the *oligarkhi,* daughter of the President's best friend and most trusted ally.

"Yes. And for that crime she was to be given to the highest bidder by her father. Oh, not for money, but for power. She chose a different path despite all of the obstacles—chose, and it killed her." She glanced at her watch. "Her mother was devastated when she left, and will be again. We have perhaps an hour before you return to the office. You must arrive after the director but not by many minutes."

Artemy set down his fork and leaned forward to listen. He ignored another round of flutters from the nearby tables.

Inessa began discussing details he had never heard. Not only of Director Murov and his daughter, but of the men who would be jealous of his sudden elevation and what forms their attacks might take. They weren't above using this crisis to sabotage Murov's new golden boy.

Then she began telling him how he must lead. The path to success was very narrow. But by the time they'd hashed it out over a quick dessert of rum baba and passionfruit sorbet, it was also clear—mostly.

Artemy had spent enough time on the front lines to know that plans lasted only until first contact with the enemy before they weren't worth the used toilet paper pumped into the Volga River.

On the street, before putting her in the car, he kissed her soundly for all to see. The timing was such that he walked the half kilometer back to the Lubyanka Building rather than calling for another car. It gave him time to organize his thoughts.

25

THE LIST OF NAMES LYING ON HER DESK LEFT CLARISSA breathless.

While he was still director, Clark had once mentioned what a great loss Miranda's parents had been for the CIA. The way this list had played out, he wasn't kidding. But he hadn't understood what they'd done, none of the prior directors had. All they'd seen was the abrupt hole left in their Russian intelligence operation by Sam and Olivia's death.

Because Olivia Chase's intelligence network had been exclusively made up of women.

Clarissa would give her left arm—well, Drake Nason's left arm—to still have assets with the quality of the unwitting moles Olivia Chase had...cultivated.

There'd been no recruiting them. No bribes that would grow over time. No payoffs to be stumbled upon due to an unbridled shopping spree or, stupidest of all, actually putting the cash into a bank.

Instead, Olivia Chase Mironova—a carefully buried

family name never used outside of Russia, except when she'd passed a form of it on to her daughter Miranda—had become their friend. The friend of every wife of every power player in the Soviet Union.

She'd spent years cultivating them. Leveraging a chance encounter that probably had nothing to do with coincidence, Olivia had built a whole constellation of top-tier access. And not one goddamn word of how she'd done it.

Sam, the handsome man of mystery, had been given a murky identity so like his real one that he would barely have to think to leverage it. Perhaps KGB, perhaps a personal spy for the Russian President himself, or maybe a military investigator reserved for the most sensitive cases.

It must have made Sam intensely attractive to the female coterie gathered by Olivia. She could imagine him at dinner parties with these women, never sharing secrets, but providing the most salacious gossip about the men who worked with their various husbands. According to his filed reports, he and Olivia would keep everyone guessing anything but the truth—that Olivia had turned the wives of the Russian elite into a spy ring.

Whatever she'd done, it had cost little more than financing Sam and Olivia to an appropriate lifestyle.

To keep them from observation, Olivia had suggested they be set up as caretakers of an obscure island in Washington State. The one they found was private, with no other residents to notice any unusual absences. It also had a runway, allowing CIA handlers and debriefing agents to easily visit unobserved for meetings.

But then they'd bought the island. Twenty-two-point-five million dollars' worth—cash. Where the hell had a couple of CIA agents come up with that kind of money? The sale of her condo and the liquidation of Clark's assets had made her comfortable, but not *that* comfortable.

Double agents? In Russia's pay?

That didn't fit what the file was telling her. She shuffled through the folders until she found the inevitable Security file.

She turned her chair to face the last of the morning sun streaming in her office window. These damn things always gave her the chills to read.

The first pages revealed that the intelligence they'd gathered had always proved actionable.

The latter pages showed no interest in any American intel beyond their own sphere of operations. Entrapment tests given to all agents—very juicy, though false, information that should propagate quickly if shared with a foreign power—never resurfaced after being fed to the Chases. In fact, twice they'd reported the person designated to slip the bad intel to them.

Honest? Or honestly dishonest? After all, they hadn't bought Spieden Island at first, instead living in the caretaker roles made up for them, paid some meaningless stipend by the land owner.

The collapse of the USSR had begun with the fall of the Berlin Wall in 1989 and finished in 1991 with the fracturing away of the independent Soviet Bloc countries.

Clarissa found their bank records in the file. By the end of 1992, the Chases were set for life. By 1994, they were truly rich. And in 1995 were able to buy the island outright. No mortgage, no bank. Paid in full. By 1996, when Clarissa herself was fourteen and discovering how awful her life could be when her mother died and her father shifted his vile attention to her, the Chases were wealthy and could have lived in luxury anywhere in the world.

And little Miranda Chase had been sitting in the middle of that with no clue how fucking lucky she was. Her screwed-up brain probably wouldn't understand even if someone explained it to her.

Now it was all hers: the island, the cash, the freedom to do anything she wanted. And there was the joke. Her idea of a good time? Crawling through the burned-out wreckage of crashed planes.

Yet there was no sign in the file that it had led to any suspicion of her parents.

Then they'd died. There wasn't a word in the file on how, but the date and location matched the *Book of Honor:* in Russia, on the day *before* TWA 800 had gone down.

Perhaps she was *too* used to operating on her own. Clarissa picked up the phone and called the Russia Desk. "Val, could you come see me?"

26

"SOMETHING'S MISSING HERE."

"No shit!" Clarissa was sick of all three of the Chases. Miranda was merely annoying, but Sam and Olivia had taken far too many of their secrets to the grave.

"Seriously, how did they die?" Val Mills had been helping her to analyze the file. Director's Eyes Only was at her discretion and she needed Val's help. When Clarissa had handed her the list of Olivia Chase's contacts within the pantheon of New Russia, she'd almost gone into cardiac arrest. *Not one! Not one of these women is still on our asset lists. What misogynistic asshole let this drop? Didn't he understand what he had?*

Now that she'd sat in the D/CIA's seat for the last four years, Clarissa had a slightly different view. To recreate the kind of connections Olivia Chase had forged would be impossible. Somehow, she'd made herself a darling of the Russian elite's *wives* during the collapse of the USSR.

Clarissa would wager that Ron Klemens had spent the rest of his tenure at the Russia Desk asking that same question and finding no answer. If any clues to Olivia's *modus operandi* had survived the Chase's death, Ron had reported no sign of it. He'd probably still been asking the question of how to recreate it when he'd died of a heart attack the year after he'd retired.

"Could the date be a typo and they really died on TWA 800?"

"It's not a typo." Clarissa had read the entry in the *Book of Honor.* Whoever had covered this up had put the truth, the *abbreviated* truth, in the book. They had also not recorded which Russian military plane crash had killed the Chases or how their corpses had ended up being fished from the ocean at the TWA investigation site.

So little Miranda's parents had died in a crash, but not the one she thought.

Clarissa did her best to keep the smile off her face. She hadn't decided whether or not to tell Miranda and, if yes, by who. But if she did, she'd make sure she was there to watch.

27

They'd been leafing through Sam Chase's reports of Olivia's activities in Russia until Clarissa's entire desk was papered with the things. It was a window into a past over a quarter-century gone.

Val Mills pulled a sheet. "Here's where the accumulation of wealth began."

Clarissa looked it over, but there were too many details and not enough contextual substance. "I was nine. I was focused on boys and multiplication tables. What's going on in Russia at this time?"

"Whereas I'm old," Val smiled but showed no signs of being pissy about reporting to a younger woman. "So ancient I was in my first year of college chasing a dual masters in Russian language and political economics—and boys. Okay, short form. In 1990 and '91 the Wall is down and the USSR is falling apart. Gorbachev eased the government's chokehold on business. A bunch of his KGB buddies start taking over and running firms. Most of this policy ends in the disaster you'd expect. The new, inexperienced-but-Western-business-minded owners fighting the entrenched communist managers and so on. Production collapses in numerous key industries, which ripples into connected industries run by other incompetents."

"Then the USSR completely fell apart." Clarissa did her best to lock in the details as Val laid them out. She spent every day buried in present-day-crises and future-disaster-mitigation thinking.

"Right. Goodbye Mikhail, hello Boris. So, Yeltsin comes to power. In the early '90s, the cash began to flow but nowhere near fast enough. All that came to a head in 1995. Debt is rising, everyone is underpaid or not paid at all. The army is selling arms and nukes on the black market so that they can eat. Teachers aren't eating at all. Yeltsin finally crawls out of his drunken-depression recluse hole long enough to create a loans-for-shares voucher system. He gives every citizen a ten-thousand-ruble voucher to invest in a company of their choice."

"And a ruble at that time?"

"In 1991, it was introduced at a buck-eighty per US dollar. By 1992, it had collapsed to about a hundred to the dollar and by 1995, it was over five thousand to the dollar, about two hundredths of a cent."

"So ten thousand rubles was better than kick in the crotch, but not much."

"Right. Unless you held those vouchers in bulk. Big bulk. For the single comrade-investor, the choices are terrible. But the more successful businessmen are still tied in hard to the Communist Party, even if they are no longer communists. They tapped the party funds to purchase great swaths of these vouchers at kopeks to the ruble. Plus several other scams, like rigged auctions and so on."

Clarissa nodded, "So, they turned millions of rubles of party money into hundreds of millions. Probably billions collectively."

"Trillions," Val corrected. "Boris pumped several trillion rubles' worth of voucher paper into the market. Its real value wasn't in rubles but in that it was effectively a share in a formerly state-owned industry. Those buyouts were a consolidation of wealth far more rapid than happened here in the US, if not as complete."

Clarissa nodded. Of the significant world countries, only Turkey, Brazil, and Mexico had worse wealth inequality than the States. How the poor survived in the hellholes of South America and the southern half of Africa, or the South-central US, she had no idea.

She tapped a finger on the stack of reports that were the Chase's finances. "And when the money begins to flow on that scale, it finds channels to flow into."

"Right. These documents shows a tiny sliver of it flowing to Olivia Chase through the women who controlled the household purse strings. Small change compared to the volume of cash deluging the pockets of the men destined to become oligarchs, but not trivial."

Clarissa then dug down and found the purchase of Spieden Island by the Chases in 1995. "Mere change doesn't explain this one."

Val whistled and sat back, drumming her fingers on the paper, the tiny vibrations transmitted to Clarissa's elbows through the glass desktop like a distant rain drumming on the roof.

"Money must have been raining down in torrents," Clarissa tried to imagine the scale and couldn't. Somehow fifty or so men had bought an entire country and become the oligarchy.

"No, this was earlier." Val snapped her fingers. "Six months before the loans-for-shares system, Russian was in full freefall. The IMF and the World Bank stepped in, mid-1995. They put up a fifteen-billion-dollar bailout. It was pumped into the companies, that cash slid straight into the oligarchs' hands—which later was also used in buying yet more vouchers. It's estimated that under a quarter of that loan actually remained in the businesses they were intended for, instead flowing straight to the owners. We're talking ten billion or so, not rubles, but hard currency."

"But what does that have to do with the Chases?" Clarissa had continued paging through their file as Val had spoken.

She stopped on a page not in any CIA report format. It was the cover page of a loan on IMF letterhead. "Holy shit!"

Val sat up, then stood to look down at the file Clarissa couldn't seem to turn toward her. She gasped, then read aloud upside down, "IMF loan to the Russian Federation for the mitigation of national debt." Then she read the handwritten note in Russian on the cover page, "My deepest regards to Samuil and Olya for making this happen. Boris. Samuel and Olivia Chase?"

"Their cover names when in-country. Fifteen billion dollars effectively passed through their hands. Goddamn sticky-fingered bastards. They were on the take." If they were still alive, Clarissa would have them thrown in a prison so deep and dark they'd no longer believe sunlight existed.

"No," Val was shaking her head. "They had to take some money. This isn't a bribe in America that had to be slipped past some watchdog. This is simple graft in Russia. If they *hadn't* taken some money, they'd have come under instant suspicion. What's impressive is how little they took. Twenty-five million, not even two-tenths of a percent, would appear abstemious to the Russians."

"Perhaps why they received a personal thanks from the Russian President."

"Perhaps," Val agreed. "It also landed when he was desperate. Yeltsin was set to lose the 1996 election to the communists. We sent in a political advisor team, even shipped over President Clinton for a glad-handing visit."

So Miranda had honest but graft-laden parents.

Who had died mysteriously...

"Val, when was Yeltsin's election?"

"July 3rd, 1996."

"And the Chases were dead less than two weeks later."

Val nodded after a moment. "That fits. The Russians couldn't risk the knowledge they had getting out. Or they needed someone to blame. Russia had asked for far more capital than that but were refused. Either way, arrange an accident to remove a problem. But why the priority on this? It's all ancient history."

"You're right. I appreciate the help in understanding this." She began gathering the documents together. "Let me know when we have anything new on today's incident."

Val nodded and left.

Clarissa tucked the Chase file back into the lockbox except for a few key pages.

Ancient history? That she was less sure about.

28

"And for what reason will you be dipped in shit?" Andi asked. "Personally, as you and I share a bed, I vote for it to be Holly."

"I didn't mean it literally," Miranda had thought she'd finally understood how analogies worked.

"Well, neither did I, except if we can do it to Holly."

"Thanks so much, mate," Holly's voice was...grim? She hadn't moved an inch since walking through the doors of the Menwith Hill Ops Floor. Holly stood, arms crossed and feet braced wide like...a really angry warrior?

Miranda did her best to parse this whole conversation, but it eluded her. Had her analogy succeeded or failed? Holly seemed to say yes and Andi no. Mike hadn't weighed in.

However, there had been the root cause of her comment before the dialogue had twisted aside like...the hookah-smoking caterpillar in *Alice in Wonderland*.

Had she fallen down a rabbit hole and would soon be forced to eat from two sides of a raw mushroom? She liked cooked mushrooms but the texture of raw ones, and the way they squeaked against her teeth when she bit into them, she found quite upsetting.

"Who is the image analyst who first observed this?" Miranda asked the tall black woman.

"That would be me," a man answered from the desk to her immediate right. "Ian Faulkner, IMINT Senior Analyst." He didn't hold out his hand, which Miranda appreciated.

"I need to see both flights from point-of-origin. As well as any information on both pilots of both aircraft." She sat in an empty chair beside his station and folded her hands to wait.

Astrid and the annoying British officer were asking why, but she ignored them. All that mattered now was that Ian didn't.

"One at a time or..."

"Both screens are fine."

Ian's desk had three monitors. Working on his left screen, he placed the AN-74MP on his center screen and the CMV-22 on his right-hand one closest to her.

The Antonov's departure was very precise, completely textbook.

The CMV-22's was not.

"Let me see the profile of the Osprey's pilots."

Ian put the two of them side by side on his left monitor. Both had very high hours in the type.

"No, someone else was flying."

Ian looked at her in surprise.

"Who else was aboard?"

"The only other pilot aboard was a Brit, Fleet Air Arm Commander Josh Osborne." Ian placed his profile on the screen. "He's neither pilot of record nor qualified in type."

Miranda scanned down through his history, an experienced helo pilot with zero hours in a CMV-22. "That's your pilot. He's highly skilled but unfamiliar with the aircraft."

"How the bloody hell can you tell that?" Group Captain Fielding was quite—

Miranda checked her emoji page, then pointed it out to Andi to confirm.

"Yes, he is *very* annoying." Andi's voice almost sounded like...

"Are you speaking with Holly's trademark amused Strine accent?" Though technically it wasn't legally trademarked that she knew of.

"My *what*? Aw cor, mate," Holly laid it on thickly.

Andi's cheeks reddened. "Kind of. I won't do it again."

"No, that's okay," Miranda reassured her. "I find it to be a very useful indicator of when she's being amused. Or about to attack someone. I haven't found a reliable indicator which of those two states she's in when speaking with a Broad Strine accent."

"Perhaps she's like Schrödinger's cat—existing in both states. Neither alive nor dead until we peek. Or, in her case, amused or deadly until she either makes us laugh or kills someone."

"I'm standing right here, Andi," Holly stated with no perceptible trace of Strine.

"You are." Miranda agreed as it was a wholly accurate statement. Then she turned her attention back to the screens.

"But you aren't nearly as annoying as the Group Captain," Andi reassured her.

Captain Fielding did not look pleased by her accurate assessment of his emotional state.

Ian had thoughtfully paused the playback, but it wasn't necessary.

"Scroll forward to five minutes before the incident. Don't jump, but you can use a ten-times scroll speed."

Even at the fast swipe Ian used, it became apparent that there was no change in which pilot remained in control. At five minutes to impact, he returned the playback to normal speed.

Moments before she asked him to jump ahead to the incident itself, something caught her attention.

"Roll back fifteen seconds on the AN-74, zoom in as tightly as you can on the control surfaces."

This process always fascinated her. Looking down from a two-hundred-and-fifty-kilometer orbit, the KH-11 Kennen satellite could resolve down to ten centimeters. If she was holding a postcard, computer enhancement might even resolve the picture if it was a simple one.

Ian nodded toward the big screens at the front of the room. He'd isolated the tail empennage and each wing separately before restarting the playback.

Actually, based on the details she could see on the control surfaces...

"Is that a KH-12?" There were rumors of a next generation past the KH-11 Block V.

There was a strange silence around her. She wondered if there was confusion about her question or something else she'd never understand.

Seven seconds in...eight... "There!" And when it ended... "And there!"

Ian put it on a loop, which made the transient movement

obvious,s—the wing ailerons wavered up, down, then resettled. Up, down, resettle. Over and over.

"What does that prove?" Fielding asked. "It's the collision that matters. Was it an attack?"

Holly rarely telegraphed the intent of physical violence, but now her fists were clenched and instead of being up on her toes ready to lunge, she had her weight on her back foot, ready to kick with the front as well.

Miranda rested a hand on Holly's arm. That's how Andi calmed Miranda herself down when she was upset.

Holly remained still, though she didn't relax. Perhaps it was some special skill that Andi had, or perhaps a skill neurotypicals possessed but was yet another thing withheld from autistic persons.

"Group Captain Fielding, you aren't a pilot." That much was a straight-line conclusion.

"Yes, I am."

Miranda wasn't sure how to respond to that. It told her one thing; she would never willingly be in an aircraft that he was piloting. Unsure what else to do, she decided to pretend he hadn't spoken, resetting the conversation back to the premise of the immediately preceding statement, her own about his not being a pilot. Then she knew where to proceed logically.

"If you observe the flight of the Osprey, it has consistently been under the control of a skilled pilot inexperienced in type. Rather than using the autopilot, he had been making constant micro-maneuvers to familiarize himself with the aircraft's handling characteristics. If he had survived another hour, I might have been unable to distinguish him from a pilot fully qualified in type; Commander Josh Osborne was that skilled."

She pointed to the Russian aircraft.

"This airplane has also not been on autopilot. I had actually assumed that it was, based on the consistency of the flight. But in that small hesitation, I see that he was neither using the autopilot nor especially skilled."

"You're making that up."

"Please let me hit him, Miranda." Holly remained still but she could feel the tension in Holly's arm muscles.

Miranda chose to ignore that as well. The touch becoming uncomfortable but she was afraid if she removed her hand that Holly would attack. Then she looked at her hand and Holly's warrior physique and decided that her touch offered minimal restraint and it was okay to remove her hand.

Once she did so, she was able to remember where she'd been.

"Air turbulence could have knocked the plane aside, and then the pilot would, in turn, have compensated. However, here we can see that the control surfaces shifted first. The recovery was not terribly efficient either."

"And the unskilled judgment?"

"His flying was *too* consistent. He is piloting with no feel for the air. Air is rarely a neat example of ideal laminar flow. It is constantly in motion and a skilled pilot will react to that with a thousand tiny corrections instilled into the body memory. The flight characteristics would present in a very different way, as anyone willing to provide a little thought can observe by these recordings."

"Rowr!" Andi made a noise like a cat. "Way to slash his eyes, Miranda."

"What?"

"That was the first nasty put-down I've ever heard from you."

Miranda slapped a hand over her mouth. "I didn't mean to."

"No. Own it! You did it so well." Then Andi leaned close to whisper. "More proof that you can do magic; I wouldn't have seen that if you hadn't pointed it out. He totally deserved it."

"But—" Miranda waved at the screen but didn't know what to say. It was so apparent.

29

Astrid had been against letting Miranda Chase into Menwith Hill. The PM had been very insistent, but it was an NSA military site that merely happened to be on UK soil, which gave Astrid the final word.

In retrospect, letting her in was worth it for that last put-down alone. Group Captain Raymond Fielding had been a constant burden. Everything was Her Majesty's government this and Her Majesty's government that—*His* Majesty's now.

That's simply not proper, Ms. Underwood.

Yes, it was a US facility on UK soil, but it served the Five Eyes intelligence network. Full data sharing between the US, UK, Canada, New Zealand, and Australia. But Fielding insisted on staking his claim to every little bit of intel territory he could manage.

Astrid had heard about Holly planting Fielding's face in the landing meadow and was very sorry she'd missed that.

But she had to hold the focus here.

"The accident, Ms. Chase." She recognized the patterns, of course.

When Fielding had radioed that there was a whole team inbound, Astrid had looked up Miranda Chase. Enough of Chase's background was classified, even to her, that her work at the NTSB must be a cover. But there was a referral on the file to call the head of the NRO directly with any questions.

That was sufficient recommendation in itself, but Astrid had called anyway.

The reason for General Elizabeth Gray's carefully worded cautions were obvious the moment Miranda had declined to shake hands or look her in the face.

Astrid's son hadn't managed his first word until he was five. She wondered how late Miranda's first word had been. It did give her hope for her boy to see an autistic person in such an important position, and having such champions as the PM and General Gray.

General Gray had also filled in a few of the details regarding her team: a SASR operator and a retired 160th Night Stalker pilot. Those were very rare breeds, times ten for being female. Mike Munroe's file was also classified, by the FBI. This had worried her until she saw the level of his security clearance; that too spoke volumes.

At Astrid's simple direction of *The accident, Ms. Chase*, Miranda had turned her back on the interesting scenario she'd instigated as if it no longer existed. Perhaps for her it didn't.

It certainly continued to exist for Fielding. His face remained bright red with near apoplexy, while the SASR agent remained poised to wipe the Ops Floor with him at the least provocation. The diminutive Night Stalker pilot turned away as one with Miranda. And Mike, standing two steps back, appeared as amused as Astrid herself.

She thought she hid it better than he did, until he offered her a conspiratorial wink.

Astrid returned it. But any joy in the moment died as Miranda's playback caught up with the collision itself.

It wasn't enough that the British PM had been hounding her for answers. Her request had been followed by others in quick succession.

The carrier captain wanted a pound of flesh in retribution—more than gunning down the Russian AN-74MP had provided. Which she wouldn't rate as a bad call, but it hadn't been a good one either.

Sadly, it hadn't been any surprise at all when the Chairman of the Joint Chiefs had phoned in soon afterward. Though his main focus had been asking her for any information regarding Russia's reaction—analysts were already casting far and wide for that.

The most worrisome aspect was that they were coming up empty. The Russians acted as if they'd taken no note of the event.

The Chairman's parting comment, however, had been about Miranda Chase: to *please* listen carefully when she spoke. He'd signed off before she could ask what the hell he meant by that.

Now it made sense, of course.

Miranda was already exposing details that her top analysts hadn't uncovered in the three hours it had taken to escalate, track her down, and get her here.

Astrid really didn't need this right now.

She had a drone in Nigeria on the verge of striking a Boko Haram leadership meeting. An intelligence intercept on Iran's latest nuclear enrichment efforts to be passed quietly to Israel's Kidon—Mossad's kill squad—for action. And—

A runner from the Russian language desk handed her a slip of paper. Paper was not a common substance on the Ops Floor.

If it was her normal Mission Director crowing about his newborn, she just might scream. He'd rousted her at two a.m. before rushing his wife, the Assistant Mission Director, off to the ER three weeks ahead of her due date. That had slammed her into the seat for the day-crew shift. If the contractions were Braxton Hicks, he was a dead man.

She read the slip.

Then read it again.

The header line indicated that the message was less than an hour old, from a code that the Russians had better *not* know the US had cracked. It was a high-level FSB code.

Arrest commander Gromovo Base. Deliver Lubyanka Building. Highest secrecy. All haste. By order of General Artemy Turgenev.

"Who the hell is Artemy Turgenev?"

Mike Munroe overheard her. "Commander of AARI."

"The Artic /Antarctic whatever? The one who survived —" Then Astrid bit her tongue. That was a very classified bit of knowledge. She'd spent all three days and nights of that disaster being whipsawed back and forth between her office and Ops Floor.

But Mike was nodding. "The purge after the loss of their stations to the Chinese. Damn but that was cold."

He'd been there? Astrid couldn't believe Mike understood his clearance if he'd let something like that slip. He should never have—

But he knew that. And he'd know her clearance level as well.

He kept watching her with that half smile. Looking so natural it might be his resting face—but it wasn't. No. He was telling her something.

It was the same message that the Director of the NRO, the Chairman of the Joint Chiefs, and the PM herself had been telling her: do *not* underestimate this team.

"What else, uh, can you tell me?"

"Without reading that message." Smart enough to not ask. "That was one of his planes?" Mike nodded toward where the others were watching the accident; she wondered why Mike wasn't.

"If he's head of the AARI, then yes."

"And the message you're holding still makes no sense?"

"Perhaps even less," Astrid admitted. What was the head of Artic operations doing ordering the arrest of a Russian Air Force officer?

"Then I'd ask who he's working for."

Astrid thought about it for a second, nodded her thanks, and headed to her station to pull up a file on a General Artemy Turgenev.

And now she understood why Mike didn't care about the accident, about the planes. He'd been listed as the team's Human Factors specialist. That was his expertise. And he'd jumped straight to the core question, making it appear effortless.

30

"Fascinating."

"Now you sound like Sherlock Holmes."

"Oh," Miranda looked from the screen to Andi. "I thought I sounded like Mr. Spock. That's what people always told me in school."

"Nope, you have too much emotion for Spock."

"Did Sherlock have emotions?"

Andi grimaced. "I think we've gotten off point. *What* is fascinating?"

Miranda turned back to Ian's screen. "Watch the piloting."

It was on a two-minute loop from first approach to the explosive destruction of the Antonov. Others had gathered around her. Astrid and Fielding watched from beside Mike and Holly.

Ian echoed his display up on the big screen.

That was good, more and more people had huddled close, standing in silence like a human wall that might topple upon her like Humpty Dumpty. Now they stepped back from the station as they shifted to look up. It left more space around her and Ian.

"Let's follow the Osprey first. The British pilot doesn't react to the emergency situation, a more skilled pilot would. As a locus on the Conjecture Sphere, we can temporarily assume that Captain Dave Walsh, the captain of the aircraft, took over the flight controls immediately upon the collision. For a matter of two and a quarter seconds, there are improvements in the situation."

Then the two aircraft rammed together once more.

"Notice that the clarity of the ocean below is dimmed during the destruction of the engine. It's the fan blades shattering. Most pieces too small to register on the satellite's imaging sensors two hundred and fifty kilometers above, but enough to form a thick haze. These probably killed or incapacitated the Osprey's captain. And we can see this after the abrupt collision. Someone survived to attempt aircraft recovery, but his control actions are incorrect. On the third spiral, you can see that if he'd had rudder control, he might have survived. But he didn't and crashed into the ocean."

Andi pointed when the replay looped around to the same point. "Look at the control surfaces here. This is a maneuver I might have tried to recover the flight. He handled the cyclic as if it was a helicopter, not a tiltrotor in airplane configuration. That supports Walsh no longer being in control and Josh Osborne resuming command. That only deepened the spiral and made it truly unrecoverable. I think you got that one dead to rights, Miranda. You're right, that is fascinating."

Miranda liked that she'd been right. *Fascinating,* after all, was a declared emotional state that she might not have attempted to label if she'd been thinking about it.

"What about the Antonov?"

"That's far more interesting. The pilot in control is not actually incompetent, but flies as if he only had a hundred or so hours of actual stick time, perhaps in lesser aircraft. The collision was caused by a sudden control maneuver that makes no sense from a pilot's point of view."

"A mistake?" Someone asked from one of the other desks. "Not an attack?"

"I'm not very good at motives, but based on prior flight characteristics, I'd say a mistake."

"Thank ya, Jesus!" someone else called out and earned a few laughs.

"Except for what happened immediately afterwards."

The room fell dead silent.

Miranda let the brief loop play several times from the collision to the Antonov's recovery and departure.

No one made any comment.

She looked at Andi, who shrugged. "I'm a helo pilot. I don't understand the implications of whatever you're seeing in a fixed-wing flight."

Miranda liked that explanation better than thinking that Andi really was in some way mentally flawed.

"Okay, from the instant of the collision, the plane behaves differently."

"Yes, it rams the Osprey," Group Captain Fielding spoke out.

Miranda was definitely never getting on a plane he piloted. "Based on aileron control and elevator control, we now have a very skilled pilot in control. After the two aircraft swung together and collided nose-to-nose, there are no discernable rudder movements."

"Because the rudder pedals were damaged?" Mike asked.

"Based on the degree of foreshortening of the nose of both aircraft brought on by the collision, I expect that their legs were pinned against their seats, perhaps even crushed."

"Bloody hell, mate," Holly whispered.

"And yet," Miranda indicated the last part of the flight and the staggering recovery of the Antonov, spinning one way, breaking the spin only to collapse into an opposite spiral. "The pilot ultimately finds balance despite that and the damage to his wing and recovers from the spin. Doing so *without* the primary control to achieve that, the rudder. It is a masterful piece of flying that I will have to practice next time I'm aloft."

"Hope you don't mind if I skip that flight," Andi's laugh had an odd tone to it.

"There won't be room. My Cessna Citation jet isn't designed to bear such loading. I'll need to run some calculations first, but the test should be within the performance envelope of my F-86 Sabrejet. It only has one seat."

"Just to be clear, if you kill yourself in the test, I'll be very upset."

"Okay."

Andi's eyes shifted into one of those uncomfortable looks that Miranda couldn't stand to focus on and turned back to the screen.

"Was it an accident or an attack?" Fielding asked. "That's all we need to know."

"My investigation is incomplete."

"What the bloody hell else do you need?"

"Information on the Russian pilots would be very helpful."

In moments, the information was up on her screen. A pair of profiles—a man and a woman.

"Wow, she's a serious looker." Mike then grunted as if Holly had just fisted him in the stomach.

Miranda didn't turn. With all of the people crowding around, she'd have to leave the room to recover.

"Not on the prowl, Hol, but not blind either." Mike managed to grunt out on a wheeze.

Miranda scrolled down to their service records. The man's hours were exactly as she'd expected. To save money on fuel, most Russian Air Force pilots flew under a hundred hours a year. Lieutenant Sergei Balakin was definitely dragging that average down with twenty-five hours per year. The woman's record was far longer, typically flying twice the hours per month that Balakin flew in a year. It was clear that Balakin had flown until the moment of the accident, perhaps to gain stick time. Yet the recovery afterward had been flown by the skilled pilot. It was still unclear who had been flying at the key moment of the collision.

Her view of the plane's control surfaces indicated that it was intentional. While that didn't feel right, it fit the evidence.

In the time it had taken her to study the flight characteristics of the incident, Miranda had overheard part of how the Ops Floor of Menwith Hill worked. Requests were called out aloud and the various analysts knew which were meant for them.

While she didn't know who she needed, apparently they would.

She raised her voice. "I need to see any other footage confirmed to be of the Russian pilot..." she scrolled up to the top, "...Natalia Ivanovna Murov."

Holly grabbed her shoulder hard enough to hurt.

"Ow!"

Holly didn't apologize or ease her grasp. Instead she leaned in until her face was close beside Miranda's, staring at the screen.

"Natalia Ivanovna *Murov,*" Holly read softly. Her voice dropped to a whisper, "I told you. Welcome to hell. This is the place where the end of the world begins."

31

MIRANDA'S HAND WAS SLAPPING LIGHTLY AGAINST HERS.

The moment Holly realized how hard she was gripping Miranda's shoulder, she yanked her hand away as if she'd rested it on molten lava.

She looked at the big screens.

Two Russian subs stalking the USS *Gerald R. Ford* aircraft carrier. Each had a deadly Virginia-class attack submarine hard on their tails ready to blow them to shit—and she'd bet they didn't know it.

A carrier group in the Med, centered on the USS *George H. W. Bush,* was snuggled up in the Aegean Sea near Crete. Eight hours sailing or a twenty-minute flight for the carrier's F-35 fighter jets from the Bosporus Straits. They were probably *exercising* halfway there even now; ready to cut off access to the Black Sea on ten minutes' notice. Block that along with the Baltic, and the only part of the Russian fleet that could mobilize was on the far end of Siberia.

Yet another screen, drone surveillance of a Malian

terrorist training camp—the kind of surveil that came shortly before a drone strike.

The SIGINT site prep for an upcoming G-7 meeting in Manila. Locating the meeting there was pushing the new US submarine bases in the Philippines right in China's face— because that tactic had always worked so fucking well. Oh, and maybe shore up a few of the Pacific trade agreements that the prior US administration had blown out of existence. No bets, the US had done its usual fine work of pissing off everyone with that move.

Threats.

Everywhere threats.

Mike huddled with Astrid over something.

Miranda's happy world of crash investigation was at full churn.

Didn't anyone see what was happening? All these smart people packed into a single pressure cooker, acting as if everything was normal and the world hadn't gone pear-shaped worse than a busted axle in the middle of the Gibson Desert.

Holly tried to breathe.

Her chest had locked up worse than a frozen bolt on that busted axle.

Out!

All she could do was... Out!

32

"Nice roof."

When she opened her eyes, Holly was resting her face against a curved concrete wall warm with the midday sun. She looked straight up. One story above her, a massive white radome ballooned outward in joined triangular sections of fiberglass or some weird composite that Miranda would be able to identify by the smell, albedo, or the magic radar secretly mounted inside her skull. Each successive dome appeared Photoshopped on the green landscape and brilliant blue of the afternoon sky.

Beside her, Andi Wu leaned against the wall, looking at her, not the bulge of the radome's enclosure. Hands stuffed in her bomber jacket pockets, looking so neat, petite, and perfect. Her jet-black hair hung to the tops of her shoulders, cut perfectly square. The jacket was made with fine Italian leather, but bore the insignia of 101st Airborne—because no Night Stalker would wear a Spec Ops badge in public. Even her mud-splattered pants were from some high-tech fabric that would dry minutes after being rinsed off.

Holly wore jeans, a t-shirt that might have once said *I'm not perfect, but at least I'm Australian* before she'd worn it to death, and a fleece sweatshirt that the stains would never wash out of. She looked and felt like she was still a poor urchin of the Outback.

"What happened?" Holly had no idea how she'd gotten here.

Andi opened her mouth.

Holly held up a hand to stop Andi, put her back to the wall, and slid down to sit on the ground. At least it wasn't Mike who'd chased her down. She wasn't ready for some dose of goddamn sympathy and civilian understanding from the man who shared her bed.

In front of her was a bucket's worth of giant golf-ball-looking radomes just waiting for God to come along with his four iron and make a divot where her life had somehow landed.

She pulled up her knees and rested her face on them.

Andi slid down to sit beside her. "Been there. Done that."

"Well I haven't!"

"Holly, my friend. Allow me to be the first to say this: *Bullshit!*"

Holly kept her face against her knees. It sucked that Andi was right. "I do *not* have PTSD."

"Uh-huh. Uh-huh." Andi sounded perfectly willing to believe her. "Then care to explain why you jackrabbited out of there like the entire pantheon of Chinese imperial dragons was about to eat your ass?"

"No!" Not this side of the next millennium.

"Okay." And Andi just sat there in silence as the cool breeze curled about the spherical radome. It was probably playing with Andi's hair.

Holly shot her legs out and leaned back—too fast—banging her head hard against the unforgiving concrete. She sat staring at the shots of light blurring her vision backed by the radomes sprouting out of the deep spring-green grass. "They need sheep here. Keep this place trimmed up a bit."

"Now you're sounding like Miranda, except she can't help herself. You're tossing out non sequiturs on purpose to avoid the core issue just like you always do."

"Shit but you're a pain in the ass, Wu."

"Spec Ops. It comes with the badge, you know that."

"Why don't you sound like this more often?"

Andi tipped her head sideways. "Well, I still think that's an avoiding-circumstances-subject-change tactic, but hey." She shrugged. "This part of me mostly died in the air. I carried a lot of shit with me from the day my copilot was literally blown up less than two feet from me, but all that changed when I hit Miranda's team. I was gone on her from Day One. That gave me a focus."

"Even while she was with Jon?"

"Didn't care. Not saying I did anything about it then, but I figured if Miranda could step beyond her genetic past, what the hell did I have to whine about? A psycho mother who drove me into Stanford Law and almost forced me into eternal servitude by her side, or should I say under her thumb, at Wu and Wu Law?"

"Trust me, your mother is *not* psycho by any Aussie standard."

"You're right. I forgot about your parents. Sorry." Andi let the silence stretch until the warm sun eased the chill of that memory for both of them. "Anyway, Mother was my role model for a successful woman until I met Miranda. She's so amazing that I had to try and be a better me around her."

"Just like that?"

"Sure, just like that. If you don't count my utter PTSD meltdown the day you met me or on the Taiwan trip or down on the Johnston Atoll or the nightmares or my assumption at lunch up at Tan Hill Inn about what she meant by me being broken or—"

"Yeah, yeah. I get the idea." Holly stared at the radomes. Inside each of those, massive antennas were accessing surveillance satellites or monitoring foreign satellites. At this very instant, any one of those, including the one shading them right now, might be snapping the image or capturing the one transmission that could—

"So what set you off?" Andi was tenacious as a dingo, another Spec Ops trait.

"It really helps to talk about this shit? I thought you said you left it in the past."

"I did...after talking about it a lot with Miranda. Don't you ever tell Mike anything?"

Holly raised her butt cheek to brush some gravel aside. It didn't help. "Once or twice."

Unlike Group Captain Fielding's attack, Holly never saw the blow that Andi back-fisted into her solar plexus.

33

THERE WAS NO BRACING, NO PREP. ONE MOMENT HOLLY HAD air and the next she didn't. Even the thought of attempting to inhale hurt too much to repeat.

Andi's shout penetrated the pain. "He loves you. And you treat him like—"

"No!" Holly managed on a wheeze. That one word cost her badly. Even Taz Cortez couldn't get past her guard. But Andi certainly had—fast and hard.

"Shit, Holly. Did you think he was hanging around for the great sex? Ain't nobody that good, not me and not even you. He puts up with all your mayhem because he loves you. Not that he's any more likely to admit it than you are." She sounded disgusted. How many times had she heard Andi and Miranda say it to each other? How much more often did they say it in private?

Holly wheezed in another breath but didn't have a lot of confidence about trying for the one after that. She could feel Andi watching her but couldn't do anything about it.

"And I thought that I was the one in this outfit who was a total mess."

"You?" Holly managed a squeak of surprise.

Andi looked away quickly, staring off at some horizon way beyond the radomes. The Yorkshire Dales rose to three sides, not as steeply as where they'd been hiking, but enough to show pastures of sheep in fields neatly quartered by gray stone walls. Here in the relative lowlands, the walls were often shrouded in a hedgerow of brush and trees. Up on the Herriot Way, nothing had grown on them except lichen.

"Trust me," a slow breath actually worked enough to let her finish the sentence, "it's not you."

"What are you so damn afraid of?"

Holly waved toward the base's main buildings. "Tell me that doesn't scare the shit out of you." Air was still coming short, but it had less to do with a stinging solar plexus and more to do with the impossible tightness across her chest. "If the folks in that room—that one, right there in front of us— make one freaking little mistake, we've got a war. A big mistake? Nukes and a *world* war."

"So, nothing to do with a guy named Mike Munroe?"

"Go to Hell, Wu."

"I probably will. But I'd rather not."

"What do you have against Hell?"

"Can you see Miranda ending up there?"

Holly wanted to laugh, would have except it would hurt too much. It was an absurd image. Miranda standing at the gates of judgment and being sent down into the fiery pit. Wasn't gonna happen. Her, Mike, even Andi, sure. But not Miranda.

"I wasn't thinking about Mike."

She held up a hand to block Andi's next verbal attack.

"Look. I'm having enough trouble thinking about him without you unloading a bunch of lovey-dovey crap on my head, okay? Just give it a rest."

"Did you two really have that good a time on vacation in Hawaii?"

"You just can't leave it alone, can you?"

Andi shrugged a *probably not*. She still hadn't turned from her contemplation of the distant hills so that Holly could see her face.

"Yes, damn you to Hell without Miranda. It was amazing. Mike was..." She wasn't used to thinking about such things and didn't have the words. "He was...great. Now change the goddamn subject."

"Only one other on the table: my original question."

Why she'd jackrabbited out of the Ops Building like a pissed-off water buffalo wanting to stampede her sorry ass? Well, she knew the answer to that well enough.

"If I asked you soldier-to-soldier to drop it..."

Andi was already shaking her head.

"Little queer bitch."

"Blonde bimbo. Now give."

Holly considered banging her head against the concrete of the radome's foundation, but it still hurt where she'd smacked it to begin with.

"Fine!" She jabbed a finger at the Ops Center. "I was on the other end of that room during an op. They were feeding me direct tasking from the Ops Floor at Pine Gap, which, just to rub it in, lies a quick jog down the Alice from where I grew up. My SASR team got tasked with offing a dictator who really, really, really deserved it. Except, during the prep-phase of the op, a drug trade handoff happened smack on top of our camp. No warning. No time to do anything but fight—fight and lose because the team was outnumbered twenty to one. Except me, because I was off scouting, checking the charges I'd set to drop a bridge the moment the target rolled onto midspan."

Andi kept silent.

"I blew the bridge to hell the moment the departing drug runners were crossing over. Didn't know they had the bodies of my team aboard. Still don't know if they were dead or not when I blew it, though they sure as shit were afterward." Holly raised a hand, palm facing Andi to make her keep her trap shut. "And yes, before you bitch about it, I've told Mike that much."

Andi eased back, showing nothing else. No judgment. No acceptance. Just passive waiting for the next piece of information. All that Spec Ops patience half felt like home and half pissed her the hell off.

"Inscrutable bitch." But Holly couldn't find much heat to put behind it. She dug her palm against her solar plexus to ease the last of the muscle knot there.

She'd never told anyone the next part, but if anyone would understand, it was Andi Wu—Spec Ops flyer who'd somehow survived the gruesome reality of having her copilot's guts splattered all over her in midflight.

"Pine Gap was in my ear the whole damn time. Kept telling me not to act. *Do Not Act.* I'm under the damn bridge deck and can hear the trucks rolling by over my head. *Complete the mission. Target due in six hours.* Shit! We'd never find the drug-runner bastards by then. So, I blew them and that bridge. Body count over fifty—plus five shot-to-shit SASR operators."

Now when she needed an interruption, Andi didn't say shit, so it kept spilling out of her.

"The body recovery team determined that my guys were all either dead or too wounded to survive without *immediate and intensive intervention,* which they bloody well weren't headed toward. Command gave me a clean record, but they didn't exactly hand out any medals either. Instead, the Governor General himself drags me aside five minutes before the memorial service back in nice, clean, everything-so-fine-here Perth."

That day, in the crystal clean of Perth, she could still taste the rotting jungle, the heavy tar smoke as the wooden bridge members burned. Could smell it now.

"He starts showing me images of the shit about the dictator—*Pine Gap Classified* stamped all over it. Turns out the bastard dictator owned the drug runners; they were local Army. Pine Gap had tracked massive payouts into his numbered accounts for bloody ever. Then he used my attack on *loyal members of our armed forces* as an excuse for a purge of the opposition—executions at a mass-grave level."

Holly closed her eyes to block it out, which only made it worse.

"Pine Gap told me none of that shit during the briefing or the action, of course. I didn't need to bloody know. Wasn't cleared for it afterward either, the GG made that damn clear. So, I'm standing there as sole survivor at the memorial. And they're droning on about *In service of their country,* and I'm thinking that my one act made it so my mates had died completely in vain because some asshole in a place just like that one," she jabbed a finger toward the ops building, "deemed that I didn't need to know."

She let her hand drop. Drained.

"What did you do?"

"What did I do?" Her own laugh came so harsh that it hurt her throat. "I resigned from the service."

Andi did that head tip thing of hers. "That doesn't actually sound like you."

"I resigned by trying to beat the shit out of the GG during the memorial service." It had taken six of her SASR brothers to pin her down. She'd resigned by walking out the gate before they could toss her in lock-up.

"Oh, okay. That fits."

After the silence had stretched for a bit, Holly looked at Andi. She still sat there. Her face calm and eyes closed with her head tipped back as if enjoying the cool spring breeze that brushed along the circular concrete wall at their backs.

"You gonna say anything?"

Andi didn't so much as open her eyes. "You get two choices, Holly. Wallow in it or put it behind you and move forward. Trust me, I've learned that one the hard way. You can try, but you'll never truly escape."

Andi didn't sound so much like she was talking about Holly. What shit-show was going on inside Andi's brainpan? Holly decided she didn't want to know at the moment. Maybe Holly would corner her later. Or maybe never.

"There's a load of ugliness going on in that building right now. We're the ones in the room this time. Your call." Then Andi pushed to her feet and walked away without looking back.

"Beating the crap out of you isn't a third option?" Holly called after her.

Like a good Spec Ops operator, Andi didn't deign to waste energy on a response beyond giving her the finger over her shoulder.

34

MIRANDA'S SHOULDER STILL HURT WHERE HOLLY HAD GRABBED it before rushing out of the room. Andi had followed close on her heels.

Mike turned from conferring with Astrid at the next station. "Earlier, did you say something about Murov?"

"Captain Natalia Ivanovna Murov. She was the pilot of the AN-74MP Cheburashka. I like saying Cheburashka, it feels happy like the little creature of Russian tales. Why did that upset Holly?"

Instead of answering, he turned back to Astrid. "The pilot was named Murov."

Astrid studied her monitor for a moment, then froze. When she finally spoke, after swallowing hard several times, her voice was a whisper. "He has a daughter named Natalia. And his wife's maiden name was Ivanovna."

"Oh. Is that important?" Miranda decided they were acting as if it was. Should she take that as a cue of actual importance? Would that be a consistent gauge she could use? Yes, it seemed reliable.

"Her father is the Director of the FSB."

"Oh." Miranda couldn't imagine what that had to do with the midair collision.

There was some heated discussion, but she didn't follow it as the room's resources provided her with three video clips of confirmed flights by Captain Natalia Ivanovna and six more possibles. After watching the three, it was trivial to dismiss four of the other six. The remaining two had a similar hand on the controls to the three confirmed flights.

She studied those carefully. Turning her attention to the other screen, Miranda watched the moment of the collision of the AN-74MP Cheburashka with the CMV-22 Osprey several more times.

"I'm missing something. What am I missing?"

No one answered. Holly and Andi were gone.

Mike was still standing by Astrid. They were staring down at a phone on speakerphone. It wasn't a video phone, so she was unsure why they were staring at it so intently. She did recognize Drake's voice but didn't listen to what he was saying. There was still something missing on her screen and that felt more important.

She turned back to the screen but wasn't seeing anything out of the ordinary.

A gentle hand slipped onto her shoulder exactly where Holly had pinched it. Miranda tipped her cheek into it and felt better than she had in a while; she knew Andi's touch as well as if it was her own.

"What did you find?" Andi asked softly.

"I don't know."

Andi pulled over a chair without removing her hand. "Show me."

The collision was playing on a loop in front of her. But

maybe Andi was asking her to explain it. "There's a..." she remembered Holly's hand clutching her shoulder, "...pinch. Something doesn't fit here, but I'm not seeing it."

"Okay. Let's break it down. What's the problem?"

"I don't know which pilot is in command at the exact moment of the collision. One isn't highly skilled and one is. The one who isn't had flown the plane for the two hours prior to the collision; an exceptional pilot flew the recovery from the collision. But I can't determine which one was flying at the moment of the incident. That would most likely tell me if it was intentional or accidental. Everyone seems very concerned about that distinction, though I don't know why."

"Because it's either an accident or an attack."

"If it's an attack, it didn't go very well, did it? Both aircraft were destroyed."

"True," Andi leaned closer to the screen and watched the collision through several iterations. "Unless that was a price they were willing to pay."

Miranda would *never* understand people. She returned to studying the planes. "See, they're flying in controlled parallel flight. They've been in this position for over thirty seconds without variation. Then...*there!* The Antonov slips sideways into the Osprey's rotor."

"If I were attacking a tiltrotor, I wouldn't go sticking my wing into its proprotor."

"But the Russians did."

"Well, they didn't do a very good job of it. They stuck their wing in and left it there until it was all chewed up with no attempt to correct outward."

Miranda watched another full loop. "No action on the ailerons to initiate a turn to port."

"Perhaps the pilot was too horrified at what he'd done and froze. That would fit the unskilled pilot criteria."

The display looped through the nose-to-nose collision, then reset to five seconds before the Antonov had veered into the Osprey.

Five, four, three, two, one, and—

"Oh!"

"What?"

"Watch the rudder." Miranda zoomed in on the vertical control surface in the plane's tail.

Andi watched in silence. "I didn't see any change."

"Exactly!" Miranda felt relief that the problem was answered and confirmed.

"I don't get—oh!" Andi turned to Astrid and called out, "It was an accident."

"How do you know?"

Andi indicated Miranda should speak. Everyone turned to look at her so she turned to look at the console before speaking. There she saw it repeat again.

"The turn was uncoordinated."

She risked a glance aside when no one spoke. No, they were all still looking at her. Miranda turned back to speak to the screen.

"A pilot, even one as unskilled as Lieutenant Sergei Balakin or Group Captain Fielding, has still learned the basics."

"I'm not a pilot. Explain it to me," Astrid insisted.

Miranda was unsure how basic to begin. "A plane has multiple control surfaces including—"

"Simple," Mike cut her off. "When you turn your car, you put on your blinker."

"Sometimes," Astrid shrugged.

Mike offered a short laugh.

Miranda certainly *hoped* it was a joke. Turn signals had been mandatory equipment since the 1960s for a good reason—to be used. Unless the Mission Director drove a motorcycle, in which case it would be 1973.

"Well, in a plane, making a turn requires two actions."

"But planes don't have blinkers," Miranda didn't understand Mike's explanation at all.

"No," he acknowledged, "but there are two actions required to make a coordinated turn. This isn't merely Piloting 101, this is learned on the very first flight, then beaten into instinct very fast. A coordinated turn requires turning the yoke *and* stepping on the rudder pedals with an appropriate amount of control to sling the tail around smoothly."

"Except this low-hour pilot," Andi waved at the screen, "when he jerked the controls and created the collision, he didn't use the rudder pedal. It was such a basic lesson that even he would have done it properly if the attack had been planned. But if he was surprised by something? An ill-trained pilot, one for whom basic controls are not instilled as body memory, may have jerked the control yoke without using the rudder pedal."

"Captain Natalia Ivanovna would never have made such a mistake," Miranda pulled up Natalia's other flights. "You can see in these key control moments," she began arranging the clips she'd excerpted first chronologically, then thought better of it and rearranged them by the decreasing severity of the situation, "would never have made an uncoordinated turn under any conditions—except incapacitation."

"How do you know that?"

"Easy," Miranda brought up the recording of the

collision and allowed it to run past the collision itself and display the recovery until she had a good side view of the tumbling plane and froze the image. "With the damaged nose and no access to the rudder pedals, she manages to recover from a highly dangerous spin showing an exceptional level of skill and knowledge of her aircraft's aerodynamics. Based on the amount of foreshortening of the plane's forward radome," she used a light pen to mark the normal extent of the nose before it had been crushed, "I estimate that the larger-sized Elta radar antenna used in the AN-74MP would have, at the risk of repeating myself, trapped her legs, perhaps crushing them. I would term that as incapacitation."

The others all winced and Mike flexed his knees as if to make sure his legs still worked.

"Are you sure, Miranda?" Drake asked from the speaker phone.

"Oh," Miranda pulled out her own phone and dialed the Prime Minister, setting it on speakerphone as that seemed to be what they always did here on the Menwith Hill Ops Floor.

The PM answered on the first ring.

"Hello, Olivia. You asked me to call if I learned anything. I did."

After a brief pause, Olivia asked what she'd learned.

"Your original instruction was to call if I learned anything, I have. You said nothing about reporting what it was." Then she realized that it was a given that the Prime Minister *would* want to know what Miranda had learned. "The collision was definitely an accident."

"That's a huge relief. I knew I could count on you, Miranda."

"It was a mistake by an under-qualified copilot, not by Captain Natalia Ivanovna Murov."

Another pause, longer this time. "Did you say Murov?"

"Yes, the daughter of the Director of the FSB. Why does everyone keep focusing on that? It wasn't her fault."

35

ARTEMY DECIDED THE GODS WERE WITH HIM WHEN HIS PHONE buzzed just as he was showing his ID to the guard at FSB headquarters.

Shirinov: G here, top floor. Gromovo commander. Excellent.

On my way up. Meet me on 3. Shirinov's security clearance wouldn't unlock access to the top floor.

For once, the elevator behaved. It stopped at the third floor and Shirinov stepped in.

"Anything new?"

"Nothing much," Shirinov handed him a sheet of paper.

"Major Alexej Pronichev. He's Czech?"

"His grandparents," Shirinov pointed farther down the page. "Moved to Saint Petersburg back when it was still Leningrad. Third generation military."

"Three years Commander Gromovo Air Base." Artemy scanned the rest quickly. Nothing special. Not incompetent but not shining either. The next sheet, the FSB's report on him, was little more interesting. Petty graft—not that his position would allow him much more than that, but so little that it showed a certain lack of imagination.

The sheet behind was a photograph of a gorgeous young redhead. Even in the photograph the power of her intense blue eyes glared out at him. He stepped from the elevator on the top floor—and almost ran down General Murov.

He and Shirinov snapped to attention and saluted. Artemy tried to read how Murov's wife had taken the news, but he gave no sign.

Murov waved their salutes and glanced down at Artemy's hands.

Artemy looked down and saw that he was still holding Natalia Murov's picture. "Uh, she was lovely, sir. I never had the pleasure of meeting her."

"Hmmm," Murov grunted. "What else do you have, Turgenev?"

"I have only just returned and glanced through the Gromovo commander's file. He's here now."

"I know. Our people were quick."

"I felt a priority code was appropriate."

"Hmmm," Murov offered no insight to his thoughts on that either. "What else?"

Artemy turned to the next page after Natalia's picture. There was too much to absorb quickly. "Shirinov?"

The man stood even straighter if possible. "The number of hazardous sorties assigned to Captain Ivanovna, er, Murov, was far above the norm for other pilots at the base."

"*Govno!*" Artemy scanned the additional attachments. "By a factor of ten to twenty in some cases." Then he realized who he'd just sworn in front of and looked up slowly.

Murov was watching him impassively.

"Sorry, sir. But only the very best pilots like Captain

Novikov, who died in the initial Antarctic crash—" *Not smooth, Artemy. His death had triggered the whole disaster there, including his predecessor's death. Plunge ahead.* "Only the very best pilots log these kinds of hours. And never so many of them in dangerous missions. It's as if she was singled out by her commander."

"Shall we go find out why?"

"Yes sir." And that's when Artemy fully absorbed where they were. In the few times he'd come here to this building with reports for Colonel Romanoff and the year since taking command first of Antarctic operations, then the whole of the AARI, he'd only heard the vaguest rumors that the Lubyanka Prison still operated.

Years ago the prison had been turned into a museum, which required special permission and escort to visit.

But there wasn't a chance that this was part of any museum; there was nothing pretty about it.

Whether or not the prison remained active had now been answered.

The dungeons of Lubyanka were on the windowless top floor, not in the basement as inmates always assumed. There would be no rescue, no escape by tunneling, no light or freedom. Those who came here would be considered fortunate to be remanded to the mines of a Corrective Prison Colony, no kinder than the gulag system they'd replaced. He assumed the rest departed by the same route as the burn bags for classified documents.

Outside the elevator, a pair of heavily armed guards sat behind a bulletproof glass wall. The narrow corridor beyond was lined with steel doors. Artemy tried not to think about others who might be behind these doors.

He stepped up to the guard station. "General Murov to

see Major Alexej Pronichev. I assume that you have a clean room for us. I don't want to have to smell this man's shit."

Artemy waved Shirinov away. Not because he didn't want the man there, but because he did. He couldn't afford to look weak by leaning on his assistant. He should have read the file before reaching the prison. But if he had, Murov might have gone to see the man alone.

After their IDs were validated, one of the guards let them through the barrier, escorting them to a small interrogation cell. Once they were seated, the guard returned a minute later with a shackled and blindfolded man who scuttled each time the chain about his wrists was yanked. He hunched as if expecting a blow, turning his head frantically side to side though he couldn't possibly see. Major Pronichev had given up hope so quickly.

The guard chained him to a seat and departed. The man flinched when the steel door banged shut. Good, he was as worried as he should be.

Artemy risked a glance at General Murov, but he sat as quietly as he always did. This was up to Artemy.

He'd never run an interrogation.

But he'd certainly dealt with any number of underlings during his years of service.

"Pronichev." No spoken rank, implying he'd already lost that privilege. "Did you know of Captain Natalia Ivanovna's family?" He kept his voice dead calm. He'd always found that unnerving as hell in a superior officer.

Pronichev began to shake his head.

Artemy couldn't imagine a commander not knowing the details of such a woman in his command.

"Pronichev." Artemy did his best to instill pity in his tone, as if to say, *Oh, I'm going to have to hurt you so badly now.*

Pronichev shifted to a shaky nod.

"How long have you known?" Artemy made a show of ruffling through the file, loudly, as the man was still blindfolded.

He held up three fingers.

"From the third day, Pronichev?" Artemy wouldn't force him to speak, yet.

Pronichev nodded.

"Did you ever rape her, Pronichev, or try to?"

That got a reaction. "I'm not insane!" the man croaked. "She is the most dangerous woman alive. And her father— No! No! I never would try to touch her."

"Alive?" It slipped out before he could stop it. Artemy risked a look at Murov, who was scowling.

"Yes. Yes."

"Where is she?"

"North Sea. Her flight is due back...I don't know the time."

Artemy now saw his path forward. "You ordered her to harass the Americans."

"No. I sent her to fly a drop to the K-329 submarine, the *Belgorod*. Special medical shipment. Then her order was changed."

"Who sent that change?"

He named a General Garin. Artemy didn't know him but Murov's tiny nod said he did.

All Artemy knew was that he wasn't in the FSB or his own AARI. Who the hell had commandeered the flight to harass the Americans?

"Did the order specifically mention Captain Ivanovna?"

"Not at first. Then he asked the pilot's name and seemed very pleased."

General Murov rose to his feet and turned to go.

It was a scenario that Inessa had suggested over dinner, that someone might be targeting Murov through his daughter. *You must dance a careful balancing act,* Inessa had explained. *You must take the initiative when it is safe, showing General Murov that you are not merely a sycophant. Yet take so little that you will not be considered a threat.*

"Did the order say she was to *attack* the Americans?" Artemy asked before the general could leave.

"*What?*" Pronichev sounded as shocked as he'd been by the rape question. "No! Flyby only. The change in order came late, after she was almost to the submarine. To *approach* the American. Not attack. Photograph and shadow. General Garin said he wanted to test how close she could get to the American aircraft carrier before a jet came."

Murov had stopped moving, then turned with his back to the door.

Artemy glanced down at the file and saw that the original medical shipment was out at the very limits of the AN-74MP Cheburashka's range. It was a risky assignment, even without the diversion.

"Why did you always send her on the most dangerous missions? Perhaps hoping she would not come back and you'd be rid of the troublesome girl with clean hands?"

Pronichev's brief nod before he caught himself signed his death warrant.

Artemy didn't bother to listen to Pronichev's hurried denials, instead following General Murov out into the hall.

36

"GENERAL GARIN NEXT?" ARTEMY ASKED AFTER THEIR SILENT ride down to General Murov's office. The report that Murov had left on his desk earlier was nowhere to be seen.

Murov stared at him without speaking.

Artemy cursed. The proper line to walk was so thin. Who the hell was Garin? Should he apologize? Inessa had said, when in doubt, keep his mouth shut. He did his best to look attentive and wait out the General. The man let the silence stretch until Artemy suspected he was headed for the cell next to Major Pronichev.

"General Garin also has a daughter."

Artemy risked a nod of understanding.

"Younger than Natalia by a few years, another startling beauty, blonde in her case."

And then it clicked. "Ah." Artemy felt that was a safe comment. The President was rumored to have two children by a mistress less than half his age—last name Garina. General Garin was untouchable.

Murov watched him, then sighed. "In answer to the

question that is so eating at your brain, I believe that he is the reason Natalia chose to join the AARI's air arm, to escape..." he apparently thought better of his words and finally said, "...Moscow. General Garin's daughter came to the President's attention instead."

And by his tone, rather than being relieved by Natalia's adroit escape, Murov had not been happy about his daughter's choice. Another piece of the sad story Inessa had told him over dinner was now filled in.

Artemy also understood that Inessa was one of the reasons Murov had chosen to trust him. General Murov may have tried to tie himself closer to the President by setting his daughter as the Presidential mistress. Yet Murov himself had recently celebrated his fiftieth anniversary with his wife Raya. Artemy wasn't even going to consider the massive double standard that represented in case the general could read it on his face.

Murov's trust was all that mattered.

Artemy had been serious about a woman twice when he was still a pilot, but neither of them had lived up to the standard of Inessa Romanoff. That Artemy had married her at the first opportunity after nearly three decades of bachelorhood hopefully spoke volumes to a man like General Murov.

"What is my next task?" Artemy chose to step back into the servant role for the moment.

The general rubbed his forehead and looked exhausted.

Artemy glanced at his watch. It was only seven p.m., a short day at the FSB. Dinner wasn't typically until eight or nine. Seven p.m. now. General Murov's daughter had died at two p.m. Moscow time; a fact reported only three hours ago. It didn't seem possible.

"The crash," he whispered it, but the general heard him and looked up. Artemy cleared his throat. "I should pursue the details of the crash."

He should have thought of it right away, but it had already been a busy evening.

"With your permission, sir, I will go to the IAC and oversee the investigation myself." The offices of the Interstate Aviation Committee lay just three kilometers away, south across the Moskva River.

Murov nodded. "Make sure they do not learn the pilot's name."

Artemy nodded in return and hurried out the door. How in the world was he supposed to do that?

When he reached his office, Artemy noticed that he still clutched the file on Pronichev and Natalia. He handed her photo to Shirinov, "Burn bag." Such a pity, the girl could have been a model as Inessa had been thirty years before.

He didn't plan to hand the text report on Natalia to anyone, but he wasn't ready to burn it yet. Instead he took a black marker pen, carefully redacting Natalia's name from each page of the report. Then he photocopied it so that her name couldn't be recovered from the document and slid the original into his burn bag. At least *he* wouldn't be the source of her name leaking out.

"I'm going to the IAC if you need me."

Shirinov was already calling for a car as Artemy left the office.

37

CLARISSA TRIED A DEEP BREATH. IT DIDN'T HELP. EVEN BY HER standards, gate-crashing a Situation Room meeting was ballsy.

That finally settled her nerves as it was *precisely* her style.

She turned in her cell phone at security and they scanned her badge. Past the watch desk, she headed for the main conference room. The Sit Room was a complex, not just the single room everyone thought—expanded significantly in 2007.

Knock or simply enter?

The question was answered when Drake stepped out and closed the door behind him. "What do you want, Clarissa?"

The watch desk operators must have notified him.

She simply pointed at one of the smaller side rooms.

The one Drake led her to had four chairs around a circular table with the fifth position taken by a single monitor and video conference station.

He closed the door, tapped the button to opaque the windows, and turned to glare at her.

"Oh, for fuck's sake, Drake. Sit the hell down."

He sat but didn't uncross his arms. At least he didn't try any *We're rather busy here* nonsense on her.

"I found something on your little protégé," she cut straight to the point. "And, no, I didn't go intentionally digging for it."

Drake's squint said that at least he had the brains to become cautious.

"Yes, I'm sure you have many people you're proud to be grooming to serve the future of the country. I'm talking about Miranda."

He shifted from cautious to threatening.

Struck close to the heart, did I, Drake? Too bad it isn't a knife.

Clarissa pulled out the pages she'd retained from the file.

"Today I learned that Sam and Olivia Chase in reality were probably the most effective agents in early 1990s Russia."

Drake pitched forward as if someone had slapped him on the back of the head to look down at the first document she set on the table. The first was the list of frequent attendees to Olivia Chase's salon.

He scanned the list fast, but not too fast to take in the quality and nature of the contacts. He offered a grunt of acknowledgement.

She laid down the cover page to the IMF's loan signed by Boris Yeltsin.

"Samuil and Olya?"

Clarissa laid down the deed of sale of Spieden Island to Sam and Olivia Chase for twenty-two million and change.

He waited.

She laid down a final sheet of paper. She'd circled the

heading—*Confirmed Body Recovery TWA 800, July 17, 1996*—and their names.

Before he could shrug, she flipped open the leather portfolio to reveal her tablet computer, keyed the password, then used the facial recognition to unlock it. Clarissa selected the photo she'd taken before coming here and placed it on the table beside the death list.

Drake read aloud very softly, "Sam and Olivia Chase. Died July 16, 1996. Crash Ilyushin Il-76T. Belgrade, Yugoslavia."

"Found that this morning in the *Book of Honor* while adding a name to the Memorial Wall."

Drake stared at her for a long moment, then whispered, "I'm sorry for your loss."

"God damn it, Nason! Don't do that shit. Remember that we hate each other's guts, please. Do *not* read how I'm feeling." Then she realized that she hadn't denied it. She rubbed her forehead. "What's the point? Yeah, the last one hurt at least as much as Clark did. Are you satisfied?"

Drake watched her with nothing showing but sympathy. He'd lost his first wife to a bunch of African jihadists who liked killing foreign doctors for sport. The sympathy was probably real, but she didn't want that chink in her armor, especially not today when it was so fresh that she was still bleeding from it.

"Just...stop doing that. I found their names. I pulled their file—Director's Eyes Only—and stumbled on this. Sammy and Olivia skimmed. But based on the notes in the file and my current Russia Desk's assessment, it was the minimum they could take without blowing their cover."

Drake looked over the pages again much more carefully before leaning back and looking at her.

"Okay, I'll bite. What do you want?"

"Jesus, do you think that little of me?"

Drake shrugged.

"This isn't some quid pro quo. It happened over twenty-five years ago. Can you imagine what this would do to her little brain if I dropped this on her? Can't say I didn't think of it, briefly, but she's such a goddamn innocent."

"Miranda is many things, Clarissa, but an innocent isn't one of them. She is painfully aware of her unique personal challenges."

"Look. You know her better than anyone, Drake. She's dealing with the Russian crash right now. Last year investigated another in Antarctica that almost killed her twice. That crazy Kidon assassin who kidnapped and drugged her a couple years before that. What happens?"

"What happens when?"

"Don't be dense. What happens if someone from Russia digs this up? What happens if they tell her and she comes apart during a critical investigation? I know how much we've come to depend on that team of hers in the middle of a crisis. Even me, and don't think that doesn't piss me off. I mean, shit, you called her before you called me."

"Actually, the British Prime Minister did. I only found out later."

"Oh, perfect. That make me feel so much better. Okay. She may not be innocent, but do you trust her to not do the dangerously unexpected if she's hit with this? Her parents loved the damn country."

"Anything to say they were turned?"

"The agency should have more agents as clean as their damned record. It fucking sparkles. Massive intel with no bribes, no coercion, no leaks, and, for the life of me, we don't know how." Clarissa rubbed at her forehead and hated even that hint of weakness in front of Drake. "It's the unknown that scares me, Drake, and right now one of the biggest unknowns in our system is how Miranda reacts if she learns about this." She tapped the file between them for emphasis. "And if Russia knows about this?"

"After twenty-seven years—"

"Don't give me that shit, Drake. Where were you twenty-seven years ago? You didn't get those four stars on your shoulders from hanging out at the Dairy Queen. Neither did the Russians. Their leadership are all former KGB buddies of the former KGB agent turned President."

Drake didn't answer her, instead he looked back down at the list.

38

ARTEMY TURGENEV WATCHED THE CRASH PLAY OUT, OR WHAT he could see of it.

Knowing how nosy and painfully territorial petty officials could be, he'd bypassed the director and all of the rest of them. As commander of AARI's Antarctic aircraft, he had been here several times before. Sometimes the information was useless, at others it answered hard questions. More of the former, less of the latter—much less in recent years as aging satellites weren't updated.

He'd detoured through the basement to arrive unobserved in the IAC's analysis section. These were the technicians who understood the data.

Artemy selected the operator's station adorned with the most crap—Soyuz models, tiny toys that might be Martians for all he could tell, and a stack of engineering magazines. Most likely candidate for genius of the group, the one who everyone tolerated to exercise unseemly behaviors. Artemy went to him directly.

Others might question a lieutenant colonel, but not a

general. Everyone had watched his arrival, then looked away faster than startled rabbits when he'd let his gaze wander over the room.

The technician, who mumbled his name inaudibly, worked his keyboard like it was an extension of his body. That was all Artemy needed of him.

There'd been no satellite in the optimal position to record the collision. Actually, there had been, but its imager had been focused on the American aircraft carrier, not the flyby. A damning oversight—for anyone except the untouchable General Garin; he should have notified satellite operations of the potential for new intelligence. The surveillance bird *had* tracked a departing fighter jet, recorded a missile firing, and then tracked the missile.

There was post-collision video of the AN-74MP Cheburashka being blown out of the sky, but little more.

Before the missile strike, the best imaging available was the radar tracking from the K-329 submarine *Belgorod* itself. The stricken sub had surfaced and was desperately awaiting the inbound Cheburashka. They were suffering from a massive outbreak of botulism and Natalia Murov had been tasked to airdrop a case of antitoxin.

Artemy called Shirinov. "Find more botulism antitoxin and get it out to the submarine."

"I'll try, sir. But I don't think any more has been manufactured. They had to work hard to gather what little was sent."

They both knew that the President, especially in the current state of affairs from his disastrous foreign relations, couldn't request antitoxin from any other country. The Americans and the World Health Organization would be only too glad to help—and announce to the world that

Russians were dying of food poisoning because the factories were in such disarray.

"Do what you can." Artemy had signed off. Men were dying on that sub because General Garin had rerouted a critical medical delivery to play chicken with an American Osprey. Worse, it was unlikely that Natalia would have had sufficient fuel to complete the delivery and return to base after the diversion.

He would tell General Murov; but do so in a way that made it clear he understood the man was untouchable.

Perhaps Garin didn't like the President screwing his daughter but refusing to acknowledge her in public. Without that acknowledgement, Garin could do nothing to leverage the affair.

Before he told Murov, he'd talk it over with Inessa— perhaps there was some way to use this information on Garin. Whether intentionally or not, he had caused the death of General Murov's only child and vastly increased the suffering on the fleet's premier Special Operations submarine.

The imaging from the *Belgorod* wasn't fantastic; all they had was a targeting radar designed for aiming torpedoes at big ships. Worse, the collision occurred three hundred kilometers from the boat. If it had occurred five hundred meters lower, it wouldn't have been visible above the curvature of the Earth's horizon at all.

Artemy had flown as a cargo pilot for fifteen years before coming to ground. He knew his dreams of *more* would never happen if he'd stayed aloft. Yet Artemy's years as a pilot let him understand details that weren't particularly clear on the image.

A standard approach from the starboard of the

American aircraft. The apparent merging into a single radar image would be the AN-74MP passing below the American plane where they could get closer because there were no long wings in the way. Then they again split, like an amoeba dividing into two bright blots on the screen, as the Antonov flew well clear to the other side.

The two aircraft held that way for half a minute but, knowing what was coming, he couldn't look away.

Then the blot that had to be the Antonov slid into the American plane. It was shockingly abrupt.

"Scroll that back. Play it again."

The technician did so.

No, there'd been no mistake. The left-hand smudge of light shone brighter near the top. Both aircraft boasted high wings, but the Antonov's wings were far larger than the American Osprey's and offered a brighter return on the radar image.

It was too abrupt. The Antonov had deliberately rammed sideways into the Americans. This was impossible!

Had the order included such an instruction?

No, Pronichev had denied that when in fear of his life.

Unless... Perhaps General Garin had contacted the plane directly. Had the President *ordered* Garin to start a war? Had Garin, a known hawk according to Shirinov, planned it on his own?

Artemy was able to count three heartbeats before the two aircraft separated again.

Tumbling apart.

The American fell rapidly below the sub's radar horizon. By the blinking brightness of the radar return, it was completely out of control in a spinning dive. One moment the wings would be reflecting radar signal back, and the next when they were edge-on, the image significantly dimmed, then bright again as the aircraft twisted downward.

"Not survivable," the technician mumbled.

No, it wasn't.

Natalia's AN-74MP fell more slowly as it struggled to survive.

Then it too disappeared below the horizon.

"Perhaps, General, if the pilot is good..." the technician ran that last few seconds several times. "Yes, the pilot is good. He should recover. Oh, he did."

Artemy did not correct his assumptions about the pilot's gender.

The tech replayed the image from the satellite. "He lived long enough to be shot down."

Artemy checked the time stamps on the two sequences. Natalia had managed to recover and fly for a full minute before the missile destroyed her flight. So, the Americans had murdered Natalia, after she'd killed their pilots.

He had the tech play the image of the missile hitting Natalia's plane again.

That was the image that put the fear of God and the President in his heart. If the man saw this, he'd go berserker.

"Scroll that back." He ordered, then watched it again. "There's something before the missile hits. Let's see it."

"Two frames, general." The tech displayed them on side-by-side monitors.

The first was blurred and only half of the Antonov was in frame, but the second was a clear image.

The Antonov.

Its nose battered in past recognition, as if it had slammed into a massive concrete wall.

Its right wing a snarl of flames. Also, the right wing was

significantly shorter than the left, parts of it dangling downward. No possibility of the plane surviving that.

"First frame. Zoom in on the pilot."

The Persona surveillance satellite didn't have the resolution of the American birds, but it did reveal the red of the bounty of her hair—the final image of Natalia Ivanovna. Without knowing her coloring, it was unlikely to reveal the pilot's sex to the pilot—just some blurred red of a helmet or scarf.

"The second frame."

The right wing was an expanding ball of flame, expanding in all directions, but definitely centered on the wing. Natalia was masked by the intense fireball reflecting off the outside of the pilot's windows.

"Third frame."

Most of the plane was enveloped by the glare. But he could still see the shadow of the tail. The right wing was *not* at the center of the new explosion. The missile hadn't blown up the plane.

The American missile had homed in on the heat source of the exploding wing. The warhead's proximity fuse had ignited close ahead of the plane and finished the destruction already happening.

"First frame again."

Natalia's image showed no white pixels that might imply she was looking forward. No, she'd been staring sideways at the burning, then exploding wing, watching her own death. What had Natalia been thinking? It gave him the shivers. Next time he was in a pilot's bar, he would raise a vodka to her memory.

"Fourth frame," Artemy asked.

Nothing but white.

The technician zoomed out.

A ball of white fire had covered any trace of the AN-74.

He didn't need to see it fall from the sky.

Artemy knew there would be no recovering the bodies or the black boxes themselves. How could you recover something you couldn't admit to?

Unless...

"Do we have a present view of the impact area?"

The technician worked his keyboard for a moment, then stopped with a gasp.

It was an image, far too stark and clear. An American destroyer was parked exactly over the impact point.

"Mark these Top Secret. All of these images, this entire incident, is now sealed by the order of General Mikhail Murov."

The technician nodded.

He'd been a lowly lieutenant long ago and remembered how they thought. Such an order from some stupid general would be treated as a *mandate* to poke around. So he leaned in close and whispered.

"And if you find anything else while looking where you'd really be better off not, tell me and only me." And he placed his card on the man's desk.

The tech stared at him wide-eyed. He was too used to threats to have his balls cut off—before being remanded to Siberia—for that to have any impact. Being given the opposite was the real shock.

Artemy hoped it would be sufficient to at least make him keep what he found to himself.

But this was Russia and he doubted it.

For now, it would be enough.

39

Artemy paused to get a copy of the two video files from the technician: the submarine's radar tracking of the collision and the Persona satellite image of Natalia's death.

Just as he was turning to leave, he glanced at the screen that the tech had left running—the image of the American destroyer searching the waters.

What if they found something? Even Natalia's body?

He would have to deal with that if it happened. Perhaps—

There was a flash across the screen. "What was that?"

"What?" the technician hadn't been facing the screen.

"Run it back. Slowly."

The cause of the flash wasn't hard to find.

A pair of Sukhoi Su-57 Felon fifth-generation fighter jets had flashed by the destroyer so close it was a miracle they hadn't collided with an antenna mast.

"What the hell are those doing there?" The tech asked the question for him.

After twenty-three years of development, Russia had

managed to build a grand total of ten of them. The Air Force hadn't let them fly over Ukraine because it would be far too embarrassing if their best stealth fighter was downed there. Two of ten, sixteen hundred kilometers from the nearest Russian base.

That would have taken time to organize and almost an hour of flight time at full thrust. Getting midair refueling tankers out there ahead of them would have taken most of that time. Call it two hours.

Four hours since General Murov had headed home to tell his wife. Two hours since Artemy himself had finished dinner and returned to the office. Had someone overheard his and Inessa's conversation at Buro TSUM? Had Shirinov leaked the word? Or...

Govno!

"I need a—"

The technician handed him a USB stick and nodded toward the screen, indicating the image was already on there.

Artemy took the stick, thumped the man on the shoulder, and barely resisted sprinting for the door. A general never sprinted. But he certainly didn't waste time acknowledging anyone he passed in the halls as he strode out to his waiting car.

40

Since the moment Miranda had named the pilot to the Prime Minister, it seemed that the Menwith Hill Ops Floor had turned busier than a Yorkshire lambing shed in mid-April.

Miranda was rather proud of that metaphor but everyone was too busy for her to ask if it was a good one.

General Mikhail Murov's profile filled a whole side screen on the wall. His daughter's military record filled another.

They acted as if the accident was the least important thing that had happened today.

Holly slid into the chair at the station beside Miranda. She propped her booted feet on the desk, tipped back her chair, and folded her arms across her chest.

"Why isn't everyone happy?" Miranda asked as soon as Holly was settled.

Mike had pulled Andi into a meeting with Astrid, the floor's Mission Director, because she was a helo pilot. The fact that she wasn't an Osprey pilot didn't appear to be an issue.

"Why would they be happy?" Holly was still scowling as she had earlier. It looked unnatural on her features.

"The collision was an accident. No fault, except for a poor action by an under-qualified pilot."

"And?"

Miranda pulled out her Castle sound level meter and took a reading. "It's quieter than my first reading, but it's…"

"More intense?"

"Yes. That's it. Why is it so intense?"

"Because Murov's daughter was killed."

For the seventh time, Miranda still couldn't understand how that was relevant.

Holly stared up at the darkness of the ceiling for a moment before turning to her again.

Miranda glanced upward, but it was just a flat, white ceiling.

"Okay, let's say that Taz and Jeremy's kid got killed."

"But he or she hasn't even been born yet. Though Taz is thirty-seven. That made the likelihood of a miscarriage twenty to thirty-five percent. That *has* fallen by eighty percent because she's past the first trimester, which brings her risk of miscarriage down to four to seven percent. Calling that *killed* is a use of language that I'm unfamiliar with."

"Okay," Holly looked around. "Let's try a different example. You know that the Chairman of the Joint Chiefs of Staff has a daughter."

"Drake's daughter? Dr. Elsie Nason? Killed?"

"Right."

"Like her mother, for giving vaccines to children in central Africa?"

"Let's pretend for a moment—"

"I'm not very good at that." Then Miranda realized that she'd interrupted Holly. "Sorry."

"No worries, Miranda." Holly glanced up at the screens. "Let's try pretending anyway. What if she was killed not like her mother, but instead during unclear conditions that involved Drake's very worst enemy."

"CIA Director Clarissa Reese?"

Holly laughed, "I was thinking more like that Chinese general."

"Oh, Zhang Ru. He was a *very* bad man."

"So you've said. What do you think President Roy Cole would do? Remember that Drake and Roy are best friends, and Drake has just lost his daughter. And it somehow had to do with Zhang Ru."

"Is there an aircraft involved?" Miranda began arranging the pieces in her mind.

"Would that make a difference?"

"I've noticed that when either Drake or Roy have a crisis involving an aircraft, I'm always called now. That didn't used to be the case. But that would mean that I knew what was happening."

"Let's assume that it did," Holly was smiling for the first time since she'd found out they were coming to Menwith Hill.

Miranda looked around the room to identify the cause. The change from a minute ago was minimal. The HUMINT analyst had delivered a cup of coffee to the SIGINT analyst; Ian hadn't left his desk for a second. Andi was apparently holding a quick class on the Osprey's performance characteristics. She really didn't see why Holly was smiling.

"Miranda?"

"Oh, okay. Drake's daughter is dead because of Zhang Ru. There's an aircraft involved; therefore I've probably been contacted." Only by pretending it was actually real could she imagine it.

"What is Roy going to do?" Holly asked.

"He'll find out what happened, then act accordingly. That's what rational people do after all."

Holly laughed again. "Damn but I wish I lived on your world."

She held up her hand for silence before Miranda could ask what world Holly lived on. Earth was the only one she knew that had a confirmed presence of life. The International Space Station didn't really count as another world.

"Okay, let's stretch it further."

"I don't know if I can. I'll try."

"Imagine that Clarissa Reese is the President. What would she do if her best friend's kid was freshly dead because of Zhang Ru?"

Miranda tried. First she had to picture Roy leaving the Oval Office, then Clarissa Reese entering. That required imagining an election campaign, a vote, and a mid-January inauguration.

Clarissa sitting at Roy's desk, no, the head of the table in the Situation Room. Her best friend's...did Clarissa have a best friend? She herself did. So a best friend like Mike or Holly, or maybe like Andi? Perhaps Mike and Holly's kid—killed—even though they don't have one and neither like Clarissa. There was so much to keep track of at once.

Clarissa Reese wouldn't keep Roy's picture of his family on the desk. Did Clarissa even have a family? With the death of Vice President Clark Winston, Miranda didn't think so.

"She'd, I don't know...bomb whoever did it?" She said it in a rush.

"Exactly!" Holly thunked her boots down onto the floor so loudly that everyone turned to stare.

Miranda had to study the readout of her sound meter until they'd returned to whatever they'd been doing earlier. The room's measurable noise level had plummeted across all frequencies except for the low thrum of the air conditioner and the high note of the computers' cooling fans, which had remained constant. She didn't look up until the noise level had risen to eighty percent of its present level. Actually because a decibel existed on a logarithmic scale, the numeric eighty percent increase in the current sound level represented approximately a hundred times more power but by percentage it was only—

"Miranda," Holly forced her attention back to...what?

They'd been talking about something. She'd been talking about so many things with so many people today. She wanted to be home on her island, visit the sheep and deer, sit out in her vegetable garden, and... But it was all gone. Burned by fire.

What if that fire had been intentional rather than lightning? What if someone had injured more of her deer and sheep than the lightning-sparked fire had? They were hers to care for and would have no defenses or even understanding of what was happening to them if they were attacked.

Her fists hurt where they were clenched onto either side of her sound meter.

If someone burned her island intentionally, she wouldn't ask Holly to hunt them down. She'd take her rifle and—

"Oh!" Miranda looked at Holly. "I get it now. Clarissa would wreak bloody havoc and not care who it hurt."

Holly held up a hand and Miranda high-fived it. "Now add in the idea that Clarissa might like nothing better than to start a war. Then she could be one of those Presidents who would be remembered forever. We remember Lincoln, Wilson, and Roosevelt, not whoever came before them."

"Buchanan, Taft, and Hoover."

"Okay, most people don't remember them."

"I do."

"Yeah, I noticed, Miranda. And no, you don't need to list all forty-six names and their vice presidents to convince me that you do."

"Forty-five names. Forty-six Presidents. Grover Cleveland served twice. First from 1885 to—"

"No, please. Don't care. I couldn't tell you Australia's Prime Ministers since the first transport ship if you threatened me with being in a locked room with Clarissa."

"The first was Edmund Barton elected in 1901. Prior to that Australia was ruled by a series of colonial governors who—"

"Please tell me you don't know their names."

"Only a few."

"Good. I feel so much better."

Miranda didn't need to look up Holly's eye roll on her emoji page. She'd seen it often enough to recognize sarcasm.

"But you get the idea."

"What idea?"

"That Murov's daughter is dead. One way or another killed by the US—collision with one of our aircraft or shot with the AMRAAM missile. Mr. Psycho Russian President looks at his best friend and says *Let me kill America for you.*"

"Actually, I've been on the phone with General Murov."

Holly's eyes grew wide but it wasn't sarcasm. Miranda decided this wasn't the time to go looking at the reference notebook for her expression's meaning.

"Last year. He struck me as a very practical man."

"And you trust your own judgment on that?"

"Well, Drake and the President seemed pleased when he didn't start a nuclear war in Antarctica."

"Oh, he was part of that mess?" She shivered as if she was once again marooned on The Ice in a dead LC-130H Skibird plane that the Russians had shot down.

"Yes. That mess," Miranda agreed. It felt like slang, like they were just two gals hanging out on the street. She rather liked that, as long as it was a clean street without too many people or too much loud music.

"Okay, what if it goes like this: *I'm a crazy Russian President with a tiny little prick. My best friend's daughter is dead at America's hands. I'm going to go nuke them!*"

"Oh, is that why he's flying Su-57 Felon jets so close to our destroyer?"

"Probably. He—*What?*"

Miranda pointed to the primary satellite feed playing on one of the big screens. "This started while you were out of the room. Everyone became very excited by it. You know..."

Miranda stopped talking. Holly was no longer sitting beside her.

41

"Damn it, Mr. President. I don't mean to complain, but what am I supposed to do with these cocky sons of bitches? Those are my men out there."

Drake was fully onboard with Vice Admiral Burkhart as his complaint filled the Sit Room. It took everything he had not to recommend to the President that the destroyer should drop both Russian jets out of the sky. He doubted that there was a single man or woman here who wouldn't back him up on that, probably including the President.

But it would be one step closer to war; one that already wasn't many steps away.

He'd been dragged back in before he'd had a chance to absorb Clarissa's news about Miranda's parents. Unsure what else Clarissa had tucked away in her portfolio and what she might choose to do with it, he'd dragged her into the meeting with the sole admonition, *Please try to think before you open your trap.*

She scowled at him with the purest hatred, which felt fine.

On-screen, the Sukhoi jets were doing supersonic flybys of the destroyer presently posted at the crash site. They passed so close they'd probably shatter a Russian ship. The Arleigh Burke-class guided missile destroyer had been made of sterner stuff, but she was out there on her own, two hundred kilometers from the carrier group. And it would not be a fun ride inside a steel can being blasted sonically.

Of course, the *Gerald R. Ford* had sent up a flight of four F/A-18F Super Hornets. They couldn't outrace the Russian Sukhois, but they could sure as hell shoot them down. They were circling a half mile above the Russians and the USS *Mason* but taking no further action at the moment. A pair of F-22 Raptors was aloft out of Ramstein and would be on site in minutes. They could outpace the Sukhois if they tried to bug out.

Burkhart had been screaming since Menwith Hill had reported the Russian Sukhois departing Gromovo Air Base fifty minutes ago.

He couldn't risk sending a second destroyer away from the carrier. The nearest ship of any serious power was a UK Duke-class frigate, but she was three hours out, just gathering way out of Inverness.

"How do we get them out of our hair *without* taking them down?" President Roy Cole glanced around the room. The years had taken their toll on him, he looked as gray and weary as Drake felt. One more year, an election, and Cole would be done with his second term. Drake had sworn to retire when Cole did, then this would all be someone else's problem.

Right now it was his.

"If they don't do anything exceptionally stupid in the next fifteen minutes, the F-22 Raptors can chase them off.

The Russians may be cocky enough to think they can outrun our Super Hornets and we won't shoot them, but after the Raptors' arrival they'll know that this isn't winnable."

"Which means," Burkhart snarled, "they're going to blast the shit out of my destroyer and run before the Raptors get there."

"They have to know that they're boxed by now. You have that second flight of four up off the carrier to cut off their retreat if they misbehave."

"Maybe," Burkart didn't sound sure. Without cutting his mike, he called out. "Tell the captain I recommend launching a third flight of four. And get another Poseidon surveillance bird up there along with some tankers. I want everyone constantly topped up if this gets ugly."

"What is he thinking?" Lizzy spoke up. His wife, also the head of the NRO, had come in with him for a meeting with the National Security Advisor in the Roosevelt Room—which had never happened as they'd all landed in the Situation Room.

"Me?" Burkhart asked. "Thought that was pretty clear. Shoot the bastards now."

"No, the Russian President."

"Are you sure he's thinking at all?" Drake countered.

He could see Lizzy bracing for a fight. She might share his bed, but General Elizabeth Gray was as fierce as any of his old 75th Ranger teammates when they'd all been testosterone-laden young bucks.

"No, I'm being serious. He isn't a man notorious for deep thinking. He sees an opportunity and reacts. And who knows what advice he's been getting."

"Here's my excuse to take on the West? He's got to know that's unwinnable."

Drake didn't bother to voice his uncertainty to Lizzy. Instead, he glanced at the President.

Cole shook his head. "I can't exactly call General Murov and say sorry about your kid, but what the hell does your boss think he's doing?"

"I've got almost four hundred people on that boat, Mr. President. It's a hell of a gamble."

"On both sides, Admiral Burkhart. On both sides."

"Mr. President," the witch's white-blonde hair was back in its usual severe ponytail. Clarissa's red power suit, that he personally thought of as her bitch suit, was immaculate. At least she had the common sense to be respectful. "We picked up something we thought you should know."

"Go ahead," Roy gave her the floor.

"Slightly over four hours ago, we tracked a chain of unusual events. We do not know what was said, but perhaps it is sufficiently significant to risk the asset, though this is one we'd very much hate to lose."

"Understood. Think carefully before moving on the intelligence. Proceed."

"The head of the FSB, a General Murov, left his office two hours earlier than normal. He traveled to his home for one hour, then he returned to the office. He is a man of deep habits and this doesn't fit at all."

"Anything else?"

"Ten minutes after he left, Izolda Garina rushed into his house."

"Why do I know that name?"

"The Russian President's mistress. Daughter of a General Garin of the Russian Air Force. The media still thinks it's a rumor, but she is confirmed." Leave it to Clarissa Reese to have pursued anything salacious.

Drake looked at the clock. Four hours since the collision in the North Sea. Dead daughter. Wife grieving and wants company. Why call the President's mistress?

"Murov's wife practically adopted the mistress Garina when her own daughter, Captain Natalia Ivanovna Murov, departed for the air force."

Drake knew that Clarissa, as usual, was damn good at her job. It explained a great deal.

"And then the mistress went and told... Oh, shit!" Lizzy looked at him aghast.

42

Artemy blundered into Murov's office before he had a chance to think it through.

Murov raised his baleful gaze to look at him.

"Su-57s. American destroyer. Your wife to Garina to the President. Only thing that—makes sense." Sprinting up the flights of stairs had winded him into mere gasps.

Murov remained frozen for several seconds but Artemy could see his mind churning behind those pale eyes. Then he spoke slowly, "From the President to Gromovo Air Base. Who was Major Pronichev's commander at Gromovo?"

Artemy closed his eyes for a moment as if to picture the command structure, though he didn't need it. He simply needed a moment to collect his thoughts without feeling as if his soul was draining into Murov's eyes.

He remembered Inessa's gaze over dinner, the pride she'd carefully shown him at how well he'd handled his first real introduction to her wider society. He'd met her inner circle at the wedding and visiting the house, but tonight's dinner had been the next step. Her gaze provided a steadiness he'd been lacking until this second.

He opened his eyes and looked directly at Murov's.

"The same man who overrode the order for your daughter's medical delivery."

"General Garin."

"General Garin," Artemy confirmed.

"A likely line from my wife to the action team," Murov agreed without showing any other reaction Artemy could assess.

"Yes sir. You told your wife, who called her friend the President's mistress, who told the President that the Americans had killed your daughter. He then ordered the Su-57s aloft, probably through General Garin."

"Current status?"

Artemy checked his watch, then cursed himself. He hadn't noticed the time when he'd bolted out of the IAC.

"I didn't want to trust the phones, so I hand-carried it. This is under ten minutes old," he guessed. He took the liberty of jamming the memory stick into Murov's computer. He then circling to the side of the desk so that they could watch the image together.

It was a satellite view of the American destroyer—and nothing but ocean around it. Had the IAC tech given him the wrong segment? Had he imagined it?

"This is—" Artemy paused to clear his throat. It didn't help and he sounded small and squeaky like the Cheburashka creature might. "It's an American Arleigh Burke-class destroyer from the carrier strike group floating to the north. It is presently positioned at the downing location of the American Osprey and your daughter's Chebu—"

He didn't have to finish as a pair of Su-57 Felons, with their distinct white-edged-and-blue-field paint design, ripped through the image. They were so close to the ship that he winced in fear of the collision though he knew it hadn't happened. Reminding himself this was a recording didn't help on the second pass either.

The shock wave of the supersonic passage must have been brutal aboard the destroyer. It actually made the nine-thousand-ton ship roll in the calm sea.

Murov reached for the phone. "I will talk to the President. You need to find out precisely what happened between my daughter and the Americans. That is of the utmost urgency."

"Yes sir." Artemy hurried out of General Murov's office. How in the name of Mother Russia was he supposed to find that out?

43

"MENWITH HILL, THIS IS SITUATION ROOM."

Miranda had been ignoring most of the calls coming in over the PA system. Because of the open communication here, requests seemed to always be rumbling about, but none were for her.

She appreciated that. Silence was apparently a matter of degree. Normally she appreciated the silence of nature, loud in its own way with wind, rain, bleating lambs and so forth, but natural. Here on the Ops Floor of Menwith Hill, the *silence* was no one demanding her personal attention. It was so little, but it was all she had to cling to.

For the last several minutes since Holly had bolted from her side to join Astrid, Mike, and Andi, Miranda had been left in peace.

She'd become intrigued by the repeated passage of the Su-57 Felons.

Others were calling their actions dangerous and crazy.

Yet there was an unnoted regularity. Miranda tried playing the ten-minute history of the flybys at a slower pace.

Using scaling tools on the screen and the known wingspan of the Su-57, she was able to estimate an airgap of under ten meters from the belly of the jet to the side of the ship's command decks. They always presented the plane's belly to the ship, which struck her as illogical. The pilot would have the poorest visibility that way, making their flyby task twice as hard.

She tried playing their passages at high speed.

Both jets were passing close to the ship at thirty-second intervals.

And they kept doing so long enough for her to see that the intervals were surprisingly regular. She doubled the playback speed once, then twice more. They were now passing close by the destroyer's upper decks almost as regularly as a ticking clock.

The jets weren't the only thing moving.

The destroyer had barely rocked at first, but now the USS *Mason* rolled very actively, tipping strongly from side to side.

She picked up her phone and called Drake.

"Yes, Miranda?" Came booming out of the overhead speakers—on a tiny time delay from when it sounded from her phone.

"Drake?" Her voice was even further delayed before it sounded into the room.

A technician hurried over, handed her a headset, then hung up her phone before returning it to her.

"Drake?"

"Yes, Miranda?" Their voices still resounded into the room, but at least the strange time delay echo was gone. Oh, he'd already been on a call with the others in the room.

"Are you aware that the Russians are trying to sink the USS *Mason*?"

"No. They would have shot her long since if that was their intent."

"Remember in March, when the Russians downed our MQ-9 Reaper drone in the Black Sea, first by dumping fuel on it and then ramming it?"

"Closest we've been to direct war in years. I'm not likely to forget."

"Watch this." Miranda placed her sped-up video on a main screen and hoped that Drake would be able to see the effect.

"What am I looking at?"

Miranda thought that was obvious. She knew tact was something she rarely achieved, but she would try. Rather than pointing out that he was looking at the Russians repeatedly flying so close to an American destroyer, she needed a different approach.

"Notice the increase of heeling motion of the USS *Mason*." He still didn't respond. "With each successive supersonic passage, carefully timed so that the shockwaves reinforce the swing, they've built up a periodicity that will soon increase to catastrophic levels. I'm unsure of the details of an Arleigh Burke-class ship's self-righting mechanisms, but I estimate another two to three minutes could place the *Mason* in severe danger of capsizing."

Vice Admiral Burkhart called out to someone on his end. "Captain of the *Mason*! Emergency turn. Starboard heading forty-five degrees."

Even as Miranda cried out a warning, the big ship heeled steeply. A hundred thousand shaft horsepower poured into the dual seventeen-foot-wide propellers and the twin rudders were thrown hard over.

The destroyer heeled even further as it turned from the bottom of a swing to port.

That wasn't the problem.

44

CAPTAIN VLAD TUSOV SET UP ON HIS NEXT RUN. AFTER THIS, everyone would say he had balls of steel. Flying blind to batter an American destroyer every thirty seconds was a test of concentration and skill like none he'd ever faced before.

Doing it in a new Su-57 made him a god.

Wingman Melnikov never came closer to the destroyer than ten meters; Tusov himself flew five meters away on each pass. Doing that on a moving target would get him into the history books. Might get him the goddamn Hero of the Russian Federation medal.

At Mach one-point-seven, two thousand kilometers an hour, he came up from the stern of the American warship. He was already thinking about how to shorten the turnaround time so that he could pass the warship on alternating sides at the depths of each heeling swing.

Command wanted the boat rocked? He'd rock it hard.

Six hundred meters out, a single second from the stern of the ship, he twisted ninety degrees until he was flying knife edge—his wings vertical, no lift except from the firing engines. The belly of his aircraft would present the greatest buffeting to the Americans this way. Their ears must be bleeding with the repeated sonic-boom shockwaves he and Melnikov were pounding into their hull.

He hoped that Melnikov's camera was capturing clean images, he wanted one for his girlfriend's bedroom wall. Kesha was already crazy about having a genuine military pilot in her bed. An image of him in Russia's greatest jet, mere feet from the American destroyer, supersonic shockwaves visible in the moist ocean air, would definitely drive her to new heights.

And if he survived that, he could only wonder to what heights the ring in his pocket might send her.

He eased another three meters closer to the ship, force increasing by the square of the distance. Let the shockwave really blast them this time.

Five seconds earlier, the USS *Mason* had begun her turn. Five-hundred-foot-long ships don't turn on a dime, but destroyers are designed for three key features with everything else being secondary: lethality, speed, and agility.

Tusov did not see the turn developing as he approached though it was well underway.

By the time he twisted sideways to present his belly shockwave to the superstructure, the destroyer had turned a mere five degrees. He was too busy imagining Kesha groaning and sex sweat slickening the skin between her breasts to notice the slight variation.

He still would have been clear, missing the protruding mount for the MK-53 Nulka decoy missile system by fifty centimeters, if he hadn't shaved in three meters closer.

The heavy-duty mount of the Nulka, designed to withstand the impact of hurricanes while still being able to launch, ripped into the composite housing of Tusov's starboard engine. The Nulka's launch tubes plowed through the hull and slammed into the front end of the Saturn turbofan. The engine stopped abruptly as it was ripped out of the Su-57's fuselage like a line of peas stripped from a pod.

The force acted like a tripwire, tipping the nose of the jet into the ship as it skidded along the outside of the superstructure. It might have slid clear, perhaps even still flying briefly on a single engine, except for the AN/SLQ-32 electronic warfare module mounted at the very leading corner of the superstructure. It was as exposed as possible to provide the widest possible range of missile tracking and jamming to protect the ship.

The Su-57 impacted the Slick-32 head-on, nine-hundredths of a second after ripping out its starboard engine on the Nulka missile mount.

Before the next hundredth of a second had passed, Captain Tusov was passing backward through the cavity left by the removal of his starboard engine as his plane accordioned against the Slick-32, then tumbled onto the *Mason's* bow. Only the destruction of the massive mount for the forward five-inch gun, which weighed as much as the jet did and was built into the deck, kept the Su-57 from sliding into the sea.

The image would be splashed all over the world news. It was a picture that Kesha would never forget. She would never let another pilot into her bed, eventually marrying a low government official who did nothing to remind her of the great pleasures Captain Vlad Tusov had once brought there.

45

CAPTAIN MELNIKOV, FLYING A KILOMETER AND TWO SECONDS behind Captain Tusov, managed to correct to port and clear the other side of the American destroyer as it continued its turn.

He'd seen his flight leader disappear on the starboard side of the American ship, but he hadn't reemerged. The ship's turn had Melnikov worrying about other matters at the instant something must have happened.

Now, though? Fire spread across the ship's foredeck. No parachute floated over the ocean. They must have shot him from the sky.

They'd actually started the war that so many of his fellow pilots had hoped for.

Now he would be the first to strike back.

The Su-57 Felon jet was one of the most advanced aircraft in the world. There were only three other fifth-generation jet designs in the world, two American and one Chinese.

Despite being on full afterburners, the Sukhoi didn't

complain as he heaved it around in a turn that he could never have managed in his old MiG. The g-force tunneled his vision until all he could see was the horizon swing past his nose as he carved the turn around toward the destroyer.

There!

He leveled the plane, tipped his head down so that the targeting computer would know he was staring at the waterline.

Five and a half seconds after spotting Tusov's crash, Melnikov fired a pair of Zvezda Kh-35 anti-ship missiles at near point-blank range.

The missiles were aligned on an identical point with an infinitesimal time delay between their launches. One would have penetrated the hull, setting up the other to punch through the gap into the bunker where the massive Mk-46 torpedoes were housed. It would have destroyed the aft third of the ship in a single flash of high explosive.

Had he done this on the starboard side where Captain Tusov had rammed into the ship and destroyed two of the ship's major self-defense systems, he might well have sunk the USS *Mason*.

But he didn't.

With the attack inbound to the intact portside, the second Slick-32 detected the incoming missiles and immediately jammed their warheads. Their guidance began drifting, their paths diverging enough that they would blow two holes through the destroyer's heavy armor plating, killing anyone within twenty-five meters and permanently deafening anyone along adjacent corridors with the overpressure shockwave. But they wouldn't destroy the ship.

The Nulka's computers detected the inbound missiles,

calculated a compensation for the heavy roll of the ship, then fired a string of four decoys.

With the Russian missile's guidance fouled by the Slick-32's jamming, the R-37 missile's onboard computer switched to heatseeking mode and destroyed the decoys launched by the Nulka.

Blinded by the flare of the double explosion, Melnikov pulled up.

He cleared the upper framework of the destroyer's superstructure by three meters.

Directly below the exposed belly of his aircraft, the Phalanx *Sea-Wiz*—slang for the CIWS, Close In Weapons System—fired eighteen 20 mm rounds into the aircraft during the fifth of a second it was overhead; one was tumbling as it passed through Captain Melnikov's hip.

He managed to pull the ejection handles and his seat jolted aloft. When the seat separated and his parachute deployed, Melnikov floated down to the ocean, but his leg fell separately. By the time he reached where it had landed, he'd bled to death. Before he could be recovered, the sharks had removed his other leg and both arms.

46

ARTEMY TURGENEV ALMOST CRIED OUT WHEN HE DISCOVERED Inessa waiting in his office. He doubted she could be of any help, but she was the only person he knew he could talk to without worrying about giving fodder for an attack.

"I'm supposed to figure out what actually happened to his daughter," he declared as soon as he dropped into the chair beside her.

"What do you know?"

"Nothing. We have a terrible radar image of the two aircraft flying together perfectly normally for a flyby. Our aircraft circled the Americans, then their radar images merged—ours into theirs, not the other way about. The next image I have is of Natalia's burning plane limping eastward. Almost simultaneously, its wing blew up and it was shot with an American missile fired a minute earlier."

"Someone must know more."

"Not our people." A memory nagged at him as he thought about that. A profile he'd assembled during Colonel

Romanoff's massive mishandling of the Antarctica situation. He dismissed the idea, but it refused to be set aside.

"What's that face, Artemy?"

He explained about the American air-crash investigator who had seemed to be everywhere during that crisis, and perhaps others before.

"A specialist in military plane crashes?"

"Yes." Artemy stared at the back of the photo on his desk. He'd replaced the portrait of Inessa that Romanoff had kept there with one of their own wedding. Two together, not the slightly chilly solo portrait of the nineteen-year-old beauty pageant runner-up that Romanoff had kept there.

"Can you call her?"

Artemy laughed. It was the most ridiculous idea he'd ever heard. She was American. They had shot down the plane of Director Murov's daughter over international waters. But...it had included the loss of one of their own aircraft. Perhaps it wasn't the worst idea on a very bad day.

He fetched the file from his locked cabinet and returned to sit beside Inessa before checking it.

"I *do* have her number. Miranda Chase of their National Transportation Safety Board. Daughter of Samuel and Olivia Chase; deceased in a plane crash when she was a kid. Must have been what got her into the field of..." He became aware of Inessa's deep silence.

She could light up a room with a smile and a regal acknowledgement of her pleasure to be among such fine people, no matter who the people were. But in their long friendship and brief courtship, then marriage, he hadn't known she could do the opposite as well.

"What else do you know of the parents?" Her voice barely reached his ears as if she'd absorbed all other sound.

"I didn't particularly focus on them. Let's see. Died on crashed TWA 747 in July 1996 that—"

"Do you have their pictures?" Inessa clamped his arm hard enough that he was glad to still be wearing his uniform jacket as padding.

He flipped through the file to no avail. But he held out a picture of Miranda Chase herself. He'd found it as part of the massive media coverage surrounding the death of a US Vice President in a helicopter crash.

"Her mother's face. They could have been twins." Again she laid her fine-fingered hand upon her heart as she had at the death of Natalia Murov.

"You knew them?"

Inessa nodded and was crying again. If she had cried for her late husband's death, she'd never let Artemy see. Yet for Natalia and this Miranda's parents...

"Some people you never forget."

47

"INESSA, IS EVERYTHING OKAY?"

Artemy jolted to his feet at General Murov's unexpected appearance in his office.

"Mikhail. I was just thinking of your daughter." She wiped her eyes with a handkerchief she slipped from her purse.

Artemy made a mental note to purchase some and make a point of carrying them in the future. Also to wonder how she could possibly know Miranda Chase's parents, yet was intent on hiding that knowledge.

"How did your dear Raya take the news?"

Murov's eyes flickered to Artemy, who shook his head infinitesimally. Not that he hadn't planned on telling Inessa about the probable link from Raya to the President through his mistress, there simply hadn't been a chance yet.

"Not well," Murov might think his tone was neutral, but he wouldn't want to be Raya Murov when this was over.

Artemy wondered if Inessa could detect the chill of displeasure in Murov's tone. If so, she gave no sign.

"I will visit her tomorrow."

"Perhaps."

Or perhaps Murov would place his wife in isolation under house arrest. Or incarcerate her upstairs next to Pronichev. He was the coldest man Artemy had ever met. His eyes traveled from Inessa back to Artemy, making him again glad of his uniform jacket—this time warding off the chill.

"I have a possible lead on determining what happened during the crash." Artemy blurted out to break the tableau. He knew better than to ask how the conversation with the President had gone, and he didn't want Murov questioning Inessa until she'd had a chance to recover.

"Explain."

After Artemy finished, Murov was thoughtful for a long moment before speaking.

"Find out where she is."

"Shirinov," Artemy called out as soon as he had the office door open to his outer office. "Track this cell phone for me. Do not let her know." A bonus of working for the FSB was that international connectivity had not been curtailed. He could watch CNN, the BBC, or CNS out of China if he wanted.

"Yes sir." Shirinov remembered to give the military snap and perfect obedience in Murov's presence.

He was back within a minute, during which Inessa exchanged a few memories of a young Natalia with her father. She elicited the hint of a smile, which Artemy would have bet a thousand in hard currency against until it happened.

Shirinov, apparently not trusting himself to speak, entered and handed over a slip of paper, departing even faster than he'd entered.

Artemy read out, "Menwith Hill Air Base in the United Kingdom."

Murov's smile had no hint of the warmth he'd shown Inessa a moment before.

"She's that good?"

If he was wrong, Artemy's reputation would be poured down the drain faster than a toilet flushed. But if he was right? He thought about the file in his hands and wished he'd delved much deeper last summer, but he hadn't. Still, she'd been involved in the loss of those Antarctic stations, surviving a bombing and a missile attack unscathed. And Inessa clearly had very close memories of her parents. Hopefully daughter like mother.

"Yes sir. I believe she is."

"Let me see the file."

Artemy handed it over. "It is only a cursory investigation I created due to her presence at the Antarctica crash site and..." He stopped speaking because Murov wasn't paying him any attention.

His attention had been riveted by a page, not the one that mentioned Miranda Chase's parents. Rather it was the one of every person she'd had known contact with while in Antarctica.

"This is accurate?"

"As far as it goes, yes sir."

Murov nodded at some decision of his own. "Call her in one minute and get her outdoors, then keep her on the phone as long as possible." He hurried out of the room.

Artemy looked to Inessa for guidance, but she merely shrugged her shoulders. Whatever he'd found, they were now in the depths of it.

48

"Well," Holly spoke into the echoing silence of the Menwith Hill Ops Floor that followed the destruction of both Su-57 Felon aircraft. "That isn't something you see much on the morning telly."

The satellite view of the encounter had shifted, but it was still clear. Miranda watched as the lone Su-57, devoid of its pilot, flew to the edge of the image. It was still climbing when it disappeared from view.

Much like what had happened to her parents' plane. The fuselage powering aloft long after the cockpit had broken away. The weight of it slammed down on her until she could barely breathe. How many thousand times had she envisioned every detail of TWA 800's final moments, and here it was recreated. With a different plane and a different pilot on the opposite side of the Atlantic, but still so impossibly real that she feared her heart would never beat again.

Miranda's phone rang loudly, shattering the silence.

She tried to imagine what shattered silence looked like.

Did it lie in chunks on the floor like broken glass? If so, would it be in shards like normal glass or the small squares of tempered glass? Perhaps the powder of sugar glass used in movie bar fights, so fine that you couldn't see it?

She managed to answer it before a second ring broke more of the silence, scattering more of it in ways she didn't understand.

Another phone rang not far away, adding to the debris of shattered silence lying about her feet.

"Hello. This is Miranda Chase. This is me and not a recording of me."

"Hello, Ms. Chase. I'm so glad that I reached you."

She never knew how to respond to such niceties, so she didn't.

"Are we private?" He didn't introduce himself. His English would be accentless to a less trained ear, but Miranda was fluent in Russian. Of course, many people were, or had it as a part of their heritage.

"I would need to investigate three separate vectors to assure that. I'm sitting among others though no one *appears* to be listening. I can't attest to the privateness of your end of this connection. Third, this is an unencrypted line and—"

"Could you perhaps step away from the others? Perhaps out of doors? It is of the utmost urgency."

"Outdoors may not prove sufficient. That would then open my end of the conversation to a wide variety of unknowns: parabolic microphones, laser sensing of vibrations my voice might induce in any nearby flexible surfaces such as windows, telescopic lipreading, direct—"

"We'll assume that out of doors will be sufficient. I will call back in two minutes. Again, please, it is very urgent." And then the connection went dead.

49

"What are you doing out here, Miranda? Needed to escape that madness?" Andi came up beside her.

Miranda had learned to brace herself for a solid shoulder bump whenever Andi approached to avoid being knocked aside, but she still didn't understand why her girlfriend did that. Or why she *didn't* do it this time.

Instead, Andi stood beside her with her fists jammed in her jacket pockets.

Miranda counted to ten and then relaxed from her braced position, though keeping a careful eye on Andi.

"You know, I never really thought about these three NSA bases." Andi barely appeared to be paying attention to her own words.

If she paid no attention, would they even be her words at all? Would they become Miranda's? Everything was turned into such a jumble. Who had told her to come outside? Someone on her phone. But who? Had they identified themselves? She couldn't even remember. The room had been so *busy*. The relief of escaping consumed her senses.

Andi kept looking around as if they weren't the only ones out here. "How many of my missions were guided from inside this building? It's super strange to think about. I love being able to see the other side of this now. All those radomes and especially the Ops Floor are fascinating—but definitely bothering Holly."

"Oh," Miranda liked knowing why Holly had acted so strangely on their arrival. Again she had to rewind the conversation to discover the missing pieces. Andi had asked if she was escaping the madness, hadn't she? "Madness is a rather dated term. The DSM 5—that's the Diagnostic and Statistical Manual of Mental Disorders, fifth edition—has significantly more detailed terms: psychosis, schizophrenia, would PTSD count as a type of madness? I suspect that right up until World War II's popularization of battle fatigue, it too would have been called a madness."

"It's also slang for a busy and confusing situation."

"I didn't think of that."

"I could tell." Andi took her hand. "I bet there was also a big section on autism."

"Yes, it has become quite a significant topic."

"I still often wonder if we neurotypicals are the ones with mental disorders and you are—"

Miranda's phone rang and she answered it, though Andi kept a tight grip on her other hand. Almost as tight as Holly's grip had been on her shoulder. "Hello. This is Miranda Chase. This is me and not a recording of me."

"So you said before," the man on the other end of the phone replied.

"I did." She felt confident assuming that his soft laugh indicated a slight joke.

"I'm having a problem with an air crash and would greatly appreciate your insights."

"I'm currently in the middle of an investigation."

"Of a Russian Cheburashka and a CMV-22 Osprey?"

"Why yes." Was the person calling her inside Menwith Hill or the Sit Room? If so, why had they asked her to come outside?

"And the flybys of a pair of Sukhoi Su-57 Felons?"

"There is little mystery there. They collided with an American destroyer during excessively dangerous maneuvers." Andi was looking at her strangely. She wished she'd selected the speakerphone but she hadn't because of the problems with her last call to Drake in the Situation Room being broadcast everywhere.

"They did *what?*" the man on the phone shouted.

She was about to hand the phone off to Andi, when a soothing woman's voice sounded in the background. "It seems that your end of the phone call isn't private."

"It's my wife. My apologies, I was simply surprised. I hadn't heard that news yet."

Another voice sounded in the background, a man's. Miranda didn't like that voice. She could almost make out what was being said, but several things happened at once.

Andi's phone pinged with a message.

Group Captain Raymond Fielding stepped out of the operations building and hurried across to the administration building.

Andi cursed, then began pulling her by the hand toward the helicopter still parked on the grass from their arrival.

"Ms. Chase," the first voice on the phone spoke again, "I'd like to ask you to proceed immediately to the helicopter in front of you."

"Why would I do that?" But she already was.

"We need to get out of here," Andi whispered in her other ear, and hurried Miranda along even faster.

"What's going on?" Miranda half asked Andi and half the unknown man on the phone.

Andi pulled the phone from her hand, "You'll have to speak later," and closed it.

"But I—"

"Uh, Fielding. We can't trust him. He'll be back with reinforcements to drag you off. I have to get you out of here. Get you to safety." Andi pushed her into the rear passenger seat and slipped off her visitor badge and tossed it into the grass along with her own. "They're electronic—traceable."

Miranda wanted her phone back but Andi had already closed the door before jumping into the pilot's seat. Within seconds, the engine was spinning to life.

Miranda dutifully buckled her seatbelt and looked out the window. No one was watching their abrupt departure.

That was good. There had been too many people, too many impressions, too many headsets and phone calls and...

She didn't like Group Captain Fielding but she hadn't mistrusted him. However, Andi knew far more about people than she did herself. And if she didn't trust Andi, who could she trust?

50

Minutes later, Andi was landing at Leeds Bradford Airport, ten miles (not sixteen kilometers) from Menwith Hill. She'd flown low and fast as only a Night Stalker pilot could, hugging the terrain as if she needed to keep in practice.

As they settled beside a hangar, a small jet landed as well and pulled up beside them. It was an Embraer Phenom 100 light business jet. Its door opened even as they turned to stop alongside Menwith Hill's helicopter.

Andi did a shutdown that Miranda felt wasn't up to her usual standard. But before she could comment, Andi had hustled her aboard the Phenom. Like most small business jets, even Miranda had to duck to move into the cabin. Apparently to get away from Fielding, Andi had to get out them of the country altogether.

There were four facing seats. She and Andi sat in the two aft seats facing forward. The man who had opened the door now closed it as the plane again began taxiing. It had been stopped less than a minute.

"Where are we going?"

Andi opened her mouth as the steward slid into the backward-facing seat across from her. The fourth across from Andi remained empty.

"You will know soon enough." His voice was deep and...nasty?

Miranda began to protest, then noticed the gun resting lightly in his big hands.

Andi flinched, leaned forward—Miranda braced for her to attack the man—but stopped when she spotted the gun aimed at Miranda's chest and dropped back into her seat like a popped balloon.

It might be a metaphor, but it made no sense to Miranda. How would a popped balloon feel?

Andi unleashed a vile curse, then turned and silently mouthed, "Oh, God, I'm so sorry, Miranda."

"It's okay," she said back silently. She knew Andi's instincts on what was achievable in hand-to-hand combat were far better than her own.

For now they could do nothing but wait.

51

ARTEMY HUNG UP THE DISCONNECTED PHONE AND TURNED TO Murov. He needed to understand what had just happened but he didn't dare ask.

Murov offered one of his chilly smiles. "You will take a plane to Kaliningrad. There is a former civilian airport there, Devau. It closed a decade ago—except for occasional FSB courier flights. Ms. Chase will be landing there in approximately two hours. It is an hour-and-a-half flight from Moscow. I can keep fists off launch buttons for that long, but I will need answers very fast after that. By whatever means necessary." Then he turned on his heel and left.

He looked to Inessa and whispered. "Did we just kidnap an American citizen?" What were the chances of the woman helping him after being kidnapped? Slim to none.

Inessa looked as if she might cry again, this time from pain. "I'm going with you."

Artemy had learned better than to argue. In fact, Inessa's gift with people might prove very useful.

For the year he'd been working from this building, he'd

always been envious of the people important enough to use the rooftop helipad. Now that it was his turn, all he could feel was dread.

"Shirinov," he called out.

"Yes sir?" The man stepped to the door.

"I need a helicopter immediately on the helipad. And a fast jet for at least two passengers waiting for me at the airport. Make sure it is civilian or unmarked."

"Yes sir." Shirinov hustled out.

Artemy offered Inessa a helping hand up from her chair. He did his best to put a good face on the situation. "I've watched so many important people use the Lubyanka helipad. I always dreamed of using it one day myself." He tucked her hand under his elbow. "But I never imagined doing so with you beside me."

"You're a good man, Artemy. Do try to remember that, whatever happens." She offered him one of her room-illuminating smiles, but it looked as forced as his own words felt. As they hurried to the elevator, she still clutched Miranda Chase's file to her chest with her other hand.

52

"Hey, anyone seen Miranda lately?" Holly looked around, but she was no longer at the IMINT console where she'd been glued all afternoon. "Andi..." she called out, but she wasn't around either.

Mike stepped up beside her. "I haven't seen either of them in a bit. I wasn't really paying attention. You don't suppose they ducked out for a quick, you know, passage at arms." He made it sound suggestive, pleasant, and like it might be a good idea if they did the same.

It almost did.

Since the destruction of the pair of Felons, they had become superfluous. Miranda had already cracked the code on the original accident and it didn't take Miranda-level expertise to explain the dog's-breakfast mess of the Felons.

Holly pulled out her phone and called Miranda anyway. It wasn't like her to leave until every T and I were crossed and dotted on the full-and-final report.

Voicemail after six rings.

Same from Andi.

Maybe Mike was right and she should just leave them alone.

But Mike's frown matched the tightness in her gut—she dialed Miranda's satellite phone. The blast of a ring close by her feet had them both jumping.

Miranda's pack was tucked under the IMINT console, and the satellite phone was blinking in the mesh side pocket.

Holly hung up and stared at the pack.

"I can't see her leaving that behind if she's going further than the bathroom," Mike nudged it with a toe as if it might explode at any moment.

Holly hurried over to the SIGINT desk. "Verity, I need the location of a cell phone number." She read off Miranda's cell.

Verity punched it in. "Out by the helipad."

"Fresh air," Mike sounded relieved. "I can just see her needing to go out and get some fresh air."

Holly might have agreed, if Miranda had answered her phone. Or her own last journey outside hadn't been an exit of blind desperation. She headed for the door—fast.

Was Miranda in a meltdown and Andi too busy consoling her to answer the phone?

Mike thought for all of half a second before following her. The only place Mike was ever slow was between the sheets. He'd taught her to appreciate that, much to her own surprise.

Out through security and the main doors there was—

"No helo. No Miranda," Mike said before she could.

She started walking, but finished at a fast trot. The grass was a foot deep. Holly began tracking back and forth across it, trying to spot the phone.

When it rang two feet behind her, she jumped again—this time landing spun half around in a fighting crouch.

Mike held up his phone sheepishly as Miranda's phone rang again.

It lay in the grass not far from the where the helo's side wheel had crushed a small patch, marking the rear passenger door. It had landed atop a pair of visitor badges.

"Call Andi," Holly told him, but already knew the answer before it rang.

It lay three steps away, close by where the helo's front door would have been.

Both of their phones in the grass—and the helicopter was gone.

53

"WHAT DO YOU *MEAN* YOU DON'T HAVE ANYTHING ON THE helo? It your own bloody bird that's gone missing."

"Easy, Holly," Mike rested a hand on her shoulder.

She'd count it as a foul mark of how much she'd come to care about Mike in that she didn't break his fingers.

"He's on our side, remember?"

Ian looked up from his screens. "I'm sorry, Ms. Harper, we aren't in the habit of keeping very expensive satellites staring at our own base."

"ATC?"

"What's that? Oh, air traffic control. It's NATS over here, National Air Traffic Services."

"Well?"

"Oh, right." Ian turned back to his console. But she could tell by his initial flurry tapering off into intermittent queries that he wasn't finding anything. "No departures out of Menwith Hill captured from any local airport radar."

"Low," Mike nodded. "How low would they have to fly to not get picked up?"

"Definitely under fifty feet here. We don't care about noise from their sweeps because we're looking up not out." Ian waved a hand toward the radomes.

"Andi was at the controls," Holly knew it was right, even if she couldn't figure out why. Probably with a gun to her head. Or more likely Miranda's because Andi would never do anything to harm a hair on Miranda's head.

She headed for Astrid's desk. The floor's Mission Director was back on the drone flying over Mali, based on the images playing on the big screens.

Holly had to actually shake her to get her attention.

"What?" Astrid didn't look away.

The drone's image joggled and Holly tried not to be sick. It was the slight shimmy that happened when a drone fired a Hellfire missile. The camera was tracking the center of a flat roof on a building surrounded by pickups and jeeps.

"I need a private line to the Situation Room."

Without looking down, Astrid picked up a handset, punched the top button beside the cradle, and handed it over.

Holly turned away as the building on the screen disappeared behind a white-out flash of light overwhelming the drone's camera. It would adjust in seconds and they'd be looking at the effect on the terrorist camp's headquarters.

"Watch officer," was how the phone was answered.

Holly stepped as far away from Astrid as the phone cord allowed. "Private line to General Drake Nason. Holly Harper calling."

"I don't show you on the call list."

"Look at the fucking origin of the call, dingo breath! Bloody Mission Director's private phone at Menwith Hill seem like maybe this is more important than scratching your balls?"

Mike might think this was funny, but she wasn't laughing with him.

The phone clicked loudly as she was patched through.

"What's up, Holly?" Drake sounded pretty calm for someone on the verge of war with Russia.

"Did you call out Miranda and Andi?"

"Call them out?"

And Holly knew. "They've gone missing with a helicopter. Their phones and badges were dumped in the grass at takeoff. They're in the wind and I can't find them."

"Did you—"

"I'm at bloody Menwith Hill, General, what do you think?"

That earned her a silence. "Look, we're kinda busy here."

"If you're brushing me off, I'll—"

"Just shut up for once, Harper. I didn't send for her or have anyone else do it. I can't deal with this right now, so it's in your hands. Anyone gets in your way that you can't run over like your usual SOP, *then* you call me."

"Knew there was a reason I liked you, General." Her Standard Operating Procedure was to ram her boot up anyone's ass who got in her way.

"Just keep me off your personal kill list, Holly, and we'll be fine."

"Deal." Holly didn't actually have one of those...well, not anymore. She'd left that behind on that rotten bridge in a Southeast Asian jungle. But she did like that people thought she still had one.

"There's something else you should know. I'll have her explain it to you. Hold for a moment." Then Drake called out to the Sit Room operator to transfer the call to Booth Four, and she was waiting in the null land of hold.

No music, no radio talk show, just dead air.

There were five booths in the Sit Room complex that looked like individual Star Trek transporter pods with curved glass doors. Each had both a standard and an encrypted telephone and room for one person. The question? Who did Drake think—

"Harper." The pure disgust dripped out of the receiver and polluted Holly's ear worse that a week-long swamp training.

"CIA Director Clarissa Reese. I thought you'd be dead by now."

"In your dreams, Harper."

"Every night. You and a fiery pit that even Dante wouldn't trespass."

"Why am I talking to you?"

Holly laughed. "I have no idea. The general said there was something I need to know."

"Did that asshole tell you what?"

"Nope." Then Holly thought about it for a second. "Something you know that I need to know about Miranda."

"Why should I tell you?"

"She and Andi Wu have gone missing. Possible kidnap."

"How the *hell* did you let that happen?"

Holly began pacing back and forth alongside Astrid's desk to the limits of the phone cord. She carefully kept her attention directed at the floor and away from the big screens.

"Okay. Okay." Clarissa actually turned the bile down to stun. "Look. I uncovered a chunk of her past this morning without meaning to. I have no idea of its relevance."

"Hit me." And as she passed by him, Mike did exactly

that. She wasn't paying attention and stumbled sideways enough to bash her hip on Astrid's desk. Astrid glared at her, then went back to demanding a BDA—Battle Damage Assessment—of the drone strike.

Holly strung the cord out sideways to get out of Astrid's range, then finally got the message. She moved next to Mike, tipping the phone away from her ear so they could both listen.

It made Clarissa's voice seem a little squeaky and tinny. Clarissa Reese as Minnie Mouse; Holly could get down with that.

"Miranda's parents *didn't* die on TWA 800. They died a day earlier on a Russian aircraft crash, a military aircraft."

"Bloody hell," Holly couldn't even rouse that to whisper level. That was going to blow Miranda out of the water if she ever found out.

"They were remarkably successful CIA operatives under deep cover in Russia. Somehow, and we don't know how, connected tightly to the wives of the up-and-comers and the already powerful—as in all of them. They were instrumental in multi-billion-dollar bailout loans from the IMF and World Bank as well. Bought that damn island of hers with skim from the deal. A lot of smart investing too, but a seriously big chunk of graft that we assess they had to take to appear legitimate to the Russians."

"Jesus." Mike tipped his head away enough to look at her.

Holly's eyes felt as wide as his looked—they hurt but she couldn't so much as blink.

"You can't tell her this, Clarissa. It'll destroy her world." Leave it to Mike to see the implications so fast.

Clarissa sighed and there was a long pause before she continued. "I thought about it."

Holly could only see red. "*You fu—*"

"For approximately three seconds," Clarissa cut her off. "Miranda has always been decent to me. Not a lot of people like that in my world."

"Whereas me?" Holly had to lighten the mood or she might forgive Clarissa being a conniving bitch—a feeling she never wanted for even three seconds.

"You can roast in hell. The sooner the better," Clarissa offered and sounded as relieved as she felt to be back on familiar ground.

"Same back at you."

There was a long silence that neither of them filled. Sharing an emotional understanding with Clarissa was something you couldn't scrub off in a shower.

So, she thought about Miranda instead. Her whole life's framework was wrong. She'd chosen her career, her passion based on a lie.

"Why the fuck did you tell me that shit, Clarissa? Setting *me* up to be the one to cut out her heart?" That was sure a version of Hell she'd never imagined.

Mike was shaking his head.

"What?" she mouthed.

Mike rolled his eyes at her, somehow indicating the kidnap site of the empty helipad outside. That meant Clarissa was telling her...in case she needed to know?

Holly had always kept her own counsel, but she didn't know what to think about this. Should she ask Mike? Is that what couples did? She'd never been a freaking couple before. Shacking up for a bit, sure. Couple? No way. *Freaking* couple. How perfect. Hundred percent *freaking* her out.

It was Clarissa who broke the silence. "I have a lot of detail, but not much of it matters. One conjecture is that Sam and Olivia, Samuil and Olya Mironova when over there, were erased for knowing too much. Once Yeltsin was secure and had won reelection, he couldn't have the people who'd helped him still wandering around out in the world— especially not if he thought they were Russians. All I know is that we lost the continued and valuable intel from the entire social group when they died. It was major."

Again a silence Holly didn't know how to fill.

Mike again took care of it. "Thanks. We'll let you know if we need anything else."

"Just...go find her."

"Damn straight!" Holly said into the already dead connection.

54

ANDI WAS PRETENDING TO SLEEP, MIRANDA COULD TELL. SHE'D propped her feet on the empty seat across from her, slouched down, and turned her face to the window. But her fists were still jammed hard into her jacket pockets. And Miranda had long since cataloged Andi's breathing rhythms and posture in sleep.

She was definitely awake and Miranda couldn't begin to conjecture the purpose behind the sham. There were only two people she could be attempting to deceive: the gunman or herself.

If it was the former, he'd shown no sign of easing his guard.

If the latter, it made even less sense.

Miranda tried pretending that she herself was Mike. What would he understand that she didn't?

Perhaps Andi was ashamed that she hadn't anticipated their capture or been able to stop it? Maybe she was worrying that Miranda could ever think less of her because there were things she didn't understand like sonic profiles of various aircraft?

Miranda looked out the plane's window. In the first part of the flight, the plane had flown in many directions. Departing northeast, turning southeast, never running above ten thousand feet.

The only theory she had was that the pilot wished to remain unnoticed in general aviation air space. Below ten thousand, he would never be required to contact air traffic control or set a unique transponder ID on its radio.

In fact, it might well be running with the transponder turned off. If so, any tracking radar that pinged it would receive back no flight information other than the bounce-back from the signal itself. Normally when pinged by a radar, a plane's transponder would respond with type of aircraft, altitude, direction, and speed of flight.

Below ten thousand feet, they would also burn significantly more fuel pushing through the thicker atmosphere. That meant the target airport was well within the Phenom 100's range.

After its initial shenanigans, the pilot had set a steady course with no discernable climbs or turns. It was a fine evening for flying. The day's thermals were already smoothing out and the engines, muted by the VIP-level sound insulation, hummed along in a strong and steady tone.

The sun had set behind them and the North Star wasn't visible yet. But the brighter stars of the Big Dipper glimmered in the dark blue sky. Enough to locate the pointer stars that made up the end of the dipper bowl and pointed to the North Star's location.

They were holding due east and now had been for over

an hour. Hamburg? Denmark? Neither made sense. Stockholm would be northeast and Copenhagen should be behind them already.

She tried reviewing the day.

There had been the incident with the Russian plane and the Osprey tiltrotor. Then the Russian jets and the Arleigh-Burke destroyer. Finally, the phone call.

Miranda had forgotten about the phone call.

This would be much easier to figure out if Andi was speaking to her. But she continued to face the growing night out her side of the plane and pretending sleep.

There had been three voices on the phone: the one who wanted to discuss the crash, his softspoken wife, and the... slippery voice in the background.

She was missing something.

The background voice. It had sounded more than slippery. It had sounded...Russian!

How had she missed that? And the first caller, he'd had a slight East European accent that she'd also dismissed because of the quality of his English.

Russia.

The plane was going to Russia.

That was at least a part of the puzzle. Thinking about the Embraer's range, she even knew which part. But, her weakest area, she couldn't think of why.

Miranda reached for a notebook from her vest pocket; she'd never made one to solve a crime instead of a crash.

When she moved her hand, the gunman shifted his sidearm to track her motion.

Perhaps the pilot was staying below ten thousand feet so that there would be no explosive decompression if the gunman had to shoot someone.

Miranda slowly returned her hand to her lap.

The gunman, just as slowly, returned his weapon to resting in his own lap, but didn't turn it aside.

Miranda wished they were still on vacation. Neither her diagram nor Andi's had anticipated the crises escalating and multiplying.

If she was still on vacation, she could be thinking about the best ways to count sheep. That was far more comfortable. She liked that idea. Until they landed, she would spend her time thinking about sheep. Or lambs. It was spring and they were very cute.

55

"You!"

Group Captain Raymond Fielding almost lost his shoes, he jumped so high. He turned to face his accuser just in time to have his back slammed into a wall a single step inside the Ops Floor door. That blonde bitch Australian had him by the throat—so tight in her fist that he didn't dare swallow for fear of ripping out his Adam's apple.

"What part did you have in it?"

"In what?" he managed to croak out.

"Your helicopter. Where the hell is your helicopter?" She eased her grip enough for him to risk speaking.

"That's what I came in here to find out."

The Aussie stared at him from a hands-breadth away for ten long seconds, then cursed under her breath and let him go.

He rubbed his throat, surprised to find there wasn't a chunk missing. "What?" Even the one word bloody hurt.

"Stolen," she told him.

"Stolen? From inside the base?"

"Yes, you British git. Stolen. Used to kidnap two of my teammates."

"Kidnap?"

"Stop repeating everything I say."

Ray looked around for Astrid. "I'd planned on asking her if she'd assigned it to any other— Actually stolen? And actually kidnapped?"

"And actually from inside the base," she confirmed.

"But who would do something like that?"

"Finally he catches a clue. Welcome to the game, mate."

Raymond rubbed his throat again as Ian Faulkner came over to them. "I found it."

"Where?" The blonde practically jumped him.

"Leeds Bradford, ten miles to the south. Tower says it came in and parked. A jet landed, onboarded the passengers, and departed to the northwest. Last they saw of them. He said we were welcome to come and get our bird at any time."

"Screw the helo, what about the jet?"

Ian nodded. "Tower gave us a tail number and model. An Embraer Phenom 100 bizjet. No sign of it since. They're staying off NATS or any other air traffic control."

Raymond scoffed. "Shows how much you know of your people. Probably kidnapped themselves, stealing my helo in the process." He turned on his heel.

"Where the hell are you going, mate?" The Aussie ground it out like some kind of threat.

Well, he'd had enough of her shit. "I'm going to find my pilot and drive him down to fetch our bird. And if you ever touch me again, I'll have you up on common assault charges, *civilian*."

He let the door close in her face. He could only pray that she'd be gone by the time he returned.

56

"I'm out of ideas, Mike." He'd dragged her outside after the episode with Fielding.

"I kinda figured that out on my own, Hol. You really got to cut down on attacking superior officers. They don't like it much."

Holly stared into the distance. "Your humongous golf balls are turning orange." The sunset had lit the radomes up like torches.

"Good for playing in the snow. Though you have to play for a higher par in the snow because they bounce and roll less."

"Why do they do that?"

"You *are* out of it, Holly. The ball is the same except for the paint job. They just hit the soft snow and stop. You lose a lot of balls in the winter because they simply disappear until the next melt."

"Right. Sorry." Holly couldn't stay still. Miranda and Andi had been gone for over thirty minutes and she was no closer to finding them. Helo to jet, an untraceable lost jet.

"What do we know about the jet?" Mike eased along beside her.

"You were there." Holly kicked at a clump of grass and wished Miranda was here to discuss the need for sheep to maintain the areas between the radomes.

"If we talk it over, we could find something we missed."

"Right. Right. I'm not thinking clearly."

Mike put a hand on her shoulder. It felt good, supportive —until he shoved her sideways so hard that she tumbled into the grass.

"What the hell?"

"Stop wallowing, Harper. You're one of the best damn soldiers on the planet. Don't take my word for it, you're the one who made it into SASR, not me. Miranda and Andi need your brain—front and center. Save the fury and rage for when we need to extract them from wherever they are."

Holly rested her face against her knees, right back where she'd started the day with Andi, then she glanced up, below the same stupid radome. Andi would be looking at her in disgust—and be absolutely right to do so. Her two closest friends had just told her to stop wallowing, even using the same damn word. That's when she knew the thought that had been making her last hour a living hell.

"You think they're still alive?"

"Sure," Mike said it so easily.

If only she could believe. All she'd seen for the last thirty minutes were their shot-up, smoking corpses.

"First, Miranda's value is what's inside her head. Other than that, she isn't a threat to a fly. There's no reason to kill her. There are a lot of reasons to want to talk to her."

Holly stared up at the radomes, fading now through dusky red.

"The Russians," she told the darkness.

"The Russians," Mike agreed.

"You couldn't just say that?"

"I figured if we both got to the same place separately, it meant it was probably true."

"They don't know what the hell happened." The only reason to kidnap an air-crash specialist was because of an air crash. Otherwise, they were about as dangerous as a librarian.

"Bingo."

Holly had to laugh, couldn't keep it inside but managed to haul it back before it slid completely into hysteria.

"What?"

"I saw this bumper sticker on a car once. It said *Back off man, I'm a librarian!* I'm going to get one of those for Miranda."

Mike laughed too. "*Back off man, I'm an air-crash investigator!* It works. Back to the Russians."

Holly slapped the ground beside her and Mike sat. "Okay," she blew out a hard breath. "Okay. Miranda, the Russians, an explanation of what happened out there over the North Sea, where are they headed?"

"Russia. Not a lot of other places they can set up a meeting. No Russians popping into Bruges for a chit-chat."

"That narrows it down for shit, Mike. Kinda big country."

They watched until the last hint of red had faded from the radomes and they were only dim white blots against the emerging stars.

"What was the jet that Ian said the tower spotted?"

Holly had to think for a minute before she came up with it, "An Embraer Phenom 100."

"Big or little?"

"Smallish."

"How small? Like what parts of Russia could it reach?"

Holly turned to ask Miranda, then fought down the nausea. "Miranda's the one who keeps all that shit tucked away in her head. Not me."

Mike pulled out his phone. "Nope, there's one other person."

57

"Hi, Mike. How's Miranda? It's weeks since we've talked. Any interesting crashes that you're working on? I'm—"

Taz didn't even have to look up at him. She simply tipped her head a little as if rolling her eyes at him from where she sat on the couch reading yet another book on pregnancy, which she propped on her rounded belly.

Jeremy cursed to himself. Mike had called him, not the other way round. And he wasn't giving Mike the chance to get in a word.

"Sorry, do you need something?" He set his phone on the desk, tapped Speaker, and folded his hands together tightly to remind himself to control his response durations.

"Hi, Jeremy. What can you tell me about an Embraer Phenom 100?"

"Did one go down? It's a little bizjet. Usually configured for one or two pilots up front plus four facing seats in the cabin. Small lavatory where you can belt in a seventh person on the cushion. It's just like Miranda's Citation M2 but one size down. They manufacture the EMB-500, that's its official designation, EMB-500 Phenom 100, in a couple variations but nothing significant. Only nine hull losses out of four hundred manufactured. It's a good jet. She's just about square with a hull length of forty-two-point-one feet and a forty-point—"

"Jeremy, take a breath."

He did. "—forty-point-three-foot wingspan. Its—"

"Jeremy," Holly spoke up. Her tone said it was a good thing they were on the phone or she'd be smacking him on the head.

"Hi, Holly. How are you? Where are you? What's—"

"Jeremy," her tone went darker.

Taz had put down her book and was staring at him with that, *Oh my God, you're a space alien* look that she sometimes gave him.

"Right. Listening now."

"The Phenom 100. What's its range?"

"Official is twenty-two hundred kilometers." Jeremy then clamped his tongue in his teeth to not overrun Holly's next question.

"How about—" Mike drawled out as if he was thinking hard "—if they're staying low? Down below ten thousand feet to keep out of controlled airspace."

"Well, that shortens the range significantly. The newer variants on the Phenom 100 have been mostly to improve climb rates so that they can get up to cruise around forty-thousand feet quickly. That's where they save the fuel. Down low? At least a ten percent hit, perhaps twenty. I've never studied that on the Phenom jet."

"So what parts of Russia are reachable from Menwith Hill?"

"Menwith Hill!" Jeremy shouldn't have shouted as it had

Taz jolting upright. He knew he was being overprotective; they still had a month to go on her pregnancy, but he hated startling her in any way.

He attempted to clamp down on his excitement.

"*Menwith Hill?*" Nope. Didn't work. "I'm *so* envious. I can't believe you guys are there! You're there, right? Right now? That is one of only three stations like it in the world. They've got—"

"We know what they have, Jeremy. We're sitting right here. Russia? Phenom 100? It's important. Someone's kidnapped Miranda and we have to figure out to where."

He couldn't even speak. Kidnapped Miranda? To Russia?

"Jeremy, are you still there?"

He should have been there, at Menwith Hill. He and Taz. Somehow they could have stopped that. Or let himself be kidnapped instead. Or—

"Jeremy!" Holly snapped out.

"Kaliningrad," blasted out on the breath he'd been holding. "That's as far as they can reach. They'd never make the main part of the country."

"Where's that?" Mike asked.

He was still attempting to draw in air to speak. At sixteen pounds per square inch of atmospheric pressure at sea level, it should have no problem invading his lungs but it simply wasn't reaching his alveoli. No air into the lungs' alveoli, no reoxygenation of spent red blood cells, he could feel himself turning blue from the inside out.

Holly answered for him. "It's an enclave that they managed to keep from the breakup of the Soviet Bloc countries. A little wedge of land between Poland and Lithuania on the Baltic Sea."

"Actually, it's a semi-exclave," Jeremy managed to find

some air. "*Semi* because it isn't wholly encapsulated in another a single other country, like Vatican City in Italy or Lesotho in South Africa. And *exclave* because it isn't its own country—still belonging to Russia though they don't share any borders. Kaliningrad is..." Jeremy couldn't remember the exact number, "...about six hundred square miles and a million people. The capital city, which is Kaliningrad in Kaliningrad Oblast, is Russia's only year-round ice-free port in Russia's west, at least before they grabbed Crimea from Ukraine back in 2014. Though after all they did in Syria, that port is pretty much Russia's too. Kaliningrad has two significant airports. One military and one international airport, the latter is mainly to provide service into St. Petersburg and Moscow. But close by the city there's a civilian air strip, Devau Airport, that's plenty long for the Phenom. The 100 is a short field specialist and would have no trouble getting in there. It's quiet there, too, because they closed the airport a decade ago. I'd land there if I was kidnapping someone." And suddenly his chest hurt again.

"How long?"

"Well, at that altitude it's a tricky balance of fuel against speed and distance. Two hours. Possibly two-fifteen."

"Shit!" There was a sound like Holly scrambling to her feet. "We've got to get moving. Thanks, Jeremy! You're the best."

"What did you say about Miranda being...kidnapped?" He was talking to himself.

"And he finally gets to the main point," Taz said softly. She leveraged herself off the couch and waddled over to stand beside his desk chair.

They'd originally set up an office for him in their DC condo's back bedroom, but that was now outfitted as a nursery. He liked this setup better anyway; he'd been too isolated from her in the office.

She slid onto his lap with slow, deliberate movements. It was crazy how big her belly had grown on such a small woman.

"I—" he raised his hands, then dropped them helplessly. "They're all the way over there. I can't do anything to help."

"It sounds like you just did."

"It wasn't enough." Miranda in peril? In the hands of the Russians? All he could manage was to bury his face against Taz's collarbone and hold on tight.

"You miss her, don't you?"

He could only nod. Those three years on her team had been the best, most exciting time of his life. He'd follow Taz anywhere; she'd made his life so much more than he'd ever imagined possible. And the tapping foot against where his hand rested on her belly told him the best was yet to come.

But he really missed Miranda.

58

"Come on, Ian. Come on. Find it. Find it. Find it." Holly knew she was being ridiculous. The man couldn't possibly work any faster.

"There's a lot of territory between here and Kaliningrad. Give me a break," Ian grumped.

He kept shifting around the images on his console. And Holly only resisted pounding on the back of Ian's chair because Mike had taken a tight hold on her arm after the first three times she'd done it.

Ian had started close in on the Devau Airport that Jeremy had suggested. There were no hangars, no control tower; in fact, no airplanes.

He'd slowed down just long enough to confirm Jeremy's memory that the airport had closed a decade earlier. It had been. But Holly would trust Jeremy's guess that Miranda was headed there. Besides, if the jet was headed to the military base or on the larger commercial airport, it would be hard to identify.

This was their best bet.

"How about a jet out of Russia into Kaliningrad?"

"I've got plenty of those." Ian did something that lit up numerous planes on a wide variety of vectors. Lithuania had closed the roads and rails across their territory that Russia normally used to supply Kaliningrad. It was part of the NATO sanctions due to the Ukraine War. Everything now had to move by sea or air, and there was a lot in the air.

"Direct out of Moscow?" Mike suggested.

"Good one!" Holly grabbed his arm and shook him side-to-side. Where else would a kidnapping be ordered from.

That cut the number of flights by about two-thirds, but it wasn't enough.

"Menwith Hill. Sit Room." Drake's voice sounded over the PA.

"Menwith Hill," Astrid answered.

"Message from CIA Director. *Meeting Miranda Devau Airport.*"

"That's it?"

"That's it." And Drake was gone.

Holly raced over to Astrid's desk. "Direct line. Give me a direct line to them."

Astrid sighed, gave her a handset, and punched for the direct line.

"Drake, Holly here. Give me more detail."

"Clarissa," was all he said.

"We don't have any," Clarissa spoke up. "A high-level asset sent in the message. All ID was scrubbed per safety protocols. Went to Russia Desk who forwarded it to me."

"We've got to send in—"

"No," President Cole spoke up. "No, Ms. Harper, we don't. We have multiple fatalities on both sides. Between ourselves and Russia, we have a quarter billion dollars of destroyed aircraft, a damaged destroyer with dozens, possibly a hundred aboard injured, and a possible war. The US will not be staging an extraction of two women in hostile territory at this time. I'm sorry. Sit Room out."

He was gone before Holly could say that he'd just lost her vote. The fact that she wasn't a citizen and he couldn't run again as this was his second term didn't matter, he had.

Before she could murder anyone, Drake came back on, using a handset instead of a speakerphone by the lack of background noise.

"I'm truly sorry, Holly. It's simply not an option."

"If we were to send in an action team to rescue them, how long would it take?"

"Four hours and fifteen minutes."

"You *do* have an action plan in place. How do I get aboard?"

"Yes, we have a plan. No, you can't get aboard because the President is never going to release them. Besides, Harper, when was the last time you were even on a range?"

Holly didn't answer. He wasn't talking about popping off a couple boxes of ammo on the shooting range she, Andi, and Taz Cortez had set up on Miranda's island. He was talking about a live-ammo, combat training range. Not since the day she'd walked out of SASR. Five years. Drake had been a 75th US Ranger, he knew exactly what he was talking about. Spec Ops skills faded fast without constant practice.

He sighed. "It doesn't matter, we can't use it anyway."

"Why the hell not?"

"Think, Harper, don't react."

"I was a staff sergeant; we weren't paid to think."

"Well try it on for goddamn size for a change," he snapped in a full-on field-officer voice.

Not the voice of negotiation and compromise, but the voice of a man who had led a team into danger from which some never returned. *That* was a voice she knew all too well inside her head. Someday she'd have to get General Drake Nason drunk and talk about how he'd survived doing that because she had never done better than holding on by her fingernails.

"We go dropping a Delta team onto undisputed Russian soil, what the hell do you think is going to happen? If our intel is right, that she'll be landing there in little more than an hour, will she be there in four hours? Or tucked away in Lubyanka Prison?"

"She's still in the air now."

"In a plane gone dark. And what the hell could we do about it if we *could* find them? Threaten to shoot them down if they don't land? They know we won't because it would kill Miranda."

"If she ends up in Lubyanka, I'll go in on my own and get her. And this is soldier-to-soldier so don't give me any crap about prisoner trades or diplomatic solutions. They just kidnapped an autistic genius and a Night Stalker, both of whose heads are packed solid with information about our most advanced weapons and tactics respectively."

Drake groaned, "Don't think I haven't pointed that out ten times already. The answer, Harper, is no. The team at Ramstein is working scenarios, but they aren't moving an inch."

"Then what the hell is moving, General?"

"Look at the bigger picture, Holly." It was the first time he'd used her given name that she could recall. Then he was gone.

Mike was standing there as she dumped the handset back on Astrid's desk.

When she shook her head, a new look crossed his features.

For the very first time she saw a sliver of a very different version of Mike Munroe—the orphanage kid who'd done his time on the street and just might have made a hell of a soldier if he'd made different choices.

She hadn't known that was in him. Maybe he didn't either. Mike was always the calm center, sophisticated and elegant and very carefully one step back from everything that happened around him.

Though it had faded to his usual urbane self, she *knew* what she'd seen there. Mike might not have the lethal instinct when needed, but he'd survived and triumphed over plenty of rough shit. She'd done it by kicking down doors. He'd done it by—

"Okay, Mike. You're the brains of this outfit. What's the bigger picture?"

He squinted at her.

"Okay, with Miranda gone, you're the brains. Besides, we both know it isn't me. Drake wants me to look at the bigger picture, which isn't Miranda either. He hinted that something's on the move, even if it isn't—as it bloody well should be—an extraction team."

Mike looked around the room, so she did the same.

They were standing in the heart of Menwith Hill's Ops Floor. Most of the West's intel passed through this room and the two others like it in Colorado and Australia. Who was passing intel on a cell phone. What increasing buzzwords were implying an upcoming terrorist attack. What Russian general got toasted on the front line in their asinine war.

Even *she* knew that their Special Military Operation in the Ukraine had been a stupid move. Of course economies always did better on a war footing, even sanctioned ones as Russia had now proved with China's help. By shifting trade to the east, even at cut-rate prices, Russia's economy was back to prewar levels. If Russia still existed by the time the sanctions were dropped, there would be a brief economic boom time—before it all collapsed under the graft and corruption again.

Her own answer? Blast the hell out of the whole lot.

What would Chairman of the Joint Chiefs of Staff, Four-star General Drake Nason's answer be?

She had no bloody clue.

Mike pointed at something. Not up on the big screen but down on a console. It was a tactical map showing the locations of warships, foreign and domestic.

The area around this morning's plane crash still had a lone destroyer lurking about.

But where the hell had the USS *Gerald R. Ford's* Carrier Strike Group gone?

Then she spotted it.

No longer off central Norway. In the last four hours it had poured on the gas and was fast coming up on the entrance to the Baltic Sea. If the carrier group blocked the entrance to the Baltic, with the sea ice not yet melted out of White Sea on the Arctic side of Russia, they would have no access to the ocean at all. Their fleet would become trapped unless they wanted to face the gauntlet thrown down by the mighty *Ford.*

"Are we going to war over this?"

Mike slid a hand around her waist and she leaned into him—she *needed* to lean into him. He didn't answer.

Holly closed her eyes for a long moment. "I wish I knew that Miranda and Andi were okay."

"You do. We got that message. *Meeting Miranda.*"

"For fuck's sake why?"

"What's Miranda good at?"

"Crashed planes. We've had a lot of those today."

Mike was again looking around the room.

Holly followed his gaze but could see what he was looking at.

"You think they have one of these?"

"For their own satellites at least..." Holly looked at the room, the people in the room.

There were a dozen simultaneous operations going on here. The BDA out of Mali was now old news. The upcoming G-7 meeting was still high on the roster, but so was a night skirmish between the Indians and the Chinese at the contested high-Himalayan Ladakh-Tibet border.

"They don't know what happened..." Holly guessed.

"Maybe they don't understand what happened today, so they grabbed Miranda to explain it." Mike started it as a question but didn't end it that way.

"They could have bloody well just asked."

"You're not thinking like a Russian."

"Big picture," it tasted like a curse. They wouldn't trust anything the West said. In fact, their pride said they could never ask. But they could take.

Well, what they could take, she could take back. But she had no idea how.

59

Holly's failed attempts to restrain her pacing annoyed everyone on the Ops Floor. She could see that. But she couldn't stop it and if she left, she might miss something. Something important.

The President had said no US military operation would be sent.

"Roy Cole is very careful with his words, isn't he?" she asked Mike then next time her pacing tracked past him.

She paused long enough to see his nod, then kept moving.

Drake told her to see the big picture.

Carrier Strike Group on the move. An Osprey and three Russian aircraft down. A beat-up destroyer. Hell, half the crew in that tin can were probably suffering from permanent hearing loss from all the sonic booms the Felons had created if nothing else. Russia, or at least the Russian President, just dying to unleash the nukes no matter what the consequences.

Out there, probably scared for her life in the middle of it

all, was Miranda Chase. Thank God Andi was with her. But Holly couldn't get to them.

The PA blasted to life with Verity's voice. "MD, SIGINT. Message intercept from Russia sub *Belgorod*. Urgent request for botulism antitoxin. Sent in the clear."

"Unencrypted?" Astrid asked in surprise.

"Confirmed. We have earlier communications, encrypted, on the same topic. It appears that the downed AN-74MP was on a medical delivery mission prior to colliding with our Osprey."

"Are there any other Russian planes aloft and headed for the *Belgorod?*"

"Negative," Ian replied from his image intelligence desk. "Nor ships."

"I've intercepted no orders," Verity reported for signals intelligence. "There's an odd message here that didn't make much sense. But maybe... One way to read it implies that all of their national on-hand stock was aboard that flight. That's only a twenty-percent confidence level, but it's possible."

Astrid punched a button and continued speaking into her headset. "Sit Room, this is Menwith Hill." And she explained *Belgorod's* plea for help. "They can't ask us directly, of course, but they sent it in the clear probably hoping we heard them."

"Position and range?" Holly recognized Drake's voice.

"Three hundred klicks northwest of *Ford's* CSG. And—" she glanced aside to a Navy control desk and received a thumbs up, "—the *Ford* has antitoxin aboard. An Osprey can be there in under an hour to make the drop. Request permission to communicate directly with the sub."

"Hold." And the connection went dead.

Holly grabbed Mike's arm. "The drop."

"What?"

"The drop!" It was clear in her head but she was having trouble turning it into words.

Mike waited her out.

"Screw Delta Force and whatever grand operation they have planned. It's dark in Kaliningrad. Nighttime. Right now. There are two planes, five bad guys, Miranda, and Andi parked on a deserted air strip."

"The moment we fly in there, they're going to shoot our asses."

Holly liked that assumed *we* a lot. "Mike, you really are the best."

He opened his mouth but she shook her head.

"I'll explain why later. You can fly a jet. You get me over the field, I parachute down. One person in the dark and they'll never notice me until it's too late. I can do this. Trust me."

Mike didn't even offer one of his uncertain shrugs. "How?"

Holly had seen something on the security screen. "Come on!" She grabbed his hand and strolled to the exit. Once past security, she sprinted into the darkness.

60

"WHERE THE HELL DID YOU GET MY HELICOPTER?" IF HE HAD A gun, he'd shoot Holly Harper with it. Instead, Group Captain Raymond Fielding could only fume. She'd landed crosswise on the road, blocking his return from delivering the pilot to Leeds. And yet, here was his helicopter again—without his pilot—and he'd almost rammed it a kilometer before the entrance.

"Look. For just a moment pretend you don't hate my guts."

"You're asking for a bloody miracle, lady."

"Yeah, well do it anyway because I don't have time to argue. My government isn't going after Miranda because it would be bloody *politically inadvisable.*"

How many times had Raymond heard that about an operation? In Menwith Hill that was far more common than being allowed to shoot the bugger they had square in the sights.

"And you want to be rid of me." Holly continued.

"In the worst way."

"I'll cut you a deal. You line me up with a jet rental. Not a charter, a rental. I already have a pilot," she slapped Mike on the shoulder.

The man didn't look happy about it but he didn't refute her statement.

"Also, I need some equipment. HALO jumpsuit with a black RAM chute, oxygen for the fall, and some weapons."

"I can't just—" But he could and she knew it. Not easy, but he could. Then he looked at her more carefully. "You're going to invade Russia on your own to free this woman. Is Miranda Chase really that important?"

"You have no idea, mate."

He'd seen the blonde as no more than an aggressive bitch to this point. He'd dismissed Mike's comment about her being former Australian SASR, but the woman *did* have the balls of steel that were unique to Spec Ops. His twin brother once had that. He'd joined the SAS and died for it in Afghanistan.

"You seriously think you can do this?"

"See any other candidates stepping up to the line?"

Raymond was sick of so many things. He was sick of feeling powerless as the British Deputy Chief of Operations at Menwith Hill—meaning the Yanks did whatever they wanted and he had to kowtow. Of how often they were ordered to abort operations.

"Astrid?"

Holly shook her head. "Nobody in Menwith Hill knows about this."

She was betting he'd like that part of it, being the only one in the know. And, damn her, she was right.

But to help her could well mean his career.

He wanted to say yes but couldn't see how to risk it.

"I know that look." Holly cut him off before he could speak. "I have an idea."

She pulled a stack of phones from her jacket pocket, sorted through, and stuffed all but one back away. She keyed in a code on the screen, scrolled up and down the phone contact list as if it was unfamiliar, then found what she was looking for, dialed, and hit Speaker.

"Miranda?" There was a mix of surprise and eagerness in the tone of the woman who answered.

"I'm sorry, Prime Minister. This isn't her. I'm one of her teammates, Holly Harper. You know what's happened to her?"

Fielding could actually get to like this woman. Well, maybe not, but he liked her attitude. Straight to the top.

"Yes, that's why I was so surprised by this call," PM Whittaker sounded calmer.

"I'm standing here with Group Captain Fielding. I'm going after her and need his assistance."

"To do what, precisely?"

"Prime Minister, this is one of those situations where the less you know, the better. I simply need your authority to get his help."

Olivia Whittaker hadn't become the Prime Minister by being stupid. She'd connect that Holly was staging a rescue, one that couldn't be on the books.

"No UK personnel?"

"Not a one will be leaving the country on my account. Civilian plane, some gear. Fielding on the Ops Floor in case I need some fast intel, like she's on the move."

There was another thoughtful silence.

"I owe Miranda my life. She saved me as PM and a colleague at great risk to herself, therefore the UK owes her as well. Group Captain, whatever Ms. Harper needs as fast as you can arrange it. Get her out of here."

"Yes, ma'am." That was one order he'd be glad to carry out.

He looked at Holly after the PM hung up. "Head for Leeds Bradford, it's ten miles south. I'm going to have to drive my pilot out to retrieve the helicopter again, aren't I?"

"Goodonya, mate!" Holly said cheerfully as she turned back for the helo. "Though he's a bit tied up at the moment. You'll find him behind Radome Four. He won't be in a tip-top mood."

He sighed. His first assessment was right, he couldn't rid himself of her fast enough.

61

"HOLLY! THAT'S A CITATION 700."

"Uh-huh!" She was going through the gear that Fielding had scared up for her. A black unmarked sedan had pulled up beside the plane moments after she'd landed the helo. The trunk had opened, but no one got out of the car. Being British, she'd bet the driver wasn't even watching out the rearview. She hauled the three big duffel bags out and dropped them with a thud on the tarmac. The moment she'd closed the trunk, the tires had chirped with hard acceleration and the car was gone.

"I've had my FAA checkride to fly Miranda's M2," Mike waved a hand at the twelve-passenger jet that had been waiting for them. No one around. Just parked with the door open. "This thing is at least four times the size. It looks like a hundred."

"A jet is a jet. Get it warming up." Gods but he was fun to tease.

"No, Holly, it isn't."

"Sure it is. I've never flown an AW109SP GrandNew

before, but I got us here." More on guts than skill, but she'd done it. Andi would have made it look effortless but she wasn't here. If she wasn't with Miranda, Holly would have given up all hope. She would admit to no one, especially not Mike, that *not* hitting a tree during the road landing to stop Fielding should be sent to the Vatican as a minor miracle.

"White knuckle the whole way, Hol."

"You or me?"

"Both." He knew her too well.

She checked the last duffel. Everything she'd asked for and more was here. She thought a little better of the Group Captain. She zipped them up and tossed the first one aboard. She hefted the other two and turned to face him. "Got a better plan, Mike?"

He wrapped his arms around her, pinning her arms to her sides. "You come back dead and I'm gonna murder you, Holly Harper."

It made no sense but Holly didn't care. She buried her face against his shoulder and let herself be held. She knew she'd never been this far out in the wind, not even when hanging under that bridge and watching all the rest of her team fall to their final end in the deep canyon below.

If Mike knew even half the holes in her plan, he'd never let her try. But she had to and they both knew it.

Yeah, his loving threat made no sense and it was about the nicest thing anyone had ever said to her.

62

MIRANDA CHECKED THE VEST POCKET WHERE HER PHONE belonged for the third time since the man with the gun had stepped off the plane. How had she missed its absence through the whole flight? Because every time she moved a finger, the man's gun had tracked the motion. But without it, she couldn't call anyone and no one could call her.

Then she'd remembered that Andi had taken it as they hurried aboard the helicopter back at Menwith Hill.

"Can I have my phone back?"

"Uh," Andi frowned. "I thought it best if they couldn't track us. I dropped both our phones in the grass before we took off. Not my best choice but it was all I could think to do. I'm so sorry."

"I hope someone finds it before the lawn mower comes through." From the air she'd seen that they'd been mowing around the back of the Menwith Hill admin building and would reach the helipad area tomorrow.

Andi's slight smile disappeared as quickly as it started.

The small plane rocked as two people stepped aboard. Were they being kidnapped too?

Perhaps not. The first was a Russian Major General by the star on his epaulet. The other was a woman perhaps ten years older than herself. Both were stooping awkwardly as they shuffled into the narrow central aisle.

"I'm Artemy Turgenev, and behind me is my wife Inessa." His English was clear but accented. It was the first voice on the phone call. He reached out a hand but Miranda kept hers clenched around the empty pocket where her cell phone belonged. Though she was sitting down, she felt distinctly off balance without its familiar weight in her upper right pocket.

After a long moment that she guessed was...awkward, he turned to Andi, "And you would be?"

"Andi Wu," Andi shook his hand and he seemed happier.

"She's my girlfriend." Miranda turned to look at her. "Is that a weak word? I don't know if it carries sufficient importance."

"It will do for now," Andi said without quite looking at her.

The new arrivals slid into the two seats, Artemy opposite Andi and Inessa directly across from herself. Inessa had long dark hair that looked very soft. It was much fuller than Miranda's own.

"Is your hair so thick naturally?"

"Yes."

"Mine isn't."

"I see that."

"You have a nice voice." Inessa's English would not have raised an eyebrow anywhere in America.

"Thank you."

There was a brief silence. She was most comfortable in silence. But Artemy, sitting stiffly in his general's uniform, wasn't and starting speaking almost immediately as if the space needed to be filled.

"First, I would like to apologize for the manner in which you were both brought here. It would be remiss of me—"

Miranda, noting that her hand had closed around her badge, which she normally kept in the pocket behind her phone, realized that she'd never properly introduced herself. "Hello, I'm Miranda Chase. Investigator-in-charge for the NTSB. I don't understand why we were brought here."

Artemy nodded his head.

She saw his right hand lift from his lap, so she held her vest tightly until it came to rest again.

"As I was saying—"

"Are you about to say more niceties?" She turned to Andi. "Is that what he's doing?"

Andi nodded.

Miranda turned back to the general. "I never understand the purpose of those. But if they make you more comfortable, that's okay."

Artemy frowned a down-frown, but Inessa smiled. She liked Inessa's smile almost as much as her hair.

"What *do* you understand, my dear?" Inessa's voice was very soothing.

"Plane crashes. I've also studied sheep and deer as they live on my island and I try to take care of them. Some metaphors but apparently not analogies. I thought I understood those but it seems, based on recent evidence, that I don't. Shall I continue or is that a sufficient start?"

"I think that's sufficient," the man said. "It is plane crashes I wish to discuss."

"Oh, good. I know about those."

"Are you aware of the incident in the North Sea that destroyed two aircraft?"

"There were two of those events today alone. I know of at least five other aircraft collisions over the North Sea. I'm sure there were many more over the English Channel during World War II but I haven't made a study of those."

"It is today's I wish to discuss." His neck above his high collar seemed to be swelling and reddening.

"Oh. I can't do that."

The swelling and reddening expanded. "And why *not?* Don't you understand your situation here?" His voice was turning nasty. If he was talking on her missing cell phone, she would have handed it to Holly or Andi by now.

Miranda looked across the aisle, and Andi nodded before turning to the general.

"General Turgenev, there are a few things you need to understand. Miranda is autistic."

"Which means what?"

"It means," Inessa rested a hand on her husband's arm, "that if you bluster or threaten, Artemy, Ms. Chase will feel overwhelmed. That would not be good for her or for us. Now be quiet for a moment, dear."

The general's neck turned redder; Miranda didn't dare look any higher to see if it had moved onto his face. She could feel his eyes boring into her. She closed her own and it barely helped. It was getting hard to breathe, as if the cabin pressure control had been set too high.

She heard the general blow out a hard breath. Then his wife told him, "That's better, dear." The plane remained silent for twenty-four heartbeats.

Miranda risked opening one eye.

Inessa sat directly across from her with her hands clasped lightly on her lap, resting on a slim folder.

Hands. She could look at hands. She'd have liked to look at Inessa's hair again, but that was too close to the eyes.

"Is it okay if I call you Miranda?"

Miranda risked a nod. She could feel her neck creaking like it was made of rusty steel cables, not elastic muscle. A metaphor! That made her feel a little better.

"Is there a reason that you can't discuss today's plane crashes?"

"Yes."

The general—thinking of him as Artemy was too personal—ground his teeth. It pushed her closer to a meltdown than she'd been in a long time. It had been even longer since a single person's attitude had so pushed at her.

So why now? There must be a reason.

She risked observing her environment with quick glances.

They sat in an Embraer Phenom 100E as the E variant had the Garmin 1000 avionics suite that she could now see in the abandoned cockpit. It was parked on a disused runway in Kaliningrad, Russia. Her arrival here had been *at gunpoint* after a very trying day filled with a great clutter of new impressions. Andi seemed to be pulling away from her, which hurt worst of all.

Aware of the nearness of a meltdown, where her only recovery would be to hide and self-stim for hours (or perhaps days after all of these events), she needed to latch onto something.

Or shed something?

There was a new concept. What if she ignored the existence of the Russian major general? There weren't four of them on the plane. Only three. It would be good practice in pretending as well. She liked dual purpose tasks.

She looked again at Inessa's hands and felt calmer yet. Yes, she would only listen to or speak to her.

Inessa repeated her question. "Is there a reason that you can't discuss today's plane crashes?"

Miranda didn't want to repeat herself; she'd already said there was. "Oh," Miranda turned to Andi. "Is this one of those implied requests for more information like with the Prime Minister?"

Andi nodded.

"Everything is so complicated. I do wish people would explain themselves. I can't discuss it with you because the information is classified. I don't know you, but I can assume that a Russian general does not have an American security clearance. As you are his wife, I would assume that you also do not have such a clearance."

Inessa's smile implied something, but Miranda had no idea what.

63

ARTEMY HAD NEVER DEALT WITH AN AUTISTIC BEFORE. HE'D seen the designation in the file now resting on Inessa's lap. He'd read a brief summary about the *spectrum* online, but had only taken away that the woman was somehow deficient. She wasn't deficient at all; she was incomprehensible, but also curiously sensible.

Now the rest of what he'd read made more sense.

She'd been kidnapped. Now his prisoner on Russian soil. And if he knew Murov and the President, she'd never see freedom again—her or her girlfriend. This was Russia. The first time they went out in public as a couple they were as likely as not to be beaten, and there were no laws to stop that. It was all the deviance needed to convict them in court and ship them to a Corrective Prison Colony.

Yet despite all that, the woman was worried about security clearances. He didn't know whether to laugh or have her shipped to Moscow.

Then he remembered the last thing General Murov had said. *I can keep fists off launch buttons for that long, but I will*

need answers very fast after that. By whatever means necessary.
It was up to him to stop a war between East and West.

Him personally.

If he succeeded, little would change. But he'd be imprisoned or executed the moment he failed.

Artemy wondered what extreme measures he could bring to bear here. He *needed* answers now, not some psychological runaround that—

But Inessa had said badgering the woman could lead to some kind of autism-driven issues that *wouldn't be good for her*—he didn't care—*or us*—and that gave him pause.

Attempts to coerce this woman would, what? Drive her into some kind of fit?

He didn't know. But if so, she was a woman strangely immune to threats or more extreme measures because once driven into an autistic episode, she'd be unable to communicate at all.

Clearly decorative, the petite Chinese girlfriend wisely remained silent. Perhaps threatening the girlfriend would work? Did lesbians even care for each other or was it simply flaunting their unclean ways that drove them together? On second thought, attacking the girlfriend might affect the woman as thoroughly as a direct attack.

He'd speak, but he couldn't think of what to say. Again he felt the major general's star burning against his shoulder. How long would it remain there after he reported failure? Days? Hours? Would he be in the cell next to Gromovo Air Base's former commander Pronichev on Lubyanka's top floor?

Perhaps he understood the President a little better. There was no way that Russia could win an open conflict with the West, the Ukraine conflict had already proven that. If you were going to be blown out like a candle, was it better to burn everyone else with you?

Except Artemy didn't want to be burned and he couldn't see a way to stop it.

"Artemy."

64

"Artemy?"

Miranda wanted to hold up her hands and stop Inessa from bringing the general into the conversation. But she couldn't because they were stiff from how long she'd been clutching her empty phone pocket. How was she supposed to pretend he wasn't here if he spoke?

"Hmm?"

She could ignore a hum, couldn't she?

"Tell Miranda what you know of the crash."

"She should be the one telling me about—"

"Artemy." And with that single word Inessa stifled the general the way Holly used to do with Jeremy. That memory made her smile—until she remembered where she was.

Miranda discovered that she could concentrate on his words as long as he spoke of the crash. He knew so little that only a few details were filled in.

The Russian AN-74MP had been on a medical delivery run when it was diverted to shadow the Osprey. It took more prompting from Inessa before he admitted that the Cheburashka had collided with the Osprey and not the other way around, but that was all he knew.

"Surely the IAC knows more."

"I spoke to them. What I said includes all they know. I need to understand how America provoked our pilot to attack when she was under orders not to." His voice was... gruff? Miranda had always liked the sound of that word, *gruff*. Too bad she didn't know what that implied about his mood.

"Who was the incompetent pilot?"

Artemy spluttered before answering. "Lieutenant Sergei Balakin. How do you know he was incompetent?"

When she explained about the uncoordinated turn before the final collision—that wouldn't be classified as secret, would it, as it was done by a Russian—she could see Artemy nodding his understanding. He proved his understanding when he explained the meaning to his wife. He was far more of a pilot than Group Captain Raymond Fielding of Menwith Hill.

"And the good pilot? She was very, very good."

Inessa sighed. "She is the problem. Captain Natalia Ivanovna Murov was a dear girl. Headstrong, but fiercely driven to be the best at everything, even as a small child."

"You knew her?"

"I know many people."

Miranda considered. She knew her team members and: Drake, Clarissa, Roy, and Lizzy, but not many more. Because of her growing focus on military crashes, she was losing touch with the people she'd known at the NTSB, even in the West Coast office. "I don't."

"What do you want to know about Natalia?" Inessa voice was so soothing.

"How she managed the final recovery with her legs crushed, no rudder control, and her right wing so severely damaged."

Inessa looked to the general for a moment before turning back.

Miranda carefully didn't look his way. Only his elbow intruded on the edge of her vision so that he hovered between being present and not.

"Like your parents, I'm afraid that is but one of many secrets she took to her grave."

"That's too bad."

The general made more spluttering noises but Inessa quelled him with a light touch on the arm. Miranda could never concentrate on anything but the contact when someone touched her lightly—a terrible feeling of there but not there. Touch should always be firm.

Miranda could see him shifting his hand to hold his wife's across the narrow aisle. It was more action than she'd ever managed when someone touched her like that.

"Her parents?" Andi spoke as if her voice was going to crack. Her eyes were wide with surprise.

Miranda had missed that. "How was Natalia Murov's death like my parents? What secrets did they take to their graves?"

"We can't know because they were secrets."

"Oh." That made sense now that Miranda thought about it.

"You're missing something else, Miranda," Andi prompted her. "This woman knew your parents."

"Oh!" Miranda turned to Inessa. "I never knew they worked in Russia."

Andi rolled her eyes.

Miranda tightened her grip on the pocket filled with nothing. "I shouldn't have said that."

65

"Your mother was the most gracious woman I've ever met."

Miranda looked up far enough to see her soft smile.

The four of them still sat in the small jet. The cool night air of Kaliningrad came in through the still open door. Miranda unzipped her vest long enough to zip up the fleece jacket she'd been wearing beneath it. The fleece reminded her of her unfinished lunch at Tan Hill Inn and her unfinished hike from the Inn back to the Keld Lodge. And her unfinished walk along the Herriot Way.

All of those incomplete threads were worrying at her like...a porcupine's quills? A cactus? Saguaro or prickly pear or—

"I knew her as Olya. Samuil and Olya Mironova."

"Mironova," Andi whispered. "Miranda. You're named for your mother."

Miranda liked that. Over the last few years, she'd felt a distance grow between her and her parents.

Sam Chase, she'd come to understand, had been

interested in her brain and the ways that it could be applied to codebreaking. And not much else. She still had fond memories of all the hours they'd spent studying cryptanalysis together before his death, but those were her *only* real memories of him. Everything else was at a distance.

Olivia Chase had worked with Miranda's therapist-governess, Tante Daniels, to teach Miranda how to function day to day. How to care for the island's sheep and deer. How to communicate with what lived inside her head. More memories of her governess Tante Daniels, but she had also been around more. Mother and Father, she now knew, were often posted overseas, though she'd never known where.

Perhaps she should have. They all spoke Russian so often at home that she'd been fluent by the time she reached junior high.

"I never knew they were *Russian* agents. I only learned they were CIA a few years ago."

"CIA?" The general practically cried out.

Again Inessa calmed him down. "No one knew until after they died." Though her look to Miranda appeared to say something else.

"But—"

"Shush, Artemy! They helped Russia in many ways; helped us survive the transition from communism to capitalism without complete collapse. They helped me, invested in me though I was so young and naive."

"You were never naive, my dear," the general managed. Miranda didn't check his neck for clenching or redness.

"Oh, but I was. Fresh from the beauty pageants, Olya is the one who suggested I start my Western fashion business. They invested money, a lot of money, in getting me started. They introduced me to the Russian society that was replacing the Soviet, who became my best customers. Many of those women you met over dinner knew Samuil and Olya when they were young," she said to the general before turning to once more face Miranda. "Olya said that I reminded them of their daughter, of you."

Miranda couldn't see how. Inessa was a beautiful, erudite woman at the center of Russian society. She was…

Inessa laughed. "Let's ask your girlfriend."

"Kindness," Andi spoke as if shocked into speaking by a massive electrical charge. "You both radiate kindness. I've known very little of that, especially when I was young, so it shines out of you both."

"Kindness," Miranda repeated to herself. "But shouldn't that be normal?"

"It should, but it isn't." Andi reached across the aisle and touched her for the first time since hurrying her aboard the helicopter at Menwith Hill. Andi's hand felt warm and safe on her shoulder.

"As your friend said. Your mother also had that quality, and it is a standard I have always striven to live up to."

The general coughed to clear his throat but didn't speak.

"Yes," Inessa acknowledged. "We need to know what happened. It is our only chance to avert a war."

Miranda looked to Andi. It made sense, but she didn't trust herself to know if that was accurate.

Andi held her hands out palm up. "I just don't know. But it can't make the situation any worse, can it?"

At a loss, Miranda fell back on her sphere-based approach to a crash. Lately each incident presented such a jumble that she was always starting in the middle somehow. Perhaps it was time to follow her traditional approach, the one that had helped her solve crashes from the very beginning.

And that way she could check each layer to confirm that it didn't include classified information.

"The outermost sphere is environment and weather. This morning was a generally clear day over the North Sea."

So far so good.

"Sphere?" the general asked but Andi shushed him.

"Don't sidetrack her. It won't help."

"A CMV-22 Osprey, that's the tiltrotor specifically enhanced for aircraft carrier operations..." she took her time spelling out each detail, verifying each sentence against what was and wasn't classified.

66

"ARE YOU SURE ABOUT THIS, HOLLY?" MIKE SAT AT THE controls of the Citation 700.

Holly had ducked her head into the cockpit, the only light anywhere on the plane came from the dimmed displays —no cabin lights that might be seen through windows or navigation lights at the tail or wingtips. All she could see out the plane's windows was more darkness with speckles of town lights below. It always bothered her that pilots trusted to instruments to know where they were. Even though she could fly and she had her helo license and knew instrument navigation was normal, her world view was boots on ground.

"Fielding reports that Ian says both planes are still there, no one has moved." *Yet,* she reminded herself.

"Are you *sure* about this, Holly?" Mike's voice was muffled by the oxygen masks they both wore.

In answer, she pulled down her mask and his—they'd both been breathing pure oxygen for the last half hour to flush the nitrogen out of their systems.

Then she leaned in and kissed him hard. It was the only answer she had.

She jerked away before she lost herself there and told Mike to turn back to the UK with both of them still aboard.

"Thirty seconds," his voice gone hoarse. Yes, he knew the thin odds of them ever meeting again.

They both pulled on their masks again.

She started her wrist timer, punched his shoulder—for which she received a very satisfying curse followed by a sharp laugh—and hurried aft into the darkened cabin. Only the emergency path lights along the floor guided her way.

Holly dropped the mostly spent oxygen bottle she'd been totting around on a seat and clipped it in. She snapped her face mask lead onto the six-pound carbon-fiber cannister already on her jump harness.

Her ears kept popping as Mike lowered the cabin pressure until it matched their altitude of thirty thousand feet. It was five thousand feet above normal maximum jump altitudes. She hadn't jumped in five years and wanted a safety margin—especially for a dangerous HAHO jump. The only thing more hazardous than a High-Altitude-High-Opening jump was the Low-Opening HALO.

The HALO was for plummeting straight down and opening the chute late to avoid radar detection and being shot out of the sky while floating down. A HAHO jump was about travel, crossing large swaths of territory while falling out of the sky.

Her ears stopped popping by the time she reached the last window on the starboard side. Closing her eyes for a few seconds to gain nerve, she opened them and yanked on the emergency exit release above the window.

The cabin filled with a shriek of passing wind, but

nothing in the cabin fluttered. Mike had dropped the pressure correctly. She yanked open the emergency hatch and belted it into the last seat.

Then she braced herself in the opening, grabbing the edges with both hands.

Below was mostly darkness.

They were sliding along the Poland-Kaliningrad border. No string of lights marked the border, no cities either. It was sparsely populated level farmland. Twenty miles off, even those lights were gone, only scattered ships lit up the black of the Baltic Sea.

Kaliningrad city and Devau Airport lay twenty-two miles, thirty-six kilometers, from the southern border. Once she jumped, that was it—she was on a one-way ticket into Russia. If Miranda's jet departed while she was aloft, it would leave Holly afoot with no support in hostile territory. If Drake wasn't sending a grab team after Miranda, he certainly wouldn't be sending one after her. It was one of those little holes in her plan that she'd been careful not to mention.

This was a one-woman invasion of Russia.

Focus, Harper.

Ten seconds.

This wasn't a jump plane. It wasn't designed for people to exit the emergency window in flight. The main door would be worse. For one, the door folded outward to form a stair. It would stick out into the airstream and either be damaged or possibly crash Mike. He was a good pilot but didn't have deep experience. For two, there was that big fat wing directly downwind of the front door.

But out this window there was still a burning jet engine, and the tail aft of that. She'd almost swallowed her tongue when she first saw the plane and knew what it would take to get out. She had to forcefully throw herself out and *down*.

Five seconds.

She slapped down the night-vision goggles, then shifted her head and upper body out into the airstream. The worst of the buffeting wind had been pushed outward by the plane's passage; she was in a relatively calm pocket of air close by the hull. Also, Mike was flying right at the edge of stall speed, as slowly as possible. But it was still a hundred miles an hour.

Three.

Two.

Just as she was about to pull herself out and pray she cleared the engine and tail, she began floating out the window.

As soon as she figured out what was happening, she heaved with all her might to add her muscles to the motion.

Mike had kicked the rudder hard over, slewing the tail sideways away from her point of exit.

Holly shot clear of the plane, passing below *and* outside of the engine and tail.

She rolled over in time to see the blacked-out plane recover—none to neatly—waggle its wings, then turn sharply to disappear back the way it had come. She waved back, though he'd never see, which left her feeling sentimental and a little foolish. Mike also began the descent down to ten thousand feet where he wouldn't need oxygen. Then he could set the autopilot for a minute and replace the emergency exit.

He'd promised to loiter offshore up to his two-hour fuel limit, in case she called for help. They both knew she wouldn't. If he had to come and try to rescue her deep inside

Russian territory, they'd both be dead within minutes. But he swore he'd do it anyway.

Jerk! He wasn't supposed to make her appreciate him even more than she already did.

She rolled once more until she lay face down and yanked the rip cord.

The Intruder RA-1 chute stopped her fall with a sharp snap and a familiar slam of harness to groin. The silence that followed was as surprising as the very first jump she'd ever made. Even with the wind's roar gone, the chute had been designed to be as quiet as possible for these specialty jumps.

Flipping down the hardened touch tablet from the front of her chest rig—new trick since she'd been in—Holly turned north. She'd preset the display with Devau Airport's coordinates. Now all she had to do was not get picked up on radar. The parachute and her gear had very little metal. What there was, like her night-vision, had angular surfaces to reflect radar aside.

Fielding had even found her an experimental FN P90 compact bullpup-style rifle entirely done in carbon fiber, right down to the barrel. The rounds in the polymer magazines were the most reflective thing on her. She'd think a little better of his British officiousness in the future.

Sixty seconds later and five hundred feet lower, she crossed into Russia.

Twenty-two miles to go.

67

"TURGENEV HERE. IT WAS AN ACCIDENT. OUR FAULT," ARTEMY said as soon as Murov answered the phone.

His response? Stony silence.

But Artemy understood that now.

He also knew he wasn't in the clear yet. It was technically an undertrained AARI pilot who had screwed up, making him Artemy's responsibility. But so far the bald truth had served him well. He stood out on the ground by the Embraer aircraft, glad to be away from the flood of information that the Chase woman had unleashed.

It was a massive dose of humble. He'd been a good pilot back in the day. Not the best, not as good as Natalia, but close. This woman had broken down every control maneuver that would have been necessary to recover a falling Cheburashka missing half a wing—something he could never have repeated either in the air or explained to another pilot. Yet as she'd explained it, everything made sense right down to the analysis of the conflicting scenarios tracing the fluid dynamics of airflow over a rudder swinging free versus pinned in place by the crushed controls in the nose of the aircraft.

Not once had she referred to any notes.

"Gromov Commander Pronichev put an underqualified copilot aboard," he informed Murov. "It would appear that your daughter was giving him much needed training that other pilots had not afforded him. He was in control at the moment of the crash—a non-verifiable control error—at least without the flight recorder that I assume the Americans have by now. When I return to the office, I will start attempts to have it returned."

"And Natalia?" He might be cold as ice, but it sounded as if Murov was pulling his own teeth—without anesthetic—to ask the question aloud.

"I have it on good authority that her recovery of controlled flight was only achieved with immense skill." Good authority because Miranda Chase's knowledge was beyond prodigious. "The expert estimates that her Antonov's right wing exploded catastrophically some seven-tenths of a second before the American missile reached her. The two events together utterly destroyed the aircraft. The final end would have been quick."

While Murov adjusted to the news with his usual silence, Artemy began walking around the British plane to stretch his legs. Inessa had remained aboard with the two Americans. In the darkness of the unlit airfield, illuminated only by the distant glow of the nearby city, he couldn't spot the two pilots and the guard. They must all be aboard the plane that had brought himself to this airport. The pilot and guard would never return to the UK, two embedded assets blown in this operation.

"And the Su-57 Felons?"

As he completed the first circuit of Miranda's plane, Artemy described how the first had been caught by the turning of the ship, exceeding safety margins. The second gunned down after trying to take on an American destroyer on his own.

"This is all reliable?"

"There's no doubt. The details are too exact, too easily verified. You would have to meet the expert to understand, but there is no question." He started his second loop around the plane.

"Good, Turgenev. Very good."

"Thank you, sir. I'm—" Artemy came to a halt in the darkest shadow past the plane's nose, on the side opposite the open door.

A heavily armed warrior in a head-to-toe black suit stood not two steps away with a battlefield rifle centered on Artemy's face. The light from the four-tube night-vision rig offered just enough green glow to see the warrior's other hand. It held a single, black-gloved finger in front of his lips, signaling for silence.

"Turgenev?"

"Yes sir?" He responded, not even daring to shift his eyes.

"You were saying?"

"Uh, I lost the thought, sir. Long day. But I'm, uh, done here." He could only hope to God that he wasn't.

"Good. He served you well?"

"She, sir." The man hadn't even remembered Miranda was a woman.

"She. I look forward to meeting her." Murov hung up.

Now it was just Artemy alone with—Death incarnate.

Turgenev made a very careful show of turning off the

phone and slipping it into his pocket before raising his hands.

"Order any planes shot down in Antarctica lately, Turgenev?" A woman's voice. Her Russian was excellent though the accent was...Australian?

"You *know* me?" Stupid question. He wasn't used to facing down the barrel of a rifle at two meters.

"Educated guess, you said your name aloud when you answered the phone."

He'd been under observation for several minutes and never noticed. "I never did. The Antarctica disaster was Colonel Romanoff." Who the hell knew about that? It was the closest held secret he knew.

"Now there was a man a six-pack short of a half rack."

She'd met him? "You were there?"

By the movement of the NVG's green glow, he could tell that the woman nodded.

"He was," Artemy decided it was best not to argue with someone pointing a rifle at his face. Besides, she was right. "Or he'd never have ignored a woman like Inessa."

He glanced toward the plane before he could stop himself. Inessa sat in clear view through one of the windows.

"You move fast, Turgenev. General's star too. Nice."

"No, I didn't. I wouldn't... She and I..." He stopped himself. He was *not* about to explain himself at gunpoint. He might piss himself, but he wasn't going to talk about Inessa.

He risked a look at the other plane.

"Don't worry about them. They're certainly in no condition to worry about us. Weapons?"

"A pen knife in my right front pocket." How many more were lurking out in the darkness with their rifles trained on him? It didn't matter, the one rifle he could see didn't waver a millimeter.

"Knife to a gun fight. Well done."

Turgenev's arms were getting tired but he didn't dare lower them.

"Is she unharmed?" The woman didn't need to nod toward the British jet or explain who she was asking about.

"Not a single hair."

"Planning to keep it that way?"

"General Murov wants to meet her."

"He does, eh? And what does General Turgenev want?"

That was a much easier question. To live.

68

"MY PARENTS WERE UNDERCOVER AGENTS IN RUSSIA? REALLY?" Miranda could ask the question now that the general had left to walk around the plane and make his phone call. His unnerving reactions were gone.

"Yes," Inessa nodded and her hair slid like a model's. "As I said before, she was splendidly gracious. Your mother ran a lovely social salon, in the old sense of the word. She hosted these cozy afternoon teas for the wives and mistresses of the rich and powerful. It was a safe place to air out our grievances and any gossip we'd overheard. Only after she died did I understand what we'd all been a part of."

"CIA agents in Russia." Miranda knew she was repeating herself, but it shifted every perspective she had about them and she didn't know what to do with that.

"Wealthy ones. Paid millions to help Boris Yeltsin retain the presidency and his pro-Western agenda. Some of it was the usual graft, some of it was investments that paid off. One of those was me and my company. I'm one of the wealthiest women in Russia because of the start your parents gave me.

The seed money was the least of it. The encouragement was the greatest gift."

Her father had only ever encouraged her to crack codes. Mother had encouraged her to control herself and behave even when to do so tore Miranda apart inside.

They'd given more to this woman than they ever had to their *damaged* child.

"They were wealthy—from spying?"

Inessa nodded, "Not exactly, but yes."

Miranda looked around the plane.

That made her think of her plane—planes. The F-86 Sabrejet had been a gift. As had the Citation M2 bizjet from the manufacturer for consulting. But she'd paid cash to replace her father's plane years ago, now lost in the fire on the island. And she'd bought the seven-million-dollar helicopter outright for Andi to fly.

She'd never had to think about money.

"The island? Even my island?" She couldn't look away from Inessa to see what Andi thought.

Inessa made an uncertain gesture. "I knew nothing of their Western life except that they had a daughter. When their plane went down in Belgrade, it was such a tragedy. I wept for days until I thought I would never cry again."

"My parents died aboard TWA 800."

"I saw that in your file," she tapped the unopened folder in her lap. "No, my dear. They died a day earlier aboard an Il-76T flying to Malta."

"My parents died aboard TWA 800," Miranda couldn't think of what else to say. "They recovered the bodies."

"It was a Spair Airlines flight carrying arms to Libya but it went down near Belgrade Airport in Serbia."

Andi gasped but didn't say anything.

"Electrical failure," Miranda had read about that one. "The ground crew who repaired it left it set up wrong, so that all of the plane's electronics ran off the batteries. When they were drained in midflight, the entire aircraft shut down: radios, instruments, and lights. It made several attempts to land in Belgrade and finally crashed into a cornfield. Eleven fatalities: nine crew and two workers."

"Yes, the workers were actually Samuil and Olya Mironova, in disguise to transit the border."

"But that accident investigation's result makes no sense. A massive electrical fault, fixed in under an hour but then done wrong? It's a mistake even a drunken tech wouldn't make. That would have to be deliberately done."

Inessa shrugged, "I know nothing of such things."

"The plane was...sabotaged." Miranda reviewed the timeline in her head and was sure of it.

"Perhaps a conspiracy to kill your parents...?" Inessa's voice drifted off as she looked at the cabin above Miranda's head.

Miranda couldn't even look up to see what Inessa was looking at.

"But my parents died aboard TWA..." Miranda couldn't complete the sentence that had been the bedrock of her life since July 17th, 1996. Though that was another anomaly. The news of their deaths had been waiting for her when she returned home from horse riding camp that day. News received within thirty minutes of the crash. Her experience since said how incredibly unusual that was—unusual to the point of ridiculous.

No one, absolutely no one would have been notified by the airline so quickly. But if the CIA had something to hide, they might have called right away. It actually explained a timing error that she'd never considered before. The satisfaction of resolving that minor detail did nothing to ease the bombshell revelation.

Inessa was leaning forward, resting a comforting hand firmly on her knee.

Miranda finally managed to face Andi. Her expression would definitely match the *shocked* emoji.

She herself was...

"But they died aboard—"

...lost?

Her reference cards pages didn't have an emoji for lost.

"Murdered on a Russian airplane for what?"

"For knowing too much?" Inessa asked. "I truly don't know."

"Is any part of my life real?"

"Your parents loved you very much," Inessa said very softly. "They often told us so."

It was one thing too many.

Miranda opened her mouth—and screamed.

69

"Oh, bloody hell!" Holly had only heard that cry once before and it had come from her own throat. Not even when the smoke had cleared and she'd spotted her team's bodies scattered in the canyon. No, it had been the moment that her brother's grasp had slipped out of hers—saving her life and taking his after she'd been the one to get them into the mess.

"Move, Turgenev. Now! To the plane."

He gaped at her.

"My life would be easier if I shot you, now move!"

He ran around the nose and stopped at the steps to wave her aboard.

"Not on my six, bloke. Not having you behind me, even armed with a mighty penknife for a sword. Go!"

Turgenev hustled up the steps as another scream blasted from inside the plane.

Over his shoulder she could see that utter mayhem reigned inside the cabin. He'd stumbled to a halt, stopped by the raw wall of pain. She shoved him hard, driving him through it into the back of the cabin.

Miranda sat in a seat, screaming her head off.

Andi and another woman were both leaning in to calm her—to no effect.

"What the bloody hell did you do to her?" She was ready to shoot all three of the cabin's occupants.

It was the woman, who must be Turgenev's Inessa, who spoke up, literally. She had to shout her words into the gaps of silence each time Miranda clawed for the breath to renew her outcry.

"Nothing. Only told her. Parents. CIA in Russia. Made their wealth here. Died in a crash. In Belgrade. Not TWA." To her credit, she kept reaching out to calm Miranda despite Miranda's hard slaps to drive her hands away.

"You dumped all that shit on her at once? No more sense than a cat walking into a doghouse."

Holly half knelt in front of Miranda. Unsure of what else to do, she yanked Miranda into her arms and held her as tightly as she could.

Her screams muffled against the utility vest over Holly's jumpsuit. She began pounding her fists against the outside of Holly's arms.

Holly squeezed her tighter, sliding her arms downward to pin Miranda's.

Finally between one breath and the next, Miranda went limp, collapsing into weeping. Her fists opened enough for her to grab onto Holly's sleeves and hold on.

Holly brushed at Miranda's hair to soothe her.

Holly's back was exposed to the unknown Inessa. *And* Turgenev at the rear of the aisle, crouched beneath the low ceiling, loomed over her. She could do nothing about either exposure.

She'd have to trust to Andi for that. Though why she wasn't helping with Miranda, Holly had no idea.

Finally Miranda's hands dropped into her lap and she began rocking against Holly.

"Damn it, Miranda," Holly whispered to her. "Oh my poor mate, you were supposed to be our pilot out of here." Another of those little holes in her plan that she'd never mentioned to Mike. The whole plan had hinged on finding Miranda alive and functional, along with a working jet. Two out of three wasn't going to cut it.

No response.

Rock. Rock. Rock.

"What do I do now, love?" she asked Miranda, knowing she was far past responding.

Rock. Rock. Rock.

70

HOLLY LOOKED UP AND SPOTTED GENERAL TURGENEV crouched and immobile at the back of the plane's low aisle. His hands were braced on the backs of the two aft seats, not reaching for the penknife in his pocket.

"AARI? You a pilot by any chance?"

He nodded.

"How do you feel about defecting? America, UK, hell, even Australia. Whaddya think, mate? Fair dinkum trade?"

"No, Artemy," Inessa said before he could respond. She had leaned in to stroke Miranda's hair.

Holly flexed a shoulder to knock her hand aside.

"I *need* a pilot."

Inessa shook her head. "I have my reasons. Ones I can't tell you, but that you would approve."

"So what do I do with the two of you?"

"Leave us here, of course, and go."

"Leave you to call in the fighter jets? They'd drop our asses."

"Miranda may be the closest thing I've ever had to a sister; we would never touch her."

Holly glanced back at Turgenev. There were a lot of emotions sliding across his face.

Half tempted by her offer to defect. Surprised by his wife's words. But also not protesting them. Perplexed but not angry. Holly could work with that. But then his jaw tightened in a determination the soldier inside her knew, even if she didn't know what he was thinking.

She thought about the pilot who had flown them here. She'd put him down with a sleepy dart and trussed him. He wouldn't be awake for another hour, more likely two, and she needed to be long gone by then.

"Andi?"

Andi raised her hands in surrender. "A jet? Are you crazy? I only ever had that one lesson in a prop plane. Never found time to get back to it."

"You flew Miranda's jet."

"And almost killed us before I found the Autoland feature. I'm betting there's no auto-takeoff feature."

"Then it's me." Five years ago, SASR gave her basic lessons in a wide variety of aircraft as a part of general operation training. Not licensed but enough to survive in an emergency, at least in theory. Time to find out if it worked?

Did she dare call Mike for help? She had an encrypted squirt transmitter that would ping a satellite and show up like a red flare at Menwith Hill. Fielding was watching for that. But it didn't offer the back-and-forth chatter needed for step-by-step instructions.

The one thing she knew, she couldn't stay here. Neither could Miranda and Andi, so she'd have to deal.

"Last chance," she looked at Inessa.

The woman simply shook her head. And did so with a smile that said she did indeed have good reasons. She was so elegant and composed, despite Holly having just invaded Russia, that she had to believe Inessa. She had her reasons, she had complete control of her husband, and she was *not* going to have him flying them out of here.

Holly turned to Turgenev, pulled out a small weapon, and shot him.

71

Fire flashed through Turgenev's body.

She'd shot him.

Everything had been so calm.

He'd been careful to keep his hands exposed so that the warrior would see he was no threat. Unable to think of anything except Murov roasting him on a spit if he returned to Moscow *without* this Miranda Chase woman.

Helpless to catch himself, he collapsed to the deck. All he could focus on was the writhing pain. His limbs shook and banged against the deck and the sides of the seats.

The torture spread out from his shoulder in waves.

As the pain eased, he still had no control of his body but he managed to open his eyes. Perhaps he'd never managed to close them.

The warrior woman stepped up and slapped an injector against his neck.

He could vaguely hear her words through the electrical overload still coursing through his system.

"Sorry about the Taser. But the sedative takes a couple minutes to kick in. Just count to a hundred, mate, and enjoy the nap."

He didn't make it to ten.

72

"SORRY ABOUT DROPPING YOUR HUSBAND," HOLLY KEPT HER Taser aimed at Inessa. "I had to cut down the variables."

The woman nodded carefully, eyeing the weapon in Holly's hand.

"Oh," she holstered the Taser but not the injector. "Do I trust you? Or would you like a couple-hour nap and wake up with your husband?"

"In which country?"

"Last chance?"

Inessa shook her head.

"Aboard the other plane then, the one staying here. You'll save me a bundle of time and keep your clothes much prettier if I don't have to drag you over there."

"I'd rather not be dragged."

Holly holstered the injector as well. "Smart woman."

"Yes, I am."

"Well, I'd love to have some girl talk, but I need to be gone."

"Yes, you do. And quickly. I'll get out of your way. Please

be gentle with my husband." She rose, brushed at her dress, and exited the plane.

Miranda was still rocking, curled up as close to fetal position as possible in a plane seat.

The general was out cold.

"Andi, help me get old Turgenev here off the plane and into a shoulder carry. Then coax Miranda into the copilot's seat."

"She won't be of any use."

"I'm praying that being somewhere that familiar may pull her out of it by the time I need her."

"I've heard worse ideas today," Andi nodded and reached for Turgenev's jacket collar.

Between them, they dragged him up the aisle and positioned him at the head of the stairs with Holly outside in the dark and Andi inside. Inessa stood to the side watching anxiously.

Holly leaned in to place her shoulder in his gut, glad that he wasn't a big man. Andi gave him a push from behind until he flopped against Holly's back like a sack of potatoes. He wasn't a small man either; she was glad the two planes were close as she staggered between them with the Russian general in a shoulder carry.

As gently as she could, she laid him in the shadows under the plane beside the other three men. Inessa caught his head and eased it down the last few inches.

"Which one is yours?"

Inessa pointed at one of the pilots. "The other two came aboard Miranda's plane."

Which is what she'd figured. Sleeper agents posted in the UK, activated on short notice to extract Miranda. She hadn't had time to check their IDs. It would be a pity to not give them as a present to Fielding.

Them she cared less about being gentle with. She grabbed the first by the Zip Ties around his wrists and dragged him over to Miranda's plane. Holly stuffed him in the rear cargo compartment. Thirty seconds later she had the other one tucked in there with him.

She slapped it shut and secured the latch. "Better hope it's pressurized, mates."

Inessa had helped as much as she could and laughed lightly.

"You're a good friend," Inessa nodded toward the inside of the plane.

Holly didn't know how to answer that.

And then something she'd heard clicked into place.

"*Meeting Miranda at Devau.*" Holly repeated the message that one of Clarissa's agents had received from a Russian mole.

Inessa nodded. "I took a great risk in sending that so quickly."

"It bloody well worked." Now it was Holly's turn to laugh. "Your reason for staying."

"Miranda's parents taught me to love my country, no matter its condition. I must fight for it. The things we care most deeply about are worth fighting for, aren't they?"

Holly's first thought as she nodded agreement was of Miranda. But she realized that if Mike had been in the same position, she'd have driven even harder to save him, and she'd have shot anyone in her way—including Turgenev and Inessa. It was a scary thought to care that much about anyone.

"Murov's going to be pissed at your husband for not

keeping a hold of her." Holly forced her thoughts back to Miranda as she double-checked the latch on the baggage compartment.

"I can take care of that."

"I'll bet you can. How about your husband? Are you safe from him?"

Her smile was electric. "Artemy isn't the smartest man but he is very wise. He knows better than to ask questions he doesn't want answers to."

Holly shook her head. "Damn but I wish we had time for that girl talk."

Inessa took her hand and squeezed it in both of hers, but her face was very serious in the dim light shining out of the jet's windows. "General Murov burned a lot of assets to capture Miranda."

Holly looked at the baggage compartment with the two people who'd been in the jet. He had. They would be... But who had gotten Miranda out of Menwith Hill in the first place?

Drake's bigger picture.

How were the pieces moving?

She nodded.

Holly didn't know how, but she knew who to ask.

Inessa squeezed her hand one more time, then strolled toward the Russian plane. "I think I'll take a nap until my husband wakes up. By the way, when you find the right person to tell, you might mention Olya's salon is reopened."

"Olya's salon?"

"A woman's social group. Your friend will know." She waved a hand toward Miranda without turning to look behind her. "Do say goodbye to my little sister for me. We may not be related by blood, but we definitely had the same parents."

"I will." Holly stepped up behind her and shot her with the injector.

She was asleep before Holly had a chance to tip back Inessa's seat aboard the Russian jet.

73

HOLLY DECIDED THAT THE LESS SAID ABOUT HER TAKEOFF, THE better.

Andi knelt in the aisle reading out the checklists.

Miranda had stopped rocking as Holly started the engines.

She fumbled her hands onto the wheel and actually fought Holly's attempt to rotate.

Just when she was ready to slam Miranda's grip aside, she made a negative, "Nuh-uh" sound and pulled her near arm up against her chest—the one Andi had to break once to save their lives.

But she kept the other one pressing forward on the yoke.

Five seconds later, Miranda pulled back and Holly helped the motion. It wasn't smooth but it was controlled.

Holly kept her hands firmly on the yoke, trying to even out Miranda's jerky motions. It was like she was remembering how to use her body one little bit at a time.

Andi leaned forward to retract the gear and some seconds later to retract the flaps.

When Holly tried to cross over five hundred feet, Miranda shoved the yoke forward again.

Between them, they silently settled in at four-fifty and headed south. Miranda was right, who knew what protections Russia had along the coast. Actually, Holly would like to be much lower but didn't dare fly lower. She needed the margin to recover if she buggered this up.

They crossed into Poland two minutes later with no fighter jets chasing them down. No missiles arcing across the border to knock them out of the sky.

With Andi's help, she radioed Mike that they were out and she had both Miranda and Andi aboard.

"Check your fuel," his voice was so rough that she wondered if he was crying. From relief? Maybe. For her? Her instincts said to shy away from that thought—fast and far. Then she spotted the fuel gauge and she forgot about everything else.

"I have a bit of a problem here."

An airplane slid up alongside her. She didn't know if she'd ever seen anything so wonderful as Mike sitting in the cockpit. A couple hundred feet away and wholly unable to help her, but right there with her.

"You're ten miles to Gdansk. You can glide that far."

"Maybe you can, mate. I've never landed a jet before."

Miranda didn't speak, but her hand reached out and lowered ten degrees of flap.

"I think maybe we're okay," Holly let him know as she watched Miranda.

"I'll take care of the tower," Mike offered. "You just take care of yourself."

"Roger that."

74

HOLLY WAITED OUT AT WHAT SHE WAS COMING TO THINK OF AS *her* spot, under the curve of Radome Four. But this time around the other side, facing away from everything at Menwith Hill. She sat with her back to the concrete and her face to the rising sun. The lawn mower still hadn't come to clear out this patch. For the moment, imagined sheep grazed on the tall grass.

It was a good day.

General Murov, or Inessa after she woke...or somebody, had convinced the Russian President to back away from the button. Instead General Turgenev had submitted a polite request for the return of any recovered remains, as well as the flight recorders. The Russians were even smart enough *not* to ask for the return of the two crashed Su-57 Felons. No one cared about the Cheburashka, but the pair of Felons—Russia's cutting-edge fighter jet—were a massive US intelligence coup. Their wreckage was probably already en route to some secret warehouse stateside being disassembled and rebuilt for testing.

No one, except the men on the submarine *Belgorod,* had even acknowledged the botulism antitoxin's delivery from the aircraft carrier. The CMV-22 Osprey making the delivery had been accompanied by a phalanx of four F/A-18 Super Hornets—it had gone off without a hitch and the CMV-22 was safely back at the carrier.

Holly wondered if the unexpected death of a General Garin, reported to be from botulism poisoning but rumored to be by a firing squad, was somehow related.

Fielding had actually thanked her when she'd pulled the two men out of the Citation 700's rear cargo compartment. They stank of shitting and pissing themselves, but a pair of RAF IDs and a desperate desire to tell everything they knew about their Russian handlers, even before a deal could be offered, said how little they'd enjoyed the flight.

"Hey."

Holly didn't open her eyes at Andi's greeting. "Hey."

"You wanted to see me?"

Holly nodded and waited until she heard Andi sitting down. She opened her eyes and looked over.

She looked as neat as ever, the pretty, slim ABC— American Born Chinese—in jeans, t-shirt, and her old 101st Airborne bomber jacket with her fists stuffed in her pockets.

"How could you?"

Andi blinked at her in surprise.

Holly sighed. So it was going to be the hard way. She slid the Taser out of her pocket and pointed it at Andi's chest.

"What the hell?" Andi started to push away, but Holly shook her head.

"I called Fielding from Gdansk. Not a single person went missing from here last night when you and Miranda were kidnapped. Every person on this base was accounted for.

They use localization on their ID badges and *not one* was near the helicopter, except for two visitor tags."

Andi didn't say a word.

"I found Miranda's phone and the visitor's tags next to where the side door would have been, but your phone lay by the pilot's."

"I was trying to get her out of here. I didn't know the plane had been hijacked. It was—"

"I brought the pilot and gunman back, Wu. Fielding and I had a little chat with them, after we'd hosed them down. They were told to *expect* you, personally." Holly reached out and grabbed both lapels of Andi's jacket in one fist to haul her close. "You didn't even try! I know how fucking fast you are, you got past my guard. And you couldn't take down an undertrained RAF mechanic with a sidearm? Bullshit!"

"I didn't want to risk Miranda getting hurt. She—"

Holly shoved her away, slamming her back against the concrete. Before she could recover, Holly rolled to straddle and pin Andi's legs and jammed the Taser up under Andi's chin, tempted to choke her with it.

"Enough talking shit, Wu. Inessa Turgenev tipped me off, said the FSB had burned a lot of assets to get Miranda. I thought she was talking about the RAF boys I'd locked up in baggage. But she wasn't. She knew. Tell me one thing, one goddamn thing. How the hell could you do it?"

Andi stared at her defiantly for ten more seconds, then she seemed to collapse. Eyes closed, shoulders slumped, abruptly half the size.

"Remember how I said you can try but you'll never truly escape?"

Holly nodded. "Thought you were talking about your past." Then she knew Andi was, just not her *military* past.

"Do you still have my phone?" her voice no more than a whisper.

Without shifting the Taser, Holly fished it out, tapped it awake, and turned it to Andi's face to unlock it.

"Text messages." Andi closed her eyes after it unlocked as if she didn't want to see. "Remember that general in Brunei?"

"The one you almost beat to death for even threatening Miranda?" As if she'd needed proof of how lethal Captain Andrea Wu could be.

"The other one."

That gave Holly pause. *The other one* had been General Liú Zuocheng, the second most powerful man in China, the head of the Central Military Commission.

She opened the text message from General Liú.

It was a series of photos, not of Andi, but of her mother. Sitting at her desk, climbing into her limousine in front of the Wu and Wu Law office building, wearing a silk nightgown as she brushed her hair at night. To the trained eye, it was clear that every image had been captured from a distance and angle only a sniper pre-scouting a target would use.

After the last photo it said, *Deliver Miranda Chase to jet at southeast corner of Leeds Airport immediately.*

"My mother. Wu and Wu Law. Then he called. He said the demand came from Russia. Highest priority. Liú threatened to *remove* my mother if I didn't deliver Miranda to the airport. I went with her. I forced them to take me too. I'd never have let them hurt her."

"Shut up," Holly tried to digest it all, but she couldn't.

"And I knew, I just knew that you would come and save us. So all I had to do was keep her alive and—"

"Shut up!" Holly drove the blunt tip of the Taser upward under her chin until Andi *couldn't* speak, though she might choke.

Expose Andi's mother? For what? The moment Holly asked the question, the answer was easy.

Wu and Wu Law were the premier Silicon Valley law firm for protecting IP, intellectual property. Every cutting-edge innovation from every bleeding-edge firm had been protected by them, and their work must be pipelined straight back to the Chinese government.

What hold did the Russians have over the Chinese that would make China willing to risk such a valuable asset, even as a mere threat? A question for another day, but one she wouldn't be forgetting.

"You knew."

Andi made gargling noises until Holly eased down the weapon. At this range she didn't know what would happen. Maybe the electrodes would punch through Andi's skin and drive straight up into her brain. Holly was half tempted to try it and find out.

"No. Not until the call. I never knew because I left. I never joined the firm. They were going to kill her if I didn't get Miranda to that plane. Just to the plane. I didn't know what else to do. I screwed up. I didn't escape my past."

Well Holly knew one thing: she'd never again trust Andi Wu to have her back.

More importantly: Miranda couldn't afford to either.

"Give me one good reason not to pull this trigger and see if you'll live."

"I would never hurt her!"

"Wrong thing to say. Count of five to convince me. Five."

Andi sputtered.

"Four."

"But—"

"Three."

"Pull the trigger! Do it, Harper! You can't make me feel any goddamn worse than I already do. I betrayed the woman I love. I didn't get how badly until I saw her walk onto that plane without hesitation because I was there beside her. Did it because she absolutely trusted me. Pull the trigger. Please!"

Holly waited through a mental count of Two and One— but they both knew she wouldn't be pulling the trigger.

"Tell me what to do, Holly. I don't know how to make it right. I swear by my oath, I don't know what to do."

"Your oath. Right, good one, Wu."

Wouldn't Drake laugh his ass off if he was here. Holly Harper finally had the big picture, and now it fell to her to be the smart one.

Mike should be the one here, but Holly hadn't dared leave Miranda alone. She'd flown them all the way back to the UK, but Miranda still hadn't spoken. Though she'd eaten when told to, she did nothing without prompting—like a well-behaved three-year-old.

Besides, Holly didn't quite trust that thin glimpse she'd had of Mike's inner soldier. Was it buried so deeply that it couldn't surface when needed?

So she'd decided to handle it on her own. Which meant she had to deal with Andi herself.

"Tell me what to do, Holly." It was little more than a mumble.

Andi's tears streamed down her face and splashed hot on the back of Holly's hand holding the Taser.

Holly flopped back to the grass, once again banging her

own head against the concrete. She couldn't even dredge up a curse.

What to do? She knew the answer. Hating it didn't help.

"You will go to Miranda right now and you'll say goodbye. Then we'll never see your face again."

Andi goggled at her wide-eyed.

"Only option."

"I think I'd rather be shot. Even with that thing."

Holly inspected the Taser, then shoved it back in her pocket.

"That option's off the table. But if you say one little thing sideways—one little thing that makes her think it was her who caused all this and not you—trust me, it will hurt a whole lot worse than death by Taser. Everyone jokes about Holly's Kill List. Don't make it real. Let's go, Wu. Now."

"I don't even get to do it alone?"

Holly shook her head.

"But she'll be devastated." Andi was pleading and it took everything Holly had to ignore that.

"That's no longer your problem. You've already made sure of that."

No. Now it would be *her* problem.

75

"MIRANDA?" ANDI'S WHISPER SEEMED TO ECHO IN THE SILENT room.

Holly stood with her back against the closed office door —against the inside. Fielding had given them the use of his office.

Mike had offered her the tiniest headshake as they'd arrived. Still nothing from Planet Miranda.

Holly waved him over, away from the table where Miranda had sat unmoving for the last few hours. She considered sending him out of the room, but if anyone had earned the right to be here for this, it was him. Besides, she didn't want to do this alone, wasn't sure if she could.

She wished she could send *herself* out of the room. Was it better for the unspeaking Miranda to be fooled into thinking Andi could remain in her life until she was calmer? Or was it better to make a clean slice and deal with the disaster all at once?

Holly had made the decision and just hoped that she and Miranda could live with it.

The inherent rightness of Andi's departure didn't make it any less painful. Holly's brother dying to save her life still hurt every day—she could only pray this wouldn't be worse.

With his look, Mike silently asked what was going on but she couldn't warn him. Couldn't bring herself to do it.

Instead he leaned beside her and they both watched.

Andi shuffled to the chair kitty-corner from Miranda's. After a long hesitation she sat. She started to reach out to Miranda, glanced at Holly, then pulled her hands back.

Holly could feel Mike twist to look at her but she couldn't turn to him.

But now, at least, he knew.

His curse sounded so low that it didn't even reach her own ears.

"I..." Andi looked everywhere but at Miranda.

Holly ignored Mike's pleading look to stop this —somehow.

"I..." Andi looked to the ceiling and out at the radomes beyond Fielding's windows.

Holly didn't know if she could stand to watch this.

"I screwed up," Andi twisted to face Miranda and blurted out, "I did something really stupid. And now I have to pay for it. I'm so sorry, Miranda. I swear by everything I care about that I'd change it if I could."

Miranda showed no sign of hearing.

Andi sat for a long minute before struggling to her feet like an ancient on her last legs. She set something on the table, then her voice dropped to a whisper that seemed to fill the room.

"I love you, Miranda."

She walked blindly toward the door.

Holly didn't move.

Andi came to a stop but didn't look up. Didn't say a word. She simply waited.

Holly had to swallow hard to clear her throat.

"Don't go home, Andrea Wu. Whatever you do, stay away from your mother."

Andi nodded without looking up.

Holly opened the door and closed it once Andi was gone.

She and Mike exchanged a look, then stepped forward together to sit to either side of Miranda. Holly quietly slipped Andi's security clearance card from the table and tucked it into her pocket.

They all three sat in silence for a long time, long enough for the radome shadows to shorten by half as morning changed into afternoon.

When Miranda reached for one of her notebooks, the move was startling. Not because it was so sudden but because it was the first motion she'd initiated herself since Holly and Mike had placed her in that chair.

She laid the notebook on the table and turned to the diagram that Andi had drawn yesterday, a lifetime ago.

Vacation → Crisis → Vacation (continued)

She scratched out the last box and replaced it with: *New Crisis.*

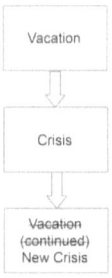

She hesitated, then put a neat line through the middle of: *Andi drew this.*

Miranda closed the notebook and carefully replaced it and the pen in her vest.

Then she lay her forehead down on her crossed arms and began to cry.

76

"Thanks for coming out to meet me. We only have a one-hour layover."

Clarissa looked around the Dulles Airport terminal and felt unclean. She didn't travel often, and when she did it was out of Andrews Air Force Base on military flights. She hadn't been in a civilian airport in years.

Val Mills had seemed at ease as the two of them had flashed their IDs at security and been escorted through. They now sat with Holly Harper at a table outside Dunkin' Donuts. She hated Dunkin' Donuts. Her father had always had a box of sugared donut holes in his office and the smell still gave her the creeps.

Yet it was hard to criticize; in the noise and mayhem of the busy terminal, it was actually a very low security risk. Picking up their conversation over three feet away would be incredibly hard.

Also Drake and President Cole were talking about awarding Holly, Miranda, and Mike the Presidential Medal of Freedom for averting war with Russia. Classified of course, they'd never be able to wear it, but the highest medal that could be bestowed on a civilian would be on their records.

It made it even harder for Clarissa to ignore Holly's request to meet here.

Curiously, *no one* had mentioned Andi.

"Where are the others?" She wasn't going to stoop to asking who that included.

"Early boarding, they're already on the plane, so I only have a few minutes."

"What's so hot that you had to drag our asses out here?"

Holly didn't even offer a jab back, which seemed odd.

"Two things. One for you, one for Russia Desk," Holly nodded toward Val.

She glanced at Val but neither of them had any more guesses than they had during the car ride in from Langley.

"First you." Holly nodded at Clarissa.

"Should I be taking notes?" Like she could actually care what Harper had to say.

"Ever hear of Wu and Wu Law in San Francisco?"

"Should I have? Isn't that Andi's last name?"

"Probably not, and it is. Well, you're going to hear about them a lot in the very near future."

"Why's that?"

"Because, Clarissa, you're going to be the one to bust their asses all the way back into the dirt."

"That's domestic. I can't touch them. You need the Feebies."

"No. You'll need the FBI, but this mess lands on your desk. Wu and Wu Law is possibly the single largest conduit of military and Silicon Valley secrets into the PRC. Especially Ching Hui Wu."

Clarissa scrabbled for a Dunkin' Donut napkin someone had left on the table. Val handed her a pen and Holly spelled it for her. This was a career-making intelligence coup if it panned out. Actually, considering that Harper was the source pretty much guaranteed its quality.

"Who's that?"

"Owner of the law firm, Number One mole, spy, whatever you people are—and Andi's mother."

Clarissa stopped taking notes after creating a deep tear in the napkin and looked up at Harper slowly. "Say what?"

"Leave Andi out of it, if you can."

"Why?"

"A favor between soldiers."

"What evidence—"

"I have a flight to catch. You've got the start you need. You're Russia Desk?" Holly turned to Val.

She nodded.

"I have a message for you."

Val reached for the pen and a fresh napkin.

"I don't think you'll need that, it's only four words. I'm supposed to tell you that Olya's salon is reopened."

She and Val looked at each other, then slowly turned to look at Holly in unison.

"Salon? That's impossible," Clarissa finally managed. "It dissolved almost three decades ago."

"I received the message from the person who did more to avert the war than anyone except Miranda could ever do. She was a member of the original salon. Like a social salon, not a hair one."

"That's how Olivia Chase did it!" Clarissa and Val almost shouted at each other. Then she caught herself.

Val's whisper of "Holy shit!" was right on the mark. Olivia

Chase hadn't manipulated the women behind Russia's most powerful men—she'd befriended them. Made herself the center of the most elite social set of women in Russia, perhaps in history.

Holly nodded. "You'll probably never meet a better person. Of course you'll probably never meet this person at all, but I will say this."

"We're listening."

"If this person ever calls for an extraction, I get first call. Not your Special Activities Division, not Delta, not even each other. Me! Personally! Are we all clear on that?"

Clarissa thought about all that had happened in the last twenty-four hours. Knew that Harper had jumped alone into Russia to save Miranda's life and come out alive.

"I can't think of anyone else who could do the job."

Harper pushed to her feet. "That wasn't a compliment, was it, Reese?"

"No way in hell, Harper."

They traded glares, and smiles. Then Holly Harper faded into the crowd as if she'd never been there.

EPILOGUE

HOLLY WAS FAST RUNNING OUT OF IDEAS, BUT MIKE HAD COME up with one more.

She'd had the silent Miranda one step from climbing aboard the team's MD 902 Explorer helicopter in the Tacoma Narrows hangar when something had snapped.

Holly caught a fist to the jaw that split her lower lip badly. Mike had ended up lying on the concrete floor holding his balls. It wasn't that Miranda had attacked them or aimed, she'd simply flipped into full blown panic and flailed out.

The moment she was a few steps away from the helicopter, she'd stumbled to a halt and sagged once more into zombie mode.

Jeremy had joined them in Dulles. So he was the one who stayed with Miranda while Holly staunched the blood flow and Mike slowly regained his feet. Holly could only hope that his familiar face would keep her calm as she dribbled more blood into the office sink and wiggled her loose tooth in the mirror.

When they'd finally tried, very carefully, escorting her aboard the Citation M2 jet, Miranda had gone without complaint. She had even gone to the cockpit, hesitating between the pilot and copilot seats.

When Holly saw that, she felt incredibly stupid. Miranda had bought the helicopter specifically for Andi to fly. Holly would smack her forehead if her jaw wasn't hurting so much. She'd take care of selling the helo very quietly and very quickly.

"Either one is okay, Miranda. Mike can fly from either side."

She'd taken the pilot's left seat, but let Mike do the flying.

The passage up to Miranda's island in the jet took fifteen minutes.

Holly had sat perched in the seat close behind the cockpit, ready to leap forward and take action. But Miranda had sat placidly as Mike first circled above the island several times, then started to descend for landing.

Miranda rested her hands on the controls for the landing itself and the two of them put it down together.

Where the hangar had once been was now a clean concrete pad. It had no walls or ceiling yet, but Mike parked the plane on it.

The four of them climbed down to stand in the knee-high grass, as deep as the fields atop Great Shunner Fell along the Herriot Way.

There'd been no talk of returning to finish the walk. Perhaps she and Mike would do it alone someday, walk the old shepherd's paths, visit pubs and castles, even visit Aysgarth Falls where Kevin Costner had survived his famous jousting scene in *Robin Hood: Prince of Thieves*.

Not this time. But plans for the future, another thing

she'd never done before with a man? She'd have to think about that later, much later.

Fielding had fetched their gear from the hotel personally.

Holly had only been back to Spieden Island once since the fire that had burned over half the area, the hangar, and Miranda's home. The rebuild had become her and Andi's domain, something they did as a couple.

Mike appeared to have no more idea what to say than she did. The normally voluble Jeremy was so worried that Holly doubted he *could* speak, even if he wanted to. They needed Taz here and her lay-it-down-like-it-is attitude. But her last month of pregnancy had grounded her in DC. They needed Andi Wu's gentle ways, but that was *not* going to happen.

So just as it had been four years ago in the Nevada desert when they came together for their first investigation, it was only the four members of the original team.

Miranda began walking slowly, across the grasses reemerging from the fire-blackened soil, toward where the house had been. The rest of them followed, more like a funeral march than all of the happy memories Holly had of her visits here.

Mike took her hand. Rather than shaking him off, she drew comfort from the contact. That too had happened here.

———

BY THE TIME SHE'D COVERED THE HALF MILE TO THE OLD house site, Miranda saw the local animals were reemerging from the woods. They'd been spooked by the plane's arrival.

There'd been a time when all they did was shuffle to the

side of the runway, but now the people no longer belonged. Her flights on and off the island were no longer a common occurrence. Her presence had slid from their animal memories.

She stopped at the new foundation and looked down at it.

Everywhere she looked, there was Andi. Sneaking down the hall to make love while the others were cooking. Standing out in the sunlight, their boots black with the ash of her burned-out house, and laughing as she began listing what they would include in the new house they'd design together. This house. This foundation.

"I can't come back."

Holly threw her arms around her and Miranda let herself be held. "I was so afraid you couldn't," Holly's voice cracked and her tears were wet in Miranda's hair.

She wondered if they were talking about the same thing.

Holly kept holding on, hard. It was very nice, but it was hard to talk with her face crushed into Holly's shoulder. She pushed her away.

Mike was smiling and Jeremy was dancing foot to foot. He finally hugged her as if he didn't know what to do with all that energy. So she hugged him briefly too. It must not have worked because his excitement was only wilder when she let him go.

"Saying I couldn't come back here, I meant the island," Miranda clarified. "I can't live here again."

"Oh right. Right." Holly nodded fiercely while wiping her eyes as if they hurt.

"What did you think I meant?"

Mike wrapped an arm around Holly and she turned into his shoulder. "She's been terrified that you had retreated into yourself and would *never* come back. To us. We all were."

"Oh, I thought about that but Andi wouldn't have liked that."

Holly twitched.

"She was always so proud of me each time I managed to learn something new."

"Until—" Holly started, but Mike stopped her with a shake. She looked at him, startled, then her skin turned even whiter than usual. She slapped a hand over her mouth, then swore and poked gently at a bloody lip.

"How did you get that?"

"Doesn't matter. Never mind." Holly waved it away so Miranda moved on, or rather back to Holly's broken sentence—unfinished sentences were still very uncomfortable things to have around.

"Until she betrayed me. Yes. That wasn't hard to figure out once I thought about it."

"When did you know?" Mike asked.

Holly appeared as startled as a fish trying to breath air. A metaphor but she didn't feel like patting herself on the back for it as tears were still streaming down Holly's face. She'd never seen Holly cry before. It was very unnerving and she had to look away.

"I should have known when she didn't kill the man with the gun. But people are confusing. It was something Andi told Inessa that made me realize what had happened."

"What was that?" Jeremy leaned in.

"Kindness. She said that Inessa and I both shared immense kindness."

"She was right," Holly declared.

"Yes, but she failed to include herself. That's when I

realized that her actions were no longer kind. They weren't unkind, instead they were very careful. That's how I knew. I didn't think about her having to leave until she did though. I wasn't ready for that." Miranda missed her. More than she'd ever missed anyone, even her parents. And now her worst nightmare had come true, Andi was gone.

She looked at the foundation again and felt a shiver run through her.

"If you don't come back *here*," Holly emphasized slightly, "what are you going to do with the island?"

"I don't know!" She had thought of little else since Holly had rescued her. And the pain welled up inside her until she was surprised she didn't burst. "Who will take care of the animals? It isn't even really mine. It's Russia's money. But I can't give it back. That was a different Russia. Or does it belong to the World Bank? Or...I don't know what to do. My poor animals!" She looked around but none of them were coming close, they were barely showing themselves at all, not even her favorites.

"Well," Jeremy looked around, "this *was* a safari park."

"Jeremy!" Holly and Mike yelled at him and Miranda covered her ears.

"I'm not saying it should be a hunting park like all those years ago. At most modern safaris now the hunting is done with cameras. Or you can call it a game preserve. Go ahead and build the house, but make it for visitors."

"Give the island to the San Juan Preservation Trust, a lot of people around here do that. With plenty of money to keep it going."

"That's good, Mike," Holly looked more...cheerful? "And what if you added a small vet clinic for students to come and study as interns."

"Oh that would be so cool." Jeremy pointed to where the garages had been before the fire. "Put the labs there. With some indoor / outdoor holding pens so that injured animals can be cared for while they heal. And you could even set up one of those raptor recovery places. After that got going, you could expand the types of animals and— I'm talking too much again. Shutting up now."

Miranda rarely initiated a hug, even with Andi. But she was so delighted by the idea that she couldn't help herself. She wrapped her arms around Jeremy's waist. He squeaked in surprise and patted her on the back.

"The Jeremy Trahn Game Preserve!"

"No," Holly said softly.

Miranda extricated herself from Jeremy and turned to face Holly.

Holly took her hands and held them firmly.

"What?" she asked Holly.

It was Mike who spoke. "The Sam and Olivia Chase Memorial Game Preserve."

She liked it. Then she looked at the house foundation again. "But if I don't live here..."

"You'll keep living with Mike and me at the team house until you can answer that question. We'll shuffle around, redecorate so that you'll be in a new bedroom. It will be okay."

"Like Andi's diagram? Do the present thing until the next one comes along?"

"Exactly."

Miranda looked around.

So many things she'd recognized were gone: the house, outbuildings, hangar, and her mother's garden. Even the copper sculpture of *Kryptos,* the hidden cryptographic codes on which Father had made her spend so many hours, had melted and deformed. Yet so much remained. The sea, the trees and fields, and especially the deer and sheep.

And she could picture it all even though she wasn't any good at pretending.

The Red Arrow passenger ferry zipping out to the island with groups of school kids. Keep the runway so that emergency supplies could be brought in. Perhaps arrange a weekly flight for caretakers. Maybe scientists.

And the vet clinic. She could make it big enough and important enough that students would clamor to come here. Each one that worked a full semester on the island, caring for the animals, would earn a special award of some sort. Not like the gray-black stars on the CIA Memorial Wall, all that remained of her parents. No, it would be a gold star with their name. Displayed prominently.

It was beautiful in her mind's eye, even though so little of it existed yet.

Holly was right. It made her very glad that she'd decided to come back, and she wasn't thinking about the island.

Maybe she was finally figuring out a form of pretending. She reached up and patted herself on the back.

For just a moment she managed to pretend that it was Andi doing it for her.

AFTERWORD

If you enjoyed <u>OSPREY</u>
please consider leaving a review.
They really help.

Keep reading for an exciting excerpt from:
Miranda Chase #14, Gryphon
(Coming winter 2023)

A list of characters and aircraft may be found at:
https://mlbuchman.com/people-places-planes

A free bonus story/scene and a recipe from the book may be be
found at:
https://mlbuchman.com/fan-club-freebies

GRYPHON (EXCERPT)

IF YOU ENJOYED THAT, YOU'LL LOVE THIS TALE!

GRYPHON (EXCERPT)

DECEMBER 13TH. EIGHT DAYS FROM ITS FINAL RETIREMENT, THE last Boeing 737-700 in his fleet went down—hard.

Nine days from his own retirement, purposely planned to follow the 737's. The way he felt, he might well be dead by tomorrow from sorrow, if nothing else.

A hundred and thirty-seven passengers (only four empty seats), two flight crew, and three cabin crew had boarded the LuftSvenska flight under their own power. They would all be departing the flight, or at least the rolling hillside of the Fjällberget ski area, very differently. DNA testing would eventually straighten out the parts that had ended up in multiple body bags. There was also the matter of eleven skiers still unaccounted for on the ground.

Rolm Lindgren glared out his window at the cold sky and did his best not to read anything into today's date—the anniversary of the airline's most infamous disaster. Easier said than done.

Not that he could do a damn thing about it from here until he knew what had happened. As if. President of the airline couldn't do a damn thing anyway except PR—and suffer a thousand headaches.

His desk offered a sweeping view from the top floor of the headquarters building. Stories below, the northern Stockholm waterfront was spectacular. But all he'd ever really cared about was looking up. There he could catch glimpses of their LuftSvenska planes headed in and out of Arlanda Airport thirty kilometers to the north. As the country's flagship airline, the King had granted permission to paint the planes flag blue with wide yellow stripes down the window line and diagonally up the tail. Distinctive from miles away.

His service boss had already called to assure him that the bird had passed all safety checks and the maintenance was fully up to date.

Then *why* had the 737 gone down?

Had it looked at a calendar?

Was it superstitious about the number thirteen like so many Swedes?

Or perhaps it knew that the diamond jubilee of the airline's founding was kicking off in two weeks—the *Seventy-five Years of Happy Customers* campaign would require a complete rebuild.

Today was also the *exact* seventieth anniversary of LuftSvenska's first crash, a mid-air collision over London that had killed all the crew and passengers, thirty-four in all. Always remembered as the second-worst disaster in the airline's history. Would it now be remembered as the third or finally relegated to a dismissal of the past? No, the newsies would make sure it was prominently remembered for a good while yet.

The newly demoted to second-worst disaster had been

the nine days *after* he'd taken over the airline—rather than nine days *before* he left it. A collision in fog between one of their departing passenger jets and a bizjet crossing the runway it shouldn't have been anywhere near. The Italian airport management and ground traffic controllers had been found guilty of that one, which hadn't mitigated the disaster.

And now...

Rolm stared at the garment bag hanging on the back of his office door. Tonight was supposed to be the first of a series of retirement dinners. How the hell was he supposed to put a good face on that? Besides, he hated wearing suits. He'd told Gertrude that in ten days, the day after he left the airline, they were going to have a suit-burning celebration. Her look said that he'd be keeping at least one to take her out to dinner at Operakällaren or Ekstedt. He hadn't conceded the win on that one yet.

Until Boeing bought McDonnell Douglas, LuftSvenska flew the MD aircraft for decades. After Boeing purchased MD, everything began slipping sideways. MD aircraft were being phased out, but not fast enough. Boeing jets were brought on board, but MD parts and Boeing parts didn't match. Machinery, engines, pilots, service people, service *methodologies,* none of it. Then someone picked up a couple of Airbus jets. Others for short-haul connectors: Fokkers, Bombardiers, a couple of BAEs, even a lone, home-grown Saab fifty-seater.

And the idiots wondered why it had all spun out of control.

Holding the fractured mess together must have made for hard years, compounded with each bad decision. Rolm could only thank the gods that he hadn't been around to see them, at least not on the front lines. Not until he'd been elevated from the rank-and-file to clean up the mess. For an entire year he'd raced from fire to fire plugging holes as fast as he could. Including the ripples of the worst crash in the airline's history—up until two hours ago.

Had he even *seen* his Gertrude in those first months? Probably not. Blessedly more tolerant than he deserved, which meant he would be keeping a dinner-out suit.

Knew that battle was lost before you even started it, Rolm. Acknowledging it didn't make him any happier.

Despite the appearances his job required, he sat far more comfortably sharing falu sausage sliced with a greasy mechanic's knife, on black bread with mustard while sitting around a half-rebuilt engine with his team.

Why had he left the line?

Because it hurt him to see what others were doing to his airline. Even as a kid fresh out of airframe and powerplant school, he could see it. He'd joined, led, then left behind the mechanics.

But he hadn't forgotten his roots like so many others before him. Not long after he'd solved the worst of the messes from the prior administration, Airbus had come around with an offer of quality planes and massive EU-subsidized discounts. Locally sourced parts, a single primary platform, and down to only two brands for the short-haul connectors. It was heaven. The bottom line cleaned up as parts and training had harmonized around fewer and fewer variables.

It had taken twenty-five years.

And in eight days it would have been done. He could have retired the day after the Boeing 737 and handed off the reins. LuftSvenska had survived the great pandemic intact and he'd made sure that it came out healthier than it had ever been beforehand. They serviced all of Scandinavia, much of Europe, and had nine prime US routes connecting Oslo, Copenhagen, and Stockholm to New York, Chicago, and Denver.

Maybe the old 737 hated him on principle.

Why *had* it gone down? Because he'd been the one to make sure it was the last of its kind at the airline?

No, the guys wouldn't have let him down. The first thing he'd done on taking over was a salary bump and double the training budget for the line staff. Every minute a plane wasn't aloft cost a small fortune. Investing in keeping the aircraft aloft, and simplifying the workload to make it happen, had paid bigger dividends than any other single action he'd taken in twenty-five years.

And now this.

It wasn't enough that the 737 had gone down in the largest single loss-of-life event in LuftSvenska's history. But rather than wrapping it up nicely and putting a neat bow on it in proper Swedish fashion, the SHK—Swedish Accident Investigation Authority in English, the "Breakdown Commission" *Haverikommission* in Swedish—had already declared the two-hour-old crash as *problematic*. They'd at least had the courtesy to let him know they were calling in the US National Transportation Safety Board.

His protest about how long that would take had been brushed aside. Apparently they had a team attending the International Society of Air Safety Investigators conference in Reykjavik. Only two hours away once they were on a plane.

He'd been a keynote speaker for the ISASI a couple years back, on a panel with United, Delta, Quantas, and Lufthansa. The other airline presidents had warned him not to stick around for the rest of the conference, but he'd ignored the advice.

It was the scariest three days of his life.

These people listened to lectures on every topic from atypical structural failures to improper software behavior to patterns of controlled flights into terrain (also known as pilot fuck-ups among his old mechanic's crowd). Each session had been about ten times as horrific as it sounded.

For ages afterward, he'd had waking nightmares every time a flight took to the air about all of the spectacular ways it could come back down: wet runways, bird strikes, FOD (foreign object debris) ingestion by an engine at takeoff... The list had been unending.

But calling in the Americans? They were so brash. They certainly didn't need paparazzi over there; Yanks were their own most vocal selves. Still, he understood SHK's reasons. With LuftSvenska phasing out Boeing aircraft over the last twenty-five years, very few of the Swedish investigators had deep experience with them, hardly anyone in Scandinavia did anymore. And even less experience with them crashing.

Maybe it was a sign he hadn't retired soon enough.

He should have stepped away when Gertrude had wanted to do that knitting cruise last spring. He could have kicked back and read a book or drunk himself blind in the ship's bar.

No, instead he'd decided to stay on until the last step of standardizing the fleet and operations was complete.

Only eight days until the last Boeing was removed from the fleet. It was already sold to the Democratic Republic of the Congo where they'd fly it until it either couldn't take off or dropped out of the sky. Which wouldn't take long to happen down there. They didn't believe in maintenance; just use it until it broke then move on. It was an ignominious ending for such a fine plane—it had performed flawlessly throughout his entire career as airline president—but a typical one in today's market.

Not anymore. Today the 737 once again counted as *his* problem, not the DRC's.

Nine days until his retirement party.

No way would this mess be done in time for Hanna Berg's takeover.

There was an idea. He could dump the whole thing in her lap and go get drunk now. Or at least hide out in his country place in Västerås. The cross-country skiing in the woods close alongside his Biskopsängen neighborhood was supposed to be very good, not that he visited there much. Gertrude had chosen it, the former biathlete Olympian who had swept him off his feet forty years ago, and still skied with a grace like she'd been born for no other purpose.

It might be very un-Swedish of him but, other than watching Gertrude, he hated cross-country skiing.

The winter sky outside his office window. It looked as if it had been carved from blue sapphire. His last time to look out this window? See his planes soaring aloft?

Only one plane in sight. It wasn't one of his.

Stockholm to Fjällberget. Fourteen minutes in the air. Driving time of three hours. That had to beat sitting in his office achieving nothing for the next three hours. And if he went, there would be no possibility of being back in time for the retirement dinner; the first good news of the day.

Ten minutes later he was in his car and driving northwest along the E4.

Why had the thing gone down?

———

"Ms. Chase?"

Mike looked up at the man who'd approached their table at the conference luncheon. And kept looking up. Not that he stood particularly tall. But it *felt* as if he did.

Not even on Mike's best days, when he was skiing every weekend and hitting the gym most weekdays to keep himself in a steady supply of cute ski bunnies, had he looked like this guy. Not quite six feet but a chest you could land a 747 on. Well, maybe only a Gulfstream 550 bizjet, but it was still ready for prime time.

Bald, black, and built. The man was a walking cliché.

He'd addressed the question to Holly, who pointed at Miranda.

Miranda had retreated in many ways over the last few months. She wore top-of-the-line Bose noise-cancelling headphones and gold-mirrored Randolph Engineering sunglasses that she probably wished were mirrored on the inside too—so that she didn't have to look at people at all.

Meg, her autism therapy dog, lay on the floor between her feet, snoozing off her small plate of raw ground meat that the conference chef had thoughtfully provided.

Jeremy was chattering away with the three delegates from the Japan Transport Safety Board in a rapid patter that wholly eluded Mike's own *konnichiwa* and *arigatou* command of the language. He couldn't come up with the polite form of either one. He hadn't scooped up many Japanese ski bunnies to practice on over the years.

The thick Australian at the table behind him sounded almost as foreign as the group of from the French BEA discussing the *chocolat* dessert.

Miranda's attention appeared to be very intent on her plate of grilled langoustine and lemon fettuccini. While she'd been staring at it without touching her fork, he'd separated the two on his own plate. Miranda wasn't a big fan of food touching each other, especially unfamiliar food. He'd also dumped all of the mushrooms onto a side plate; she didn't like their squidgy texture.

When Holly had Miranda's attention focused on the newcomer, Mike quickly switched their plates.

Holly, who always noticed everything, typically nodded her approval when he did something like that. But she hadn't noticed while too busy admiring Mr. Shoulders.

Since when did he need her approval? Since when had pathetic become a line in his job description?

Miranda tapped the button on her left earmuff, turning down the noise-cancellation on her headset without removing them.

"Ms. Chase?" He had a bass voice low enough to make Vin Diesel sound like a tenor.

"I'm Miranda Chase," her sunglasses focused on the man's left elbow.

"I'm Tad Jobson. That's short for Tad Jobson. Pop wasn't big on fancy names. He claims it comes from me being just a *small tad of a thing* when I was born. Mama has more than few things to say on that any time he brings it up—mostly along the you-try-passing-a-watermelon-out-of-your-body-and-see-how-you-feel lines. Either way, I'm your new rotorcraft specialist." He flashed a big smile.

Miranda turned into an absolute statue long enough for Tad Jobson to look up and around at him and Holly.

When she snapped back to life, Tad didn't jump, but he sure twitched.

"I...have a..." Miranda stopped again, stuttering like a robot with a short in its power supply. No, her team *didn't* have a rotorcraft specialist—anymore. Even after months, Miranda hadn't integrated her partner Andi's abrupt departure from the team and her life.

"Mr. Jobson—" Mike started.

"Tad. I'm Mike Munroe." His handshake didn't crush down on Mike's as he'd expected.

"Tad, why don't you have a seat for a moment? Maybe eat some lunch." He had to get Tad away from looming into Miranda's personal space. He was back far enough for a normal person, but Miranda was anything but.

Mike had seen something else. It was still a new factor, but he was getting to know it better and better.

Meg the dog had come up out of a deep sleep the second her master had frozen. Short enough to do so, she stood and stepped out from under Miranda's chair. Mike snagged the handle on the back of Meg's harness and lifted the gray Glen of Imaal Terrier. Easier than it looked as she was a solid little scamp. As soon as she was high enough, she stepped forward and Mike released her onto Miranda's lap.

After a long few seconds, one of Miranda arms came around the little dog. And then as if nothing had happened, she picked up her fork and inspected her plate. Carefully avoiding the grilled langoustines that Mike had placed neatly around the edge of the plate, she twirled up some of the olive oil-and-lemon pasta—without mushrooms—and began eating.

"What the...?" Tad had sat down in the only open seat at their table. The seat next to Holly.

Mike hadn't thought that through very well, had he?

Gryphon (excerpt)

———

Available at fine retailers everywhere:
Gryphon
(Coming winter 2023-20224)

*And don't forget that review for **O**SPREY*
They really help.

ABOUT THE AUTHOR

USA Today and Amazon #1 Bestseller M. L. "Matt" Buchman started writing on a flight south from Japan to ride his bicycle across the Australian Outback. Just part of a solo around-the-world trip that ultimately launched his writing career.

From the very beginning, his powerful female heroines insisted on putting character first, *then* a great adventure. He's since written over 70 action-adventure thrillers and military romantic suspense novels. And more than 125 short stories, and a fast-growing pile of read-by-author audiobooks.

PW declares of his Miranda Chase action-adventure thrillers: "Tom Clancy fans open to a strong female lead will clamor for more." About his military romantic thrillers: "Like Robert Ludlum and Nora Roberts had a book baby."

His fans say: "I want more now...of everything!" That his characters are even more insistent than his fans is a hoot. He is also the founder and editor of *Thrill Ride – the Magazine*.

As a 30-year project manager with a geophysics degree who has designed and built houses, flown and jumped out of planes, and solo-sailed a 50' ketch, he is awed by what is possible. He and his wife presently live on the North Shore of Massachusetts. More at: www.mlbuchman.com.

Other works by M. L. Buchman: (* - also in audio)

Action-Adventure Thrillers

Dead Chef
One Chef!
Two Chef!

Miranda Chase
Drone*
Thunderbolt*
Condor*
Ghostrider*
Raider*
Chinook*
Havoc*
White Top*
Start the Chase*
Lightning*
Skibird*
Nightwatch*
Osprey*
Gryphon*

Science Fiction / Fantasy

Deities Anonymous
Cookbook from Hell: Reheated
Saviors 101

Contemporary Romance

Eagle Cove
Return to Eagle Cove
Recipe for Eagle Cove
Longing for Eagle Cove
Keepsake for Eagle Cove

Love Abroad
Heart of the Cotswolds: England
Path of Love: Cinque Terre, Italy

Where Dreams
Where Dreams are Born
Where Dreams Reside
Where Dreams Are of Christmas*
Where Dreams Unfold
Where Dreams Are Written
Where Dreams Continue

Non-Fiction

Strategies for Success
Managing Your Inner Artist/Writer
Estate Planning for Authors*
Character Voice
Narrate and Record Your Own
Audiobook*

Short Story Series by M. L. Buchman:

Action-Adventure Thrillers

Dead Chef

Miranda Chase Stories

Romantic Suspense

Antarctic Ice Fliers

US Coast Guard

Contemporary Romance

Eagle Cove

Other

Deities Anonymous (fantasy)

Single Titles

The Emily Beale Universe
(military romantic suspense)

The Night Stalkers
MAIN FLIGHT
The Night Is Mine
I Own the Dawn
Wait Until Dark
Take Over at Midnight
Light Up the Night
Bring On the Dusk
By Break of Day
Target of the Heart
Target Lock on Love
Target of Mine
Target of One's Own
NIGHT STALKERS HOLIDAYS
Daniel's Christmas*
Frank's Independence Day*
Peter's Christmas*
Christmas at Steel Beach
Zachary's Christmas*
Roy's Independence Day*
Damien's Christmas*
Christmas at Peleliu Cove

Henderson's Ranch
Nathan's Big Sky*
Big Sky, Loyal Heart*
Big Sky Dog Whisperer*
Tales of Henderson's Ranch*

Shadow Force: Psi
At the Slightest Sound*
At the Quietest Word*
At the Merest Glance*
At the Clearest Sensation*

White House Protection Force
Off the Leash*
On Your Mark*
In the Weeds*

Firehawks
Pure Heat
Full Blaze
Hot Point*
Flash of Fire*
Wild Fire
SMOKEJUMPERS
Wildfire at Dawn*
Wildfire at Larch Creek*
Wildfire on the Skagit*

Delta Force
Target Engaged*
Heart Strike*
Wild Justice*
Midnight Trust*

Emily Beale Universe Short Story Series

The Night Stalkers
The Night Stalkers Stories
The Night Stalkers CSAR
The Night Stalkers Wedding Stories
The Future Night Stalkers

Delta Force
Th Delta Force Shooters
The Delta Force Warriors

Firehawks
The Firehawks Lookouts
The Firehawks Hotshots
The Firebirds

White House Protection Force
Stories

Future Night Stalkers
Stories (Science Fiction)

SIGN UP FOR M. L. BUCHMAN'S NEWSLETTER TODAY

and receive:
Release News
Free Short Stories
a Free Book

Get your free book today. Do it now.
free-book.mlbuchman.com